A DEVIL OF A TIME

TIME

A Tom Wilkins Mystery

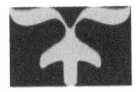

ROBERT HOWELL

WWW.STORYWRITER.CA

ISBN 978-1-9994235-3-7

Cover artwork by Lily Meyers - @lilymeyerslily on X.

Editing done by Laurie Carter – editor extraordinaire – lauriecarter.com

Author Website: www.storywriter.ca

This book is a work of fiction. Names, characters, businesses, organizations, places, events, and incidents either are the product of the author's imagination or are used fictitiously. Any resemblance to actual persons, living or dead, events, or locales is entirely coincidental.

CONTENTS

INTRODUCTION

It was a late winter midnight when Tom Wilkins' phone rang. Being the junior detective at a large Private investigation firm, he was the one who was called at all hours to take on a new case. But this one was to be different from any other case he had ever been asked to solve.

He is informed that this client is a regular of one of the senior executives of the firm and that he had asked directly for Tom to work this case. When he meets the client, he is shocked to find out that he is the Devil himself, and the job was to locate a missing demon. And not just any demon. Asmodeus, the most powerful demon, second only to Lucifer himself in the hierarchy of hell.

Knowing that a mortal would not be able to handle a demon, the devil tells Tom he will assign him an assistant, who will meet him later. Sure enough, when Tom returns home, lying in his bed in a state of undress is the most gorgeous woman he has ever seen. When he tries to evict her, she informs him that she is to be his assistant and calls herself a demoness. In reality, she is a succubus, and little does Tom know she has a double assignment – To protect Tom and to seduce him to taint his soul so that one day the devil can claim it.

Every step of the way, they encounter the forces of Asmodeus, whose plan is to take over the rulership of both Hell and Earth. From human, to demon, to golem, the forces appear undefeatable. However, with the help of his own family, his brother the priest, his cousin the monk, and his mother the nun, Tom and the succubus work together to prevent Armageddon. No one expected, though, that love could interfere with all they tried to accomplish.

It is not until the very end that Tom finds out the real truth of all that has happened.

CHAPTER 1

Shrill ringing pulled Tom Wilkins out of the most wonderful dream he had ever had. But even as the tropical air and warm sands of Bora Bora dissolved into the real-life cold and dark of the late-winter midnight metropolis, he knew that if the window had been open, the honking horn, even at this hour, would have woken him long before the incessant racket of the phone.

Nothing to do but answer it. Being the new guy meant being on call, and that meant answering the phone at all hours for any new case that came up. Of course, changing the ringtone on his cell phone should have been a priority. Maybe a song or even an old rendition of the telephone ring would be better than the shrill noise the device emitted now. But when he received the phone from the company, he had never bothered to adapt it to his personal preferences.

The other priority should have been having slippers near his bed, or a night table he could have placed his phone on, so he wouldn't have to walk to where he kept it plugged in. The cold floor on his bare feet made him curse his neglect, but allowed him to get to his adjoining office space with less of the sleep cobwebs cluttering his thinking processes.

"Hello, Tom Wilkins." He managed to make his voice sound sharp and crisp, yet his self-satisfied smirk soon disappeared when he realized the voice on the other end wasn't fooled.

"Good evening, Mr. Wilkins," came the sultry reply of the night shift secretary. "Sorry to wake you up, but Mr. Potenkins has asked you to come in tonight to meet with one of his clients.

A certain case has come up, and he explicitly asked for you. Unfortunately, it can't wait until morning, so could you please come as soon as you have showered and changed? I will have coffee and bagels here, so don't take the time to eat." With that, the line went dead, and Tom was left standing and staring at the receiver. It was just like Amy not to give him a chance to respond.

The trip into the office was quick and quiet, morning rush hour still being several hours away. After parking his '98 Mustang in his reserved spot, Tom pushed open the well-lubricated, massive bronze doors of the Greystone building with ease and strode across the lobby to the elevators with purpose. At least that was the impression he was trying to leave for the cameras that recorded every movement twenty-four hours a day.

Although originally built in 1910, the large building was completely redone in 1997, including the installation of high-speed elevators. The offices of P.I. International occupied the two top floors, a total of twenty-two thousand square feet. With a local staff of fifty-two, the company was part of the largest investigating organization in the world, encompassing seventy-five offices in forty-seven countries and a total staff of almost four thousand, not including part-time workers and subcontractors. At first reluctant to work for such a large organization, Tom had come to love the level of resources such an enterprise made available.

After only six months, he had handled over fifty cases and had been able to bring to a successful conclusion all but two, which were currently with the police. Although the cases had mostly involved simple research, there had been a couple that were much more involved and had even necessitated the use of his firearm, which made him quite happy to have kept up his practice at the firing range. Tom owned a variety of weapons, but usually carried with him only two pistols, the Browning classic Hi-Power, a 9mm with a ten-round magazine, and, strapped to his leg, a small .357 magnum Smith and Wesson special with a two-inch barrel. Before passing into the offices, he had to take out his weapons and place them on a tray to pass through the metal detectors. His weapons were returned, without the ammo, on the other side. Ammo would be returned on his departure. A security measure that had been added several years ago.

The elevator opened into the Lobby of P.I. International. Immediately facing anyone who entered was a large marble reception desk that had to be built in three separate sections and then put together in place. It was a classically beautiful desk, but it served a double purpose. It could stop bullets. Like all the walls and glass doors of the lobby area, everything was bulletproof. Incidents were rare, especially with the addition of the metal detectors, but the owners of this investigation company took no chances. Especially since they had taken on several government contracts, some of which had involved international terrorism.

"Messages, Amy?" Tom asked as he leaned his strong, lean, twenty-eight-year-old frame on the reception desk, flashing a large smile of bright white teeth.

"You might be able to make those young girls who work the daytime swoon, but it won't work with me, Mr. Wilkins," the thirty-nine-year-old senior secretary said as she handed Tom his call slips. "Mr. Potenkins expects you to handle his client with the utmost professionalism. Since the client is already waiting in your office, I suggest you do not keep him long."

As Tom received the client file from Amy, he could not help but tell her, "Now, Amy, you know I only have eyes for you. I still say you should be modeling for *GQ* or maybe *Playboy*."

"Any more talk like that, Mr. Wilkins, and I will be forced to report you." The smile on her face was well hidden so as not to betray her pleasure.

"What else can you tell me about the client? I only know that he's a VIP, and yet none of the senior detectives seem to want this case, or I wouldn't have been called in."

"The file contains all you require to know about this client. Anything else, and he will fill you in himself. I can tell you that he is very impatient and doesn't like being kept waiting, so you had better move it, mister." Although her tone was severe, she smiled at him as he left her desk.

Still perplexed, both about the new client and about Amy's continuing coolness towards him, Tom walked the long corridor to his private office, the one furthest from the reception. He knew that being the junior, even with his excellent case record, he was the one called for assignments and cases others didn't want. But to be called in by one of the senior partners and asked to handle one of his clients as a personal favor was unusual. Well, there was nothing to do but meet with the client and take on the case, no matter what it was. You didn't say no to a senior partner. Not if you wanted to keep your job.

Even though he had one of the smaller offices in the company, it was still quite spacious, and as Tom entered, he marveled at its size, as he had every day since he started. His eight-foot mahogany desk faced him as he walked in, and he spotted his new client standing off to the right of the desk, looking out the large picture window.

Even though Tom had not made a sound as he entered, the client spoke. "I always enjoy the night sky when the clouds hang just so, don't you, Tom?"

"Don't you find that the clouds block the beauty of a star-filled sky?" Tom answered the question with one of his own.

"I guess that depends on one's idea of beauty." Turning to face Tom was a man who could have been anywhere from early thirties to late forties. He moved with the agility and strength of a large predatory cat. He had slightly greying temples around thick locks of jet-black hair, which surrounded a face with few imperfections. It was his eyes, though, that truly caught Tom's attention and surprised him the most. They had black pupils and yet seemed to hold a wealth of knowledge, should anyone dare to ask, but at the same time, those eyes drilled into Tom's with an almost unbearable intensity.

"I see that you don't flinch from my gaze. That is good, Tom. If we are to work together, I will need you to be able to look hell in the eyes and smile back."

"You have me at a disadvantage, sir, in that I've just been handed your file and don't know you. You obviously know me, though, but I will introduce myself nonetheless. I am Tom Wilkins." He held out his hand.

Taking his hand and shaking it firmly, the client responded, "Of course, I know you, Tom. And who can say, maybe one day I will change your future, and you will become one of my clients. But I get ahead of myself. My name here is Natasha Lucifer.   Allowing himself nothing more than a raised eyebrow at this unusual name, Tom walked over to the liquor cabinet. "Would you like a drink, Mr. Lucifer?"

"Sure. I will drink the same as you normally do, Tom, a Remy Martin VSOP straight up."

Frowning, Tom felt inadequately prepared, not having read his client's dossier. Clearly, his client had read up on him. Tom was slow and deliberate in his actions, trying to give himself time to think. After handing over the drink, Tom went behind his desk and sat down, planning on taking his sweet time studying the dossier before speaking further with this person. His surprise at finding the file empty must have shown on his face.

"Sorry, but my file is very hush-hush," the client was quick to say. "I know you like to be more informed before taking on a case, but it could not be helped. By the way, your shoulder seems much better. Back at one hundred percent?"

Although once again caught completely by surprise, since almost no one knew he had partially separated his shoulder playing basketball the other day, Tom refused to show it. He was damned if he was going to let this client get the better of him.

"That is much better, Tom. No surprise this time. Good. You will have to keep your emotions in check on this case. The particular ... person I want you to find feeds on raw emotion."

"Oh, so this is just about a person search, or are we talking about a missing person?"

"He is definitely classified as missing, and I would not say 'just.' He has been absent for two days, and he must be located as soon as possible."

"Have you tried the police?"

For some reason, the client seemed to find this quite funny. Between laughs, he managed to say, "Believe me when I tell you that if I went to the police, they would not believe me."

Refusing to be put off, Tom continued with his usual questioning in cases like this.

"Do you suspect there may have been foul play?"

"Absolutely, there has been, but he is the one who has been committing it."

"I'm sorry, Mr. Lucifer, but I'm not following you. Maybe you should start from the beginning. Tell me everything from the time you noticed him missing. By the way, do you have any pictures?"

"Actually, I do have a picture of him, but I doubt it will help you."

"Let me be the judge of that."

Pulling a large book seemingly out of nowhere, Natasha opened it to a pre-marked page, turned the book towards Tom, and pointed at a picture.

"This is him. However, he won't look like this in the here and now."

The picture depicted a hideous creature with three heads, one a bull, one a ram, and the other some type of subhuman, maybe an ogre-like creature from the books of fantasy Tom had read as a youth. It had the feet and legs of a cock, and it rode on what appeared to be a fire-breathing lion.

"Either you're showing me the wrong picture, or I've become the butt of someone's joke."

"I assure you, Tom, it is neither. Let me explain. The world you have perceived to be normal for all of your life is only one aspect of reality. The Christian/Judaic/Babylonian versions also exist, to an extent not even believed by most of the Catholic Church. I say most, as the pope, cardinals, and several of their functionaries are fully aware of the real battle going on between good and evil. Asmodeus, the creature you see here, is a reality. He was one of my personal assistants and was good at his job until he went rogue.

"His Christian-denoted name, by the way, is Sammael, one of the original fallen angels. Of course, some have mixed him up as being Satan himself, but that is blatantly absurd since I am not he, and he is not me, as you can see."

"You're claiming to be the devil?" Tom demanded.

"No need to claim what is, Tom. The facts are the facts."

At this point, Tom's disbelief got the better of his tongue. "And Jesus will come riding into this room any minute to send you back to Hell," he said, his words dripping with sarcasm.

"And the rest of us will ascend to Heaven, I presume."

"Well, normally you might have been right," Natasha answered with a small chuckle. "As I said at the beginning, I had a devil of a time getting here. I had to get special permission from Heaven, and believe me, that isn't easy. The paperwork alone will keep my imps busy for a month. But that is neither here nor there. They permitted me because they know the damage an out-of-control Asmodeus can cause, both to humans and immortals alike."

Looking around for cameras or hidden co-workers, Tom turned to the client and said, "Look, Mr. Lucifer, I don't know who put you up to this, but—"

"I guess it is time for a little demonstration, or should I say demon-stration. Of course, I did not expect you to believe me right away. Still, I did personally request you, due to your open mind on things supernatural. I do know about your previous studies in the paranormal and the O'Brien case, where you all but insinuated that a mythological creature, a pixie, I believe you said, was involved in the theft of documents. By the way, pixies don't steal. They may play games and move things around, but to steal something is beyond their minuscule intelligence level. It was a brownie who took that document as part of an agreement with the owner's brother-in-law, but that is another story. I do usually get the details on all interactions between creatures of my realm and humans. Still curious, though, about why you became so open to the possibilities of the supernatural.

"Anyway, time for that demon-stration. I will do something simple first. I will allow you to see the way I can see when I wish, through walls, barriers, even clothes. Watch that wall. Good. Now tell me what you see."

Turning to where Natasha pointed, Tom said, "I only see a wall ... Wait, the wall is fading. I now see the reception desk, oh, which is also disappearing. Now I see Amy, and she's only wearing her bra and panties, and now she's … Okay, that's enough. You've convinced me that you're some kind of supernatural creature," said Tom, deliberately turning his head away from the *Playboy*-like scene and moving to block the client's view as well.

Laughing, Natasha stared into Tom's eyes and said, "If I truly wanted to see her naked, you couldn't possibly stop me, Tom. However, there are far too many beautiful women for me to look at to worry about a middle-aged secretary, even if she does keep in pretty good shape. By the way, I can only look at people like that who have sinned sufficiently for me to look into their personal lives. She has been sleeping with a married man. Naughty, naughty, wouldn't you say?"

"If I were to buy what you're saying, that would mean I have also sinned sufficiently, since you know a lot about me, for example, my shoulder injury."

"Truth be told, Tom, that was pure detective work and nothing more. As you know, this firm investigates all its employees, and I was in a position to read all the files, which is how I came to select you. Since I never know when I may need the services of someone such as yourself, once I had picked your file as one who could one day be of use to me, I … well, I have kind of had you watched. Ergo, one of my creatures was at the basketball court when you got hurt. Simple, really."

"If you are so powerful, why can't you just zap up your demon with the blink of an eye?"

Lucifer sighed deeply. "That is the embarrassing part. You see, I kind of accidentally told him to get lost. Unfortunately, when I said it, I put the force of my will behind it. This gave him the power to do just that: get lost. He took on a human form, popped out of hell, and we haven't been able to find him since. We were able to trace him to this city only because he made the mistake of trying to rape a nun. And of course, being pure, she was able to see him in his natural form. She reported the incident to her superior, and eventually, the news made its way to the Vatican. That took two days, though, and now we are on the hunt again. We do not believe he has left this city.

"Now here is where you come in. We need someone to try and trace his movements for the last few days. He is known as the demon of lust, which is, after all, one of the seven deadly sins. After his encounter with the nun, I think he will try to stay in one of the slimier parts of town and stick with the prostitutes and easy women found there. After a session with him, the woman will know she has been with something strange, human form or not. We need a human detective to hunt him down. If one of my servants, or even one of Heaven's servants, were to get too close, he would know it. The repercussions of a fight now between two or more of the major demons, or demons and angels, could be catastrophic, and it would take a couple of the major demons to properly subdue him. It could even set off the apocalypse. Contrary to popular belief, I do not want the Earth destroyed. I want to rule the Earth, and I need people on it to rule. Heaven, of course, would prefer to get this demon off the streets and back in Hell.

"I will see to it that your employment will not be affected by a negative decision here, Tom, but I am sure you realize that this case could make your name or kill you. Are you up to the challenge?"

Doubts still played in Tom's mind, and he sat studying his pen for a while to think things through. Lucifer seemed to know what was going through Tom's mind, for he kept his silence during this time. A lot of what Lucifer had said made sense, and Tom was even beginning to accept the fact that this character could be who he said he was. Too many things fell into place.

Either the owners of this company knew this guy was who he said he was, or they had some reason to humor him. It stood to reason that they expected Tom to do the same.

Looking up once again, Tom said, "I need to know how to recognize him if I see him, how to track him once I have made contact, and what to do with him when I do find him. After all, you must have some plan to avoid that apocalyptic battle you mentioned."

"That's the spirit. And you are right about that, so once you find him, you must not try to capture him. He would destroy you with a thought. Let's start with recognition. I will put a spell on you that will allow you to see him for what he is, no matter the human form he is wearing. Once you do spot him, the same spell will give you a limited ability to track him. The spell will put a small stench of evil on you. That is another reason why I selected you. You are a very good person at heart, so Asmodeus will not spot this small bit of evil attached to you. He will just think you are a naturally bad person."

"Will this stench, as you call it, be permanent?"

"No need to worry about that. It is one of the agreements I had to make to be allowed here. It will be lifted from you when this case is finished. As I mentioned, fighting Asmodeus would be … well, I would not recommend it. Still, you will need some protection. I have got dispensation for an assistant for you. I will make arrangements for a meeting. Once you have tracked Asmodeus down, you must contact us and lure him to a prearranged rendezvous where we can trap him without a major battle."

"And just how am I supposed to do that?" Tom blurted out.

"Well, the luring part is for you to figure out. Contacting us will be easy enough. Either your assistant can do it, or you just have to summon me by calling my name three times. My true name, that is."

"And that is …?'

"Oh, you must figure that out for yourself. I am not allowed to tell you. Sorry, those are Heaven's rules. But I am sure you are smart enough to find the answer. Amy will have all the rest of the information you will need about Asmodeus and the investigation to this point. Now, stand still while I set the spell on you."

Pulling out a red glowing sphere from somewhere in his cloak, Satan murmured a few words under his breath and then let go of the sphere. It floated there for a few minutes and then settled towards Tom. He expected to feel pain, or at least an uncomfortable sensation; however, as the sphere slowly sank into his head, he only felt a slight feeling of pleasure that quickly subsided as the orb was completely absorbed.

"I suggest you get right to work. There is one little thing I should mention. The more women he has, the harder he will be to handle. So, you should try to get to him as soon as possible. Another week or two and we might have a real devil of a time trying to contain him, so to speak. Good luck." And with that, the devil disappeared, leaving Tom wondering if it had all been a drug-induced illusion. The problem was that Tom didn't take drugs. Still, the Devil's comment about being curious as to why Tom was open to the idea of supernatural occurrences brought back to memory his first paranormal experience.

CHAPTER 2

Tom was ten when he had his first supernatural encounter. Of course, no adults believed him, but the friends who were with him at the time would remember it always.

Boys will be boys, and this was a typical pre-teen boys' outing. A friend had told a friend who had told a friend who had told Tom's friend, Andy, about a haunted house. It was about an hour's bike ride from where they lived, and it meant leaving the city proper, but it was something the boys just could not resist.

Being from a devoutly Catholic home, Tom had been taught that ghosts do not exist and that you never disobey your parents. So, how to be able to go with his friends without lying to his mother or father, since he knew his parents would say no to an outing that far away, with only three other boys his age? Then it hit him. They would pack a lunch and just say they were going for a long bike ride and then having a picnic in the park. Tom was sure there had to be a park near the haunted house, so he would not be lying. He just wasn't going to say which park they would be at.

It worked like a charm. His mother liked the idea of the boys being out in the fresh air of early summer, and going on a picnic would be ideal. She even packed a lunch for both him and Andy. George and Steve were bringing their own.

They set out early that morning with the sun shining brightly and not a cloud appearing anywhere in the sky. George commented that it would have been more fun if there had been a thunderstorm, but was quickly reminded by Andy that they would not have been allowed on this "picnic" if it were raining out.

What should have taken under an hour took well over two as the boys stopped countless times to investigate different things—a pond, a quarry, an abandoned theatre, which they were unable to enter, but not for lack of trying. Then there was the ice cream wagon that they could not possibly pass by without sampling the big old oak tree that just begged to be climbed; and the high school football scrimmage with all the loud crashes from opposing players' helmets. Although it was only a practice and they quickly lost interest. Still, it was almost noon by the time they arrived at the place marked on the map they had been given.

The boys were not disappointed when they finally saw the house through the iron-grated fence. It was an old mansion, three stories high, with stone gargoyles attached to the front soffits. The boarded windows outnumbered the glass-paned ones, the front door had plywood nailed across it, and there were the standard no-trespassing signs on the front gate. To make it even better, clouds had started to form seemingly out of nowhere, and it looked like a storm was coming. Then Andy had the great idea of eating their lunch inside, so the boys brought their backpacks with them.

Climbing the fence was easy, and soon they were making a tour of the grounds, looking for an easy way in. At first Tom was reluctant because of the no trespassing signs, but his friends convinced him that since so many people had already visited the house, the signs were only meant for thieves and vandals. As they did not plan on stealing or vandalizing anything, it would be okay to go in. It helped that Tom wanted to be convinced. He had never been in a haunted house before.

Access presented itself in the form of a basement window whose covering piece of plywood had somehow lifted away from the frame. Moving it aside, they realized that this was the point of entry used by other would-be ghost-hunting boys like themselves. Smart boys that they were, each had remembered to bring a flashlight. Only George, though, had been able to sneak out a high-powered lantern-type light, so he led the way.

Slipping in through the opening, the boys discovered that someone had conveniently left some wooden crates by the window, so getting in was easy, and leaving would be just as easy. The four regrouped, and George shone his bright lantern around the room. There was a lot of dust, and they saw the footprints of the last group that had been there. What was funny was that the footsteps entering were close together and obviously made by boys about their age, using caution going in. However, the steps leaving looked like the boys were in full flight, running as fast as they could, appearing to almost jump onto the crates to get out the window.

Steve made a comment about the last group being a bunch of fraidy cats, and they all giggled, albeit nervously, and slowly started walking in the same direction as the footsteps. Only one door led into this room, and leaving the room, they entered a hallway that seemed to run a lot longer than the house appeared to be from the outside. There were doors off the hall, but most were locked, and behind the open ones, the rooms were empty. At the end of the hall was a wooden staircase that brought them up to the next level. The door at the top opened easily, and as they entered into what appeared to be the main foyer of the house, they could see where the footsteps they were following became all mixed up and then ended—like the previous visitors had encountered something and then run off.

They spread out somewhat, walking around the large and magnificent foyer, seeing old portraits hanging on the walls and antique furniture in unbelievably good condition, like a two-seat chair with oak legs, covered in a paisley cushion, a roll-top desk, and a beautiful grandfather clock. To one side was a hall that looked like it led to the kitchen, and in front of the main door was a circular staircase leading up to what must be the bedrooms. They all thought that this would be a great spot to eat their lunch.

Steve had brought a blanket, so they spread it out in the middle of the hallway floor and started eating. As they were finishing their meal, they heard banging coming from upstairs. Looking in that direction, they saw a shadow making its way down. The boys jumped to their feet and began throwing everything into their packs, getting ready to run—everyone except Tom. Curious by nature and afraid of little that was supernatural—since he'd been told over and over that ghosts didn't exist—Tom felt he had to go meet this so-called ghost and see what it was.

From the stairway came a baritone voice. "Leave this place at once. The master is coming."

Tom continued to walk towards the spirit, feeling no fear. As he got closer, the spirit became agitated. "Go, go. Hurry, he is coming. You must not let him catch you here."

"Who is 'he' that you are talking about?" Tom asked.

"He is the master and will harm you. Please go now while you can."

"We are not here to do anything wrong. We just want to see this old house. We are told it is haunted." Tom reached out, figuring he would pull the sheet off this impersonator, and they would all have a good laugh. Instead, his hand went right through the specter, and he partially fell on the steps, banging his hand hard and making quite the loud noise.

All was quiet for a moment, and then they heard this gosh awful screech come from the uppermost part of the house, a door slamming open, and banging like someone heavy was running down a flight of steps.

"Now you have done it. The master is coming," warned the spectral image in front of Tom. "If you value your lives, I suggest you run as fast as you can. I will try and slow down the master." With that, the specter turned back towards the upstairs and disappeared. They then heard a voice yell, "No master," and a screech, and then the banging footsteps resumed coming towards them.

The boys needed no other prompting. As fast as their little legs could carry them, they were out the entranceway, down the steps to the basement, and scrambling out the small basement window, Tom along with them. Across the lawn and over the fence, they jumped on their bikes and drove like the devil was on their tails. It was only when they were ten minutes away that they slowed down and realized that the sun was shining brightly and they had covered almost half the distance home.

The boys never told anyone about their encounter, as the adults would not have believed them, and the other boys would have called them fraidy cats for running away.

CHAPTER 3

Hitting the intercom button, Tom asked Amy to come to his office. Being the only secretary on the night shift unless there was a major case at a critical point, Amy not only covered reception, which was obviously quiet in the wee hours of the morning, but also handled all the necessary secretarial work.

Pad and pencil in hand, she strolled into Tom's office with a smug expression on her face. "So, what did you think of your client?" she asked with an air of innocence.

"You knew all along who he was and didn't say anything," Tom accused.

"Of course, I didn't say anything. You wouldn't have believed a word I said even if I had. Besides, my orders are strict when it comes to this particular client." She squared her shoulders and looked him in the eye. "Now, I am sure that you didn't call me in here to discuss my prior knowledge."

"Okay, be that way," Tom shot back. "I need you to check current police files on prostitution here in New York. Mainly, where the flesh trade is heaviest, especially in areas where prostitutes tend to disappear without anyone caring. We could be talking about anything from escort services to massage parlors to street corners. Then pull police reports on recent missing persons—mainly female—murders, unidentified bodies, or strange sexual occurrences. We'll try to correlate the two and find a pattern. Also, bring me the case file now. The client said it contains information on the situation to date."

For once, Amy seemed speechless and had quite the puzzled look on her face.

Tom couldn't repress a little sense of satisfaction. "So, you don't necessarily know everything, do you, Amy? I'll tell you what. You start getting that information for me, and I might even indulge you and tell you a little bit about the case. If, that is, you're a good little secretary."

Amy raised an eyebrow and pursed her lips into a thin line of disapproval. "Your condescending attitude does not become someone of your insignificant stature, Mr. Wilkins. I will have the information for you shortly, and you can keep your case business to yourself."

She turned to go, but Tom couldn't let her leave without one parting volley. "By the way, that butterfly tattoo is most becoming."

In spite of herself, Amy stopped and glanced around to see if her dress was riding up. Tom just watched with a self-satisfied smile on his face.

After the door closed behind her, he began to marshal his thoughts. Tom knew that dealing with supernatural clients and enemies meant he was going to need a little supernatural help of his own. There were times like this when he was glad his family had strong religious beliefs. He, of course, being the exception—until today that is.

Using the auto-dialer on his desk phone, Tom called his brother's personal emergency cell phone, the one that people in his profession were not supposed to have, but that John always carried.

"Hi, John? It's Tom," he said, the moment his brother picked up. "I hope I didn't catch you at a bad time, but I need some help."

"Hi, brother," came the response in a hushed voice. "You did kind of catch me at an awkward moment. I'm in confession. And, yes, I know it's not usual at this time of morning, but when it comes to the night people, I have a hard time saying no."

"Sorry, John, I didn't mean to bother you, but this is important. I need to see you."

"You do sound desperate," said John, responding to the urgency in his brother's tone. "Why don't you come over in about an hour? I'll have coffee ready."

"That sounds good, but I might need confession and some advice even more."

"You need confession?! I'd better get something even stronger then. I'll have some good Napoleon brandy for you. See you soon," he said, and without waiting for a reply, disconnected.

Tom considered what to do next and decided to start his own internet search on demons. First, he punched in Asmodeus. After ruling out the official homepages of the band Asmodeus, Tom came across the New Advent website, which offered the Catholic Encyclopaedia definition: "Asmodeus: Demon first mentioned in the book of Tobias. The name was probably derived from the Hebrew root meaning 'to destroy.' That particular definition only talked about his relation to Sarah and her seven husbands and how God allowed the demon to kill Sarah's husbands on the night of the nuptials because their motives had not been pure. Only when Tobias, whose advances were sanctioned by God, married Sarah, was the demon vanquished."

"Well, not much help there," thought Tom aloud. "There is no one here for me to marry."

Another website offered a similar definition but added that the Angel Raphael was sent by God in answer to Sarah's prayer. It was the angel who told Tobias to court and marry Sarah to break the curse. Raphael eventually pursued Asmodeus to Egypt and there bound him "hand and foot."

In the book of Solomon, this website went on to say, "Solomon asked for the demon Asmodeus to aid him in building the temple. The demon appears and predicts that someday the kingdom of Solomon will be divided:

"My constellation (is like an animal which) reclines in its den in heaven; some men call me the Great Bear, but others the Offspring of a Dragon. Moreover, a smaller constellation accompanies my constellation, for the high position and throne of my father is always in the sky. So do not ask me so many things, Solomon, for eventually your kingdom will be divided. This glory of yours is temporary. You have us to torture for a little while; then we shall disperse among human beings again with the result that we shall be worshiped as gods because men do not know the names of the angels who rule over us."

— Testament of Solomon 5:4-5

And further, Asmodeus was also known as Ashmadia, which most likely originated from the Persian Aeshma-deva (the demon of wrath).

Another website referred to Asmodeus as the Overlord of Hell, but of course, Satan himself had disproved that theory. Then there was the site that stated he was the demon of longing, passion, and rage, and the enemy of marriage and spousal union.

After another twenty minutes of searching, Tom felt that he wasn't going to find what he wanted online. As he closed his internet access, Amy returned with three folders: two thick, one thin.

"The police reports are as of last week," she cautioned. "We will only have the updated reports when the police administration office opens in the morning."

"Thanks, Amy," Tom said to her retreating back.

The thin folder was the case file. It had very little information to go on. Just the report on the attempted rape of the nun and the description of Asmodeus, which differed little from what he'd found on the internet. He put aside the police report for later and picked up the other two folders. The thicker one contained all the areas of prostitution in New York City. The size of the flesh trade being plied in the city astonished Tom. Yet when he looked at some of the dates on the files, he saw that quite a bit of it was old information. Still, the list of massage parlors, strip clubs, and street corners where sex could be bought was a long one. From Queens to the Bronx, Harlem to Manhattan, each district had its own little sex area. Comparing some of the older lists with the current ones, Tom saw how much New York had been cleaned up by the last few administrations. Still, he realized he had a lot of work to narrow this down. However, that would have to wait till later in the morning. More important was his meeting with his brother.

Tom loved working at night. It meant no traffic, no gridlock. The drive to the church where his brother served took little time. It was a medium-sized church with lots of stonework and stained-glass windows. Although it was in a neighborhood that bordered a poor district, there was no graffiti and no broken windows. The lawn was well-manicured with hedges and wrought iron gates surrounding the entire property, but at such a height that they could be easily scaled by teens. Yet nowhere was there any sign of vandalism.

He arrived with time to spare. His brother was waiting for him anyway. Trust John to be early for his own funeral and waiting at the archway for St. Peter to arrive.

Clasping his brother warmly, Tom said, "Forgive me, Father, for I have sinned."

"Yes, I know you started when you were born and haven't stopped since. Now forget the "father" bull, at least until we get to the confessional. You know I should not be giving you confession, being a family member. I could get Father Augustus to come in. I'm sure he'd do it on such short notice, being that he owes me big time."

"No, my brother," Tom interjected. "This is something that can't get out. I'm afraid I've gotten myself into a little bit of a bind and will need divine intervention if I am to survive with life and soul intact."

"Wow, you almost make it sound like you've made a deal with the devil himself." Father John chuckled until he saw the expression on his brother's face. "Hey, that was supposed to be a joke. Why aren't you laughing? You can't mean to say—"

"Yes, John, I am afraid I do. At least I think I may have made a deal with the devil; I'm just not sure. Is it a deal, or was I trapped into it is a question of semantics."

"I think you'd better sit and tell me the whole story."

Even in his state of mind, Tom could not but stare in awe at the inside of the church, with its sweeping cathedral ceilings, solid oak benches and pews, and the immense multi-pipe organ against the side wall, as John led his brother to the back of the church and through the black velvet drapes to the family meeting rooms. There was a section with a table and chairs where all could sit and discuss, and a smaller area with two comfortable La-Z-Boys and a small coffee table. It was to the latter that Tom was led. Already upon the table were a half-full brandy decanter and two glasses.

After settling into his chair and sipping on the quite excellent brandy, Tom leaned back and looked over at his brother. He found John staring intently at him, as if looking to see if he had already sold his soul, as if that could be visible like a second skin.

"Truth be told, brother, the story is quite simple," Tom began. "I was assigned a new client, had little choice but to agree if I wanted to keep my job, and well, it turns out that this new client is ole big horns himself."

John, in the middle of taking a sip of his brandy, barely managed to keep from spitting it up, and even choked a little before getting himself back together. He finally managed to say, "You never cease to amaze and shock me, Tom. It must be a special talent you have."

"Oh, but it gets even better. You see, it's a missing personage case."

"A missing personage, you say? I gather we're not talking about a normal run-of-the-mill person, or you would have expressed it that way. Who or whom are you supposed to be looking for?"

"Asmodeus."

John stood up. The drink fell from his hand and he made some quite unconventional noises as he tried to speak.

"Well, this is the first time I've ever seen you at a loss for words," Tom remarked. "Maybe you should get a towel and clean up the brandy before it permanently stains the carpet?"

"Yeah, right, let me get something."

John was gone for a few minutes before returning with a damp cloth, a briefcase, which he did not explain, and a more composed comportment. After wiping up the mess, he poured himself another drink, sat, took a long sip, and uttered a deep sigh. Turning to his brother he said, "You are in deep shit, Tom."

"Tell me about it. What I need from you is advice on how to protect myself from him when and if I find him. And I do think you should give me confession to clear my soul." Tom then proceeded to tell John about the entire conversation with Lucifer.

"You see, I need to know if this 'stench' he put on me will eventually take my soul, and if it is removable. I mean, after all, I didn't have any trouble entering this church so it can't be that bad, can it? I also need to know the real name of the devil."

"When it comes to dealing with the devil, everything is bad. Well, I guess I might as well tell you something that few, even in the Church, know, considering your recent encounter. Yes, the Church has hidden a lot of the activity that has gone on through the years between itself and the minions of the dark one. Yes, we, and I use that collectively when I speak of the Church, have used the threat of Satan and his demons as the stick part of the carrot and the stick to help keep our congregations from sinning, and of course to keep them coming back to church.

"But there has long been a deeper and darker relationship. As the horned one has told you, there really is a line of communication between the Vatican and the minions of him below.

Few know about it, but because of the three years I served in the Vatican as scribe to his holiness, I became privy to a lot of Church secrets. After a while, it became too much for me, and I asked to be sent back home to become once again a simple parish priest. I see God had his reasons for this. It put me in a position to possibly be of assistance to you.

"I am not saying that I can do too much. There are many of the Church's secrets that I have sworn never to reveal. One of which is Lucifer's real name, but believe me, you can figure that out on your own. However, there are other ways in which I can help. You do have the right idea about confession. First, I am going to run a few tests on you to see the extent of control and influence placed upon you. Follow me." With that, John stood and held out his hand to his brother.

"Your hand is still quite wet. Since you had to get wet to clean up this mess, you feel I should be wet too, or what?"

"No, Tom. I just dipped my hand in some holy water. Since you are not steaming now, nor feeling a burning sensation, I think it is safe to assume that the devil's touch has not left anything permanent. Now, do me a favor. Reach over to the table there and pick up that crucifix. Good, now give me three Hail Marys."

Tom complied.

"Okay. The first round of tests is done. But maybe we should do what they did in the Middle Ages. Torture you until we get a confession."

"Very funny, brother. If you keep that up, I'll spend the rest of the night calling you Father, Father."

"You don't have to get nasty. I just wanted to put a little levity in here."

"One minute you're telling me I am in deep shit, the next you're making jokes about it? Boy, our mother sure did raise one deranged priest."

"Leave our mother out of this," John said with a grin on his face. "That reminds me, did Mom tell you she plans on taking the vows next spring?"

"Really!? Now that is just great. My brother has become my Father, and now my mother is going to become my Sister. When she was studying under Mother Superior Sandy, I thought she was just using this as another way of dealing with Dad's death. I didn't believe she was serious about becoming a nun."

"Well, she will be finishing her studies, and of course, the Church would love to have someone of her accomplishments in its fold. Now let's conduct a few more minor tests."

The testing continued for another half hour and included holding and reading from the Bible, standing under the large Crucifix up on the altar, and other similar tests, ending with a confession.

Once again seated in the lounge, John looked at his brother knowingly. "There is something further you are not telling me, Tom. Cough it up."

"I never could beat you at poker. Satan promised me an assistant, which I wanted to refuse, except he didn't give me much choice. It will be someone demonic in nature since he said that I am being assigned this assistant for my protection. How is he going to get this demon to me without the usual bureaucratic problems that he insinuated his kind must go through to travel amongst us?"

"That is a good question. First, you must understand a lot of the mechanics of the relationship between the Church, Heaven, and the minions of the underworld. Simple demons walk among humans daily. These, though, have no real powers or influence unless invited by a person, and even then, what they do have is quite limited. When Asmodeus escaped hell, it must have caused quite a ruckus both at the Vatican and upstairs. However, since this was not an actual move by Satan to start Armageddon, we did not see the Angels coming to Earth on their fiery chariots.

"I'm surprised, though, that I was not notified that there is a high-level demon in my area. Even though I'm no longer with the secret society of the inner circle of the Vatican, I am probably one of the few Church members in this area who know about the truth. Unless, when the Devil got his special dispensation, he didn't necessarily declare where on Earth he was going.

"Anyway, that is neither here nor there. He is the father of deceit after all. And by the way, he has often traveled to our realms without permission. He probably had to get special leave this time because of the fear of having two major forces of evil on Earth at the same time."

John suddenly paused. "Sorry, just thinking aloud. What we must figure out is the form of this demon you will be assigned. It probably can't be another of the major demons like Lilith. She was Asmodeus' lover for a time. Maybe he would assign a half-demon, one with human blood. That would solve two problems. It could still be powerful enough, but with human blood, it would not be considered one of the upper-echelon demons. And with human blood, it could very well have the ability to take human form, solving the problem of explaining its presence to others. Of course, it could be a shapeshifter like Asmodeus, but I think the human blood profile would fit it best. When are you going to meet with this helper?"

"That's the odd part. I was never told. Probably when I get into the office later. So, what can you give me to protect myself?"

"Funny you should need this at this time. I had already been preparing some things for you and had been waiting for the chance to convince you to carry this stuff. Knowing what I know, I wanted to try to protect my family, but couldn't think of a way to get you to take these things without spilling the beans, so to speak. I guess God does work in unusual ways.

"First, do you still carry the Browning classic 9mm and the small .357 magnum Smith and Wesson special?"

"Of course, those are my two favorites."

"I thought so." John reached for and opened the briefcase, which Tom had been curiously eyeing off and on during the conversation. He first pulled out two cloth bags, each a little larger than a standard sandwich baggie. He reached over and placed them both in Tom's hands.

"Don't open them just now. Those bags contain silver bullets prepared specially. First off, the silver casings were soaked for two years in water blessed by the Pope and left resting at the feet of various saints whose remains are stored beneath the Vatican. The gunpowder inside was prepared at an Abbey in France, sent to at least eight different cardinals to be blessed, and then encased in silver shells on Easter Sunday. These should slow down even the toughest of demons."

Once again, John reached into the case, this time pulling out three white candles of the sort often seen in churches for various blessings. Along with this, he handed Tom a parchment that appeared quite aged.

"We all know that the Lord of Flies is the great deceiver. There is the chance that he will still try to claim your soul in the end, or at least refuse to remove the stench. Although I could probably remove most of it with great difficulty and pain to you, it would be better if he took back what he gave you. These candles and this scripture will help ensure that he does. I do hope you remember your old Latin. When you call on the Devil to release you, make sure these candles are lit and are set in a triangle with you in the center. That way, he can't reach you. Read the first two paragraphs before he comes. If he refuses to honor his word, tell him you will read aloud the third and final paragraphs."

Tom's eyes became saucer-sized as he finished reading the paper. "This is a call to arms to St. Peter standing at the gates of Heaven. Would he really come?"

"You had better hope it does not come to that. It could mean the beginning of the end if St. Peter were to face the Devil on our level of existence.

"Now here, of course, is some holy water—I'm sure you know what to do with this—and always carry this bible with you."

The Bible was small and easily fit into the breast pocket of Tom's suit jacket.

"Last, but not least, when you do meet your assistant, try to convince this creature to come here with you so we can assure ourselves that it will not be able to turn on you at an inopportune moment. I will figure out a way to get it into the church without causing a good/evil conflict."

Tom pocketed all the articles his brother had given him and then stood up. "Thanks for everything, brother, but I must leave you if I want to get a couple of hours of shut-eye before morning. I get a feeling that this coming day is going to be a long and dangerous one, and I want to have my wits about me. As much as I know what you have given me will be of help; my strongest assets have always been the use of my noggin and my instincts. I don't want my head addled in the day to come."

"Of course, my brother. Allow me to bless you one last time before you leave."

CHAPTER 4

The pre-traffic calm allowed Tom to get back to his apartment in short order. He figured to catch a few hours of sleep before returning to the office. By that time, the police reports should be ready. Living on the third floor of a non-elevator building, Tom tended to take the steps two or even three at a time. Even at 4:00 in the morning. He loved the fact that his apartment was all by itself at the end of the hall. Although the building had been semi-converted into a condo complex, when the sales did not go well, the developers ended up renting the units. This unit became available last year when the previous tenant shot his wife in a domestic dispute. His mistake was that he mostly missed her, just causing a minor flesh wound in her hand. She, however, did not miss his head with the cast-iron skillet and was now living happily on the insurance money somewhere in the Dominican Republic.

As soon as he opened the door, Tom knew something was not right, but could not place it. He had a specialized Abloy lock that was almost impossible to pick, so no one without a key could get in without breaking down the door, and since he had needed his key to get in, obviously, the door was still in place. He always left two lights on, one on the stove hood in the kitchen, the other one on a lamp in the living room, and from where he was in the entrance hall, he could see that both those lights were still on, while no others were on that he could see. The stereo was still on and playing music at low volume, as he usually left it. But just as he thought, this case must be getting to him, Tom

realized what it was. He always left the stereo at his favorite hard rock station. But what

was coming out of the stereo was music from Air Supply, and from where he stood, he

could see the stereo had been changed from radio to CD player. He didn't own any Air

Supply CDs.

Pulling out his trusty Browning, Tom edged his way down the hall. Another

reason he had chosen this apartment was because of its open concept, and that served him

well now. As soon as he passed out of the hallway, he had a complete view of the

kitchen, dining area, and spacious living room. Nothing in sight there. He could now see

down the hall leading to the two bedrooms and office, and saw that the light in the master

bedroom was on, but dimmed. Keeping an eye on the spare bedroom in case of an

ambush, Tom moved towards the master, making sure his back was against the wall. As

he passed the spare bedroom, he reached in, grabbed the door handle, and pulled it shut,

thus making sure no one could sneak up on him from there.

Decision time. Burst into the room with the gun ready to fire? Roll into the room

using the somersault spring-up? Try to sneak around the corner? Tom decided just to

enter quickly, pistol at the ready.

Bursting into the room, moving the Browning from side to side, the vision that

caught his eyes surprised him, causing him to lower the pistol and stare with mouth wide

open. Lying on his bed in just a bra and panties was one of the most beautiful women he

had ever seen in this state of undress, for that matter, in any state whatsoever.

"I think you have the wrong weapon in your hand if you want to play with me," came the sultry voice from his queen-sized bed.

Finally, regaining control, Tom demanded, in a not-so-demanding voice, "Who are you and what are you doing in my bed? For that matter, how did you get in here?"

"Slightly flustered, are we? I would not have taken you as the easily flustered type. I always thought that you private dicks took everything in stride, and nothing got to you. Speaking of dicks put the gun down and come on over here. I have something to show you," she added as she reached for the front clasp on her bra.

Moving quickly, Tom grabbed the blanket at the end of the bed and threw it over the beauty before she could finish her action.

"On second thought, I don't care who you are; I want you out now. Get your stuff and leave before I throw you out."

"Oh, I love a rough man who gets physical. Do you like it rough, too? This could be fun."

"Look, just get out now before I call the police."

"But I can't leave. My boss sent me over here, and he would be angry at us if I left. You would not like my boss when he gets angry."

"I don't care how your boss gets. I will deal with him the same way I will deal with you, by throwing him out."

Sitting up, but making no move to further undress, the buxom babe looked directly into Tom's eyes and, with a slight but familiar-looking smirk, said, "I think you would have a hard time throwing my boss out. You see, he drips fire and brimstone when he gets angry."

"So that is who sent you. I should have known. Already, he is trying to corrupt me. Well, sending over some two-bit whore with implants is not going to tempt me. You can tell him—"

Tom did not get a chance to finish the statement as the "lady" in front of him had changed into something, well, that was a bit difficult to describe, part luscious woman, part animal, part something indescribable, and she had become seemingly larger than life as she stood on the bed. Ripping off her bra, lifting and holding her breasts, she looked down upon him and, with steam coming out of her mouth, bellowed, "These are real, and they are all-natural, and if you want to live, you will never, ever say that again." Then, suddenly in the blink of an eye, she was standing before him, fully clothed and completely human in appearance, and in the sweetest voice, as if nothing had happened, said, "And as for being two-bit, well, believe you me it would cost you plenty to have me."

Walking away from him and out the bedroom door, she looked over her shoulder and said, "Now, if you will join me for a drink in the living room, we can get down to the business of catching Asmodeus."

Standing there in stunned silence once again, Tom was beginning to wonder if he would ever be able to keep his composure while working on this case. Sighing deeply, he followed the demoness into the living room and watched as she poured two cups of coffee from the pot that he was sure had not been on when he came into the apartment.

"I believe you should stick to coffee since we have a lot of work to do."

"Well, I had intended on catching a couple of hours of shut-eye before going into the office. The reports I need won't be ready for a few hours anyway. Besides, we humans do need some sleep, you know."

"Really? Well, answer me this, Tom. Do you feel tired about now?"

Before answering, Tom thought about how he was feeling and realized that not only was he not tired, but he felt refreshed, like he had just had a full night's sleep.

"That is one of the benefits of the spell my boss put on you. Eventually, you will get tired, but you should be okay for at least a few days. So, let's discuss the case. What have you found out so far? By the way, my name is Laura-Luss, hyphenated, not first name last name," she finished, holding out her hand as part of the introduction.

Tom ignored the outstretched hand, walked by her, and over to the kitchen to pour himself a coffee.

"Don't be like that, Tom. We do have to work together, and you will find that I grow on you. For that matter, because you are cute, I will let you grow on top of me, if you get what I am saying. And there is no reason to be afraid of my touch. Shaking the hand of a demon will not affect you in any way, at least not unless the demon wants it to, and in that case, he would not have to touch you to destroy you."

"Look, I don't know why Lucifer sent you instead of a real demon, but ..."

Laura-Luss did not let him finish his sentence as she started shifting, and this time growled. But once again, in the flash of an eye, she was back to her womanly form, albeit with steam still coming out of her ears.

"You will find, Tom, that making me angry by insulting me is not in your best interests. As for why Satan sent me, well, there are a few reasons. First off, I have human blood, thanks to having a human grandfather whom, unfortunately, I never met. I think my grandmother, who, of course, was a demon, kind of accidentally killed him while they were making love. Of course, that bout of sex caused a pregnancy. The second reason would be that I have many abilities that can be of help in this case, the least of which is my control over men. And thirdly, well, Asmodeus happens to be my great-grandfather."

Tom surprised himself with his lack of reaction to this last bit of news. Then again, maybe the whole situation was numbing him to everything.

"How do I know that when you are with him, you won't turn on me?"

"Simple, if I did that, my boss would kill me. Literally. And believe me, demons can die, and it is not pleasant."

"Yet would not family bonds make you hesitate at a crucial moment?"

"You really must look up more about demons, my pet. We don't have anywhere near the same family connections that humans do. Let me tell you some of my genealogy, and you might understand a bit more. My great-grandparents are Asmodeus, as I already mentioned, and Lilith. My grandparents include Yukki-Onna, a strikingly beautiful demoness who lured many a man to his death, and Shadow, who is, of course, the son of Asmodeus and Lilith. My mother is Lilus, the daughter of Shadow and Yukki-Onna, and my father is Linkus, a half-human and descendant of Mara, the Hindu agent of death. I have seen my grandparents maybe a dozen times over the last hundred years, and my parents even less than that. The only reason that most demons don't kill their offspring right off is that that would make our master very angry indeed. We demons don't exactly have active reproductive systems, even if we indulge in the flesh to an extraordinary degree. So, any new demons, Satan makes sure are nurtured to adulthood, which doesn't take long for us.

"And yes, we are in theory capable of love, but it is extremely rare, and can cause us to lose our powers and be banished to the depths of Hell. Not an exciting proposition, even for us demons."

"Okay, what you say does make sense in a demented sort of way. Still, how do I know that as soon as Asmodeus is captured, you won't turn on me just for the fun of it?"

"You don't. That's what makes this so exciting, don't you think?"

"Well, exciting is not exactly the word I had in mind. Still, if I'm going to be working with you, at least make yourself useful and clean my apartment. It's the cleaning people's week off, and I won't have time."

Turning beet red and getting ready to explode, voice amplified considerably, Laura-Luss started telling Tom that she was not a cleaning lady until she saw the smile on his face.

"I warned you it is not wise to make me angry, Tom Wilkins. I might just decide right now to pack you up into a little ball no bigger than a basketball and play some hoops with you. I don't think you would enjoy that, beside the point that you would most likely not survive it."

"I'm sure your boss would reward you well for that trick."

"That may protect you for now, Tom, but eventually he will have no further use for you, and at that point, I might just ask to have you to do with as I please, as my real reward for a successful completion of this case."

"I do need to know at what point you will explode, Ms. Laura-Luss. There might be many situations in the coming days where not keeping your cool could completely blow it for us. If some guy on the street makes a comment you don't like, and you make use of your powers, well, beside the fact that you would probably tip off Asmodeus that we are on his trail, you might make some other supernatural powers angry, and we don't want to draw that kind of attention to us at an inopportune time. Now I am asking you, can you keep your temper under control, or do I call your boss and tell him to take you back?"

"For your information, Tom, I do not have a temper," replied the demoness, visibly working to keep herself under control. "However, I am a demoness, and we will do what is in our blood."

"Then I suggest you work on getting in touch with your human blood and learn a little control, or you can just go right back to your boss and tell him I refuse to work with you."

Suddenly Laura-Luss became all sugar and sweet. Putting on an "I am just a sweet innocent little girl" expression that Tom found more worrisome than her regular attitude, she turned to Tom and said, "Of course, I can keep myself completely under control, just like a good little nun if you so desire." Then, suddenly changing back to a seductress and shedding clothes as she walked towards Tom, she continued, "But don't you prefer the nymphet demoness instead?"

Not allowing himself to become disconcerted again in her presence, Tom simply said, "If you want to be filled in on the case to this point, you can sit down and join me for coffee. If it is sex you want, you can go out on the street somewhere and find someone who is attracted to you because I am not." Then, turning back to the coffee machine, he poured himself a cup and went and sat in the living room to wait for Laura-Luss.

A minute later, a cup of coffee also in hand, Laura-Luss joined him, taking the sofa facing Tom, rather than trying to sit beside him. Now she was attired in a pair of beige slacks with a brown blazer and cream top. Tom was not going to allow himself to be drawn into the discussion of how she changed clothes so fast. He just chalked it up to her demon powers and let it go.

Letting her sit for a while without saying anything, Tom took the time to study her. He realized now that no matter what form or state of dress she took, her facial features remained the same. She had high cheekbones, a nicely sculpted nose, deep green eyes, a strong chin, and delicate ears. One would even say her face was classical. The type of face that would look good with almost any style or color of hair. The kind of face that he was normally attracted to.

"So, what do you have, or are you just going to sit there staring at me until the sun rises to see if I turn into a pumpkin or something?"

Her comment allowed Tom to pull himself back from where his thoughts were leading.

"We have very little so far. Other than some basic research I did on the case subject, I have pulled out a list of all the red-light areas in New York, and have ordered police reports from the last seven days to see if there has been any increase in violent or sex crimes, or any unusual occurrences or reports. When I get into the office, I plan on calling a friend of mine at a local paper to see if he's received any calls about supernatural or strange events, at least ones out of the ordinary, as he gets these crazy calls all the time. This is New York after all."

"That's all you have done?"

"Well, Ms. Laura-Luss, I've only been on the case for a few hours, and it is the middle of the night, so most people are not available to be questioned."

"And where have you been getting your research information?"

"Well, I started with the internet, but that didn't tell me much, so I went and visited a priest."

Laura-Luss laughed out loud at that last comment, and rather than being offended, Tom found her laugh appealing and could not get upset about what she was laughing at.

"Why would you go to a priest to learn about demons? Other than a few well-appointed officials at the Vatican, most would not only not believe you, but would try to get you taken away to be examined at the local crazy house."

"It just so happens that I know a priest who is well-connected at the Vatican and was quite helpful. Maybe I will take you to meet him soon. However, since I have someone in front of me now who must be an expert in the field, why don't you enlighten me? Tell me what you know about Asmodeus, or rather what I will need to know to track him down and get him captured—and hopefully be able to survive the encounter."

"Okay, start by forgetting almost everything you have read in the Bible about him. The only accurate facts are that he is a very lustful demon and loves drawing in married women. However, now I believe you are on the right track in looking into the seedier elements of society. There is less chance that he will bring attention to himself. At least that is what he will be thinking. By now, I'm sure he knows that someone is on his trail.

"Asmodeus is very crafty, but not quite as crafty as he thinks he is, and that's something you might be able to use to your advantage. As long as he thinks he's outsmarting someone, he won't try harder.

"He is also probably the most powerful of all the demons. Few outside of Satan, God, or some of the High Angels can defeat him one-on-one. His main weakness is his need for flesh, and I am not talking about food. That is where I may be able to help. I can be the perfect bait, as long as he doesn't get too close to me. If he were to touch me, he would be able to recognize me no matter what shape I wore."

"That is his only weakness, lust?"

"That's about it, sweetheart. One other thing, though. Once I get close enough to him, I will probably be able to track him after that, no matter where he goes. Almost like a bloodhound. His scent, shall we say, will lead me to him as long as I follow to where he has gone within twenty-four hours."

Resisting the temptation to comment on the bloodhound statement, Tom asked the relevant question. "What do you mean by follow him wherever he goes? Like, do you mean he can disappear or something?"

"Oh, I thought you knew. Asmodeus has the capability of, shall we say, teleporting himself from one place to another. He will try not to do it too much, as it might attract other demons. But like I said, once I've gotten close to him, if he teleports, I will be able to track where he has gone."

"And this works how? Is it like he's gone, reappears in say Paris, and you know exactly where he is?"

"Not really. I will be able to get a direction and approximate distance. We will then have to use human transport to get to that area and try to track him down. Of course, once I am within a few miles of him, I will be able to take you to his exact location."

"Since you said to take human transport, I assume you can't teleport me with you to him?"

"It's even more complicated than that, lover-boy. My teleporting abilities are limited to myself and where I can either see visibly, or sense psychically, a matter of a few miles at most, and of course, the ability to return to Hell; however, if I return to Hell by that method, others will know my whereabouts. But Asmodeus does have the capability to take someone with him if he so desires."

"Are there any other little bits of information I might find useful if I can find out before he surprises me with something? You know something that might save my life?"

"Oh no, not really, other than that his regular demon powers are stronger than pretty well all other demons."

"What do you mean by regular demon powers?"

"You know the same old stuff."

"Just pretend for a minute that I know nothing about demons, which I don't. What can I expect from him?" The irritation in Tom's voice became evident.

"Where do I start? For one thing, most demons have the power of possession. In most cases, the person either must be willing or extremely evil. On occasion, an innocent is possessed when certain circumstances come into play. However, Asmodeus does have the power to take some by force. Even for him, however, it is a very difficult thing to do and will call unwanted attention to himself. If he is desperate enough, though, he will do it.

"Then there is the power of divination, also called seeing into the future. Fortunately, even the most powerful of demons can only see a few seconds into the future, and even that only when he is concentrating on it.

"He can also bind you using the air around you and then toss you quite a distance. And don't get into a staring contest with him. He could use his will to get you to do things. Not really possession but more a draining of your will and a desire to please him on your part, something like the vampires in movies."

"What tools do we have to fight him?"

"You have me for one thing. However, that is why my master told you not to try and handle him on your own. You must find where he is, somehow convince him not to leave long enough for you to get help, and then stay out of the way."

"Easy enough for you to say. If Asmodeus catches on to me, I am history, but being his great-granddaughter, he probably wouldn't hurt you."

"Asmodeus is a demon, Tom. Family means nothing to him. If I got in his way, he would do all in his power to destroy me. Plus, there is a much greater chance he would discover me following him before he senses you. No, we are both equally at risk from him. I can just fight him for a little longer than you can. But if help doesn't arrive soon enough, my fate would be the same as yours."

"Then why are you doing this?"

"Because when my master commands, all obey. Besides, this gives me more power in the world of demons if we are successful. Now you tell me, why are you doing this? Why not just drop the case?"

"I have a contract to honor. As long as I am not breaking the law or any morals, then I am obliged to do it. Also, I don't like the idea of a demon as powerful as everyone tells me Asmodeus is walking amongst us. Sooner or later, he will cause mass destruction. I want him off the streets."

"Bravo, the man wants to be a hero. I will tell you one thing, Tom. Heroes end up dead!"

"No, I am not trying to be a hero. Believe me, the minute I see him, I will be doing everything in my power to get help and then get out."

"It is going to be time soon to go to your office. I suggest you make yourself a big breakfast. Satan's mark does allow you to get by on much less sleep, but your body demands you pay the price by consuming calories. I figure a dozen eggs, a pound of bacon, and a loaf of bread toasted should hold you until lunch. Meanwhile, I am going to take a nap. We demons don't necessarily need sleep, but thirty minutes occasionally feels good. I guess it is a reminder of our mortality."

Tom did find that he was getting hungry, and while Laura-Luss dozed on the couch, he started preparing a meal, and as the odor of cooking bacon reached his nose, he realized that he was not so much hungry as ravenous. In the end, he ate all that the demoness had told him, as well as a large container of yogurt and two quarts of milk.

Thirty minutes to the second later, Laura-Luss sat up and watched as Tom finished the last of his meal. Seeing her awake, Tom asked, "Can I expect to have to eat this way three meals a day? I will gain a hundred pounds on this case at this rate."

"No, Tom, you will probably eat like this four meals a day. But you will not gain any weight. Your body is doing this to compensate for the lack of sleep. Now, maybe we should head to your office."

CHAPTER 5

Traffic was the usual horrendous early morning fare, but it seemed to Tom that they had arrived all too soon. He still had not decided on the best approach to explain Laura-Luss to the staff. Since she was probably going to be with him every day until the case was over, that might be a little too much to be just the daughter of the missing client. In the end, he decided to say nothing and let them guess and talk. They would no matter what he said anyway.

"I want you to behave yourself inside, Laura-Luss. We can not afford to have people talking too much. Even though our staff has been taught the importance of client confidence, talk can happen. If word were to get out about you, well, in New York, some people make a living by selling information. Once someone gets hold of information, they usually know where to find a buyer. I'm sure Asmodeus knows that he's being hunted and must have put feelers out. So please be .... well, try not to let your natural demon habits show."

Now dressed in a business suit, skirt, blouse, and blazer, Laura-Luss looked like the model of a businessman's assistant.

"Is this satisfactory, Mr. Wilkins?" she asked in a demure voice. "Now, just who are you going to tell them I am?"

"I will try to avoid explaining you at all if I can, but if worst comes to worst, I will say that you're my client's assistant, going over documents with me, which of course would be the truth. Now I am going to have to call you something other than Laura-Luss or Hey, Demoness. Do you have another name?"

"For the purpose of this case, you can call me Ms. Luss. I am sure that name won't sound too strange."

"Good enough, Ms. Luss. Let's go in and get to work. Hopefully, the reports will be in, and we can come up with a lead right away."

Walking to the reception desk, Tom said good morning to the receptionist, picked up his messages, and proceeded down the hall to his office, Laura-Luss by his side all the way. Other than a raised eyebrow, the receptionist did not give any impression that Tom walking in with a beautiful woman was anything out of the norm.

Tom was happy to see the extra files on his desk as he entered his office. It meant that police administration was not always an oxymoron. Waving Laura-Luss to the chair facing his desk, Tom pulled one of the files off the top and handed it to her.

"This file has all the unusual cases the police are working on now. It should be divided into robberies, sex crimes, homicides, and so on. I've only asked for files from the last month. I assume he hasn't been here longer than that?"

"My boss may be known as the Father of Lies, but when the truth serves his purpose, that is what he uses. In this case, it is important you know the facts, so when he said Asmodeus has only been here for a few days, or a week at the most, he was not lying."

"And I am supposed to believe you? Well, be that as it may, there may be some things even your boss doesn't know. I have a suspicion that Asmodeus has been planning his departure for a while and setting things up. Since you are my local demon expert, I would assume you would be able to see traces of his type of action if it appeared in any of these files."

"What makes you think he's been planning this? I am just dying to find out how a superior human brain can know more than Satan himself." Sarcasm just dripped from her words.

"Well, my dear demoness, anyone with a brain can figure it out. I guess that is why you have such a hard time with it. It's quite simple. So far, both you and your boss have told me that Asmodeus is crafty and sneaky, with a devious intelligence. I'm willing to bet that he purposely goaded Satan into casting that spell or whatever that allowed him to leave Hell. He probably had some of his personal minions helping. I am correct in saying that most of the major demons have humans who worship them and whom they can communicate with from time to time?"

For once, Laura-Luss did not have a comeback. Sitting in amazement, she realized that Tom was probably right. Why hadn't Lucifer thought of this, or if he had, why had he kept this possibility from her?

"From your silence, I gather I've guessed correctly? Now I need to know from you how he goes about contacting his human helpers, and is there a way we can trace these contacts?"

"I ... well, maybe you are on to something, but there would be no way that I can think of to trace this. Humans worship and pray to the likes of Asmodeus, and he can hear them calling to him if the ritual is done correctly. Once that is accomplished, he can then talk to them if he so chooses, which is rare. For the humans, it would almost seem like a dream, or in reality, a nightmare, but the force of his presence would, in most likelihood, convince them to follow what he says. Once he arrived here, of course, he could then talk to them as one human would to another."

"And if he talks to a human, that won't harm the human in any way?"

"Well, other than probable migraines and earaches, no, nothing permanent. Wait, maybe there is something. It has been known that when a high-ranking demon talks to a human without being cautious, it can, on occasion, cause eardrums to shatter. That could be something else to look for."

"Okay, then I will have someone check into the local clinics and hospitals to see where there might be an increase in ear incidences. Meanwhile, by going through the police reports, do you think you can spot something that would appear to have the hand of Asmodeus on it?"

"It is possible, but there's a lot here. What is that list you have?"

"This is a list of the known red-light districts, massage parlors, and hotels that deal in the flesh trade. Once you pick out a few possibilities, we'll compare them to this list and see if there are any correlations."

Picking up his phone, Tom called for one of the secretaries to do a hospital data bank search for an increase in incidences of ear problems. He also asked her to bring in the large marker board with the city map on it.

"You have access to hospital programs?" asked Laura-Luss in a surprised voice.

"We have many such programs. Sometimes I'm surprised myself by some of the various government and private programs we have access to. I guess that comes with working with a large organization."

"Isn't this stuff illegal?"

"Technically, no. Most of this information is public domain. We just have better computer programs designed for us to put all the data together in whatever format we need at the time. I'm sure our computer programming budget must be astronomical."

"Well, lover-boy, I guess we should get to work."

Ignoring the taunt, Tom opened the files on his desk while Laura-Luss studied the file on her lap. Tom had offered her another desk, but she had refused, saying she was more comfortable like this. Tom was sure she preferred it this way because it tended to show more of her body. Once again, Tom was thankful that his office was at the end of the hall where few had reason to pass.

"Would anyone like a cup of coffee?" came the perky voice of one of the many young hostesses employed by P.I. International. Concentrating on the files, as he was, Tom had failed to hear her approach. Feeling it was best not to get Laura-Luss too involved with the staff, Tom was about to wave her away when Laura-Luss spoke up.

"Please, yes. I would like a large coffee, three sugars, and two creams. And you, Mr. Wilkins, your usual just cream?" Laura-Luss asked Tom, looking at him with an oh-so-innocent look.

Groaning inwardly and knowing that now there definitely would be gossip, Tom answered yes just to get the hostess out as soon as possible. When she left, Tom turned to Laura-Luss to say something, saw that she was studiously ignoring him, and decided it was safer just to let it drop for the time being.

After about half an hour, Laura-Luss pulled out a few sheets and closed the file. She took a sip of her coffee and realized it was now cold, the taste on her mouth making her pucker. At the same time, his computer gave a little ping, indicating he had received an internal office email. Opening his inbox, he saw that the hospital report he had asked for was in. Displaying it on his screen, he was able to see three areas that seemed to have a higher-than-normal number of ear problems. Getting up, he went over to the map and, using a black magic marker, circled these.

"Have you found anything there that might be of use to us?" he asked the demoness.

"Maybe. There was an incident where a teenager sacrificially killed his younger brother. He claimed that he was directed to do this to call forth a demon. He doesn't name any demon, and normally, we might even be able to ignore this as typical of a large city, but he said he had succeeded and even described Asmodeus in his hellish form. What is interesting, though, is who directed him to do this. A man who had symbols tattooed on his arms, symbols often found on altars to Asmodeus, from what I was able to get from this kid's description.

"Second was a gang rape. No, it is not what you're thinking. This group of ten women claimed that someone took them hostage and raped them, and that although they were not tied up, they felt powerless to escape. Again, not particularly noteworthy, except that he raped all of them repeatedly, one after the other, continuously over five hours. I do not know of any man alive who can perform like that, not even Ron Jeremy at his best. Of course, the police just laughed it off, either figuring they had made the entire thing up or maybe wishing they had been able to perform like that.

"The last one that might fit is the most unusual. Three prostitutes, while locked in jail, vanished, only leaving behind a note saying their master had called for them. Police are doing an internal investigation, having decided that someone in the department must have helped them, even though the exit cameras failed to show any of the three departing."

When she gave Tom the three locations, he circled them with a red marker, adding the incident with the nun that had originally directed Satan to New York. Next, they compared it to the list that Tom had narrowed down of areas that were known centers for prostitution.

"It just doesn't make any sense," said an exasperated Tom. "We have the area here with a higher level of ear problems. In the same area, separated only by a few streets, we have our police report incidents, and yet, there are no known flesh trade areas near there. I must be missing something."

"We could be wrong about him hanging around sex trade areas. Maybe he just has someone go get the girls for him or orders them like pizzas," joked Laura-Luss.

"That's it," exclaimed Tom, turning to his computer.

"What, you get a whore with a pizza here in New York?"

"No, but you can get a prostitute on order. I remember reading something in yesterday's *Daily News*. Something about the police investigating an internet-based prostitution ring. You could literally order a girl by email. Once an appointment is made, they give you an address near where you are, and there you go."

Turning back to his computer, Tom punched a few keys and moments later ... "Okay, let's see. Yes, here it is. I think it's time for you to get a job, Ms. Luss. They happen to be hiring."

"Now wait a minute. I may be a demoness, but I have no intention of hiring myself out."

"What, a demon with morals?!" Anyway, you won't have to work. Once inside for the interview, just use your powers of observation and hearing. With those ears, you probably can hear extremely well. Listen to any special orders, or any of the girls talking about unusual customers."

"And what will you be up to while I am doing this?"

"I will be calling in to try to set up a little fun. I will tell them that I live in the Murray Hill area, just where all these incidents are located, and ask if there's a place near me that I can visit. Once I set up the appointment, I'll stake out the place and see who comes and goes."

CHAPTER 6

Stakeouts were the most boring part of any case, and this one was no exception. Even though Cindy's Beautiful Escorts lived up to its name and reputation, and the prostitutes that had come and gone over the last number of hours were well above the industry norm in looks, Tom was having a hard time keeping his mind on the job. His thoughts kept slipping to the last conversation with Laura-Luss.

If he did not know better, he would have thought that Laura-Luss was a prim and proper acolyte of an order of nuns, one step away from sisterhood, and doing her best to protect her virginity, as well as her virgin eyes, virgin ears and any other part of a body that could still be considered pure and chaste for a creature that was several centuries old—which the demoness had accidentally let slip as being the case. Even when he finally got her to agree to the inside job after over half an hour of arguing, she was quite reluctant and pouted the entire trip to the agency.

He had been concerned that she would blow the cover just to spite him; however, once she walked into the agency, she seemed to be an entirely different er ... person. Watching her from the car, Tom saw her change into the exact type who would work at a place like this: sexy, alluring, and extremely hot. Even knowing who she was, it was almost enough to turn him on.

Tom had waited the full hour they had discussed and then called the agency to set up his rendezvous for that night, verifying first through their website that Laura-Luss was available. He had booked early to ensure that no one else had a chance to pick her. Once given the address, he had immediately set off to start the stakeout.

And here he was, bored out of his tree, trying not to let Laura-Luss' attitude bother him. His "appointment" with his chosen call girl was not long off, and still nothing noteworthy had happened. It was beginning to look like he would have to enter the hotel room and meet with the demoness in order not to blow their cover. He was sure she would love the opportunity to try to seduce him. He would have to be sure not to let her embarrass him while trying to maintain his cool.

With his appointment only a few minutes away, Tom decided to arrive early and see if he could sense anything out of the norm—that is—out of the norm for a bordello.

As per the instructions he'd been given after surrendering his Visa number, Tom went to the reception desk and asked if his room was ready. He'd been told to ask for room 425. The man behind the courtesy desk looked more the part of a bouncer than a hotel host. Still, he was efficient and produced the key as soon as Tom confirmed his reservation with his credit card. What a country this was, he thought, where you could use a credit card to pay for illegal merchandise.

Passing up the elevator in favor of the dimly lit stairs, Tom climbed them two at a time, all the while listening for unusual sounds, footsteps, voices, or anything that would indicate his quarry might be nearby. Arriving at the fourth-floor landing, he eased open the door to the main hall and looked in both directions. Still nothing. Yet why was he getting this creepy feeling that kept telling him to look over his shoulder? One thing Tom had learned in his months with this agency, and years before working cases solo, was never to ignore a feeling. But nothing seemed to substantiate this concern.

Walking the empty hall to room 425, Tom carefully unlocked the door and, taking a final look over his shoulder and seeing nothing, entered the room. He eased the door closed behind him and made sure to turn the deadbolt lock. Even though he was taking the chance that he might not be able to get out of the room as fast as he might want to, he felt it was justified, balanced against the possibility of having someone grab him from behind.

There was a short hallway, then a turn leading to the main room. As Tom stopped to look around the corner, a voice said, "Why don't you join us? We have been waiting for you and have gone to a lot of trouble to greet you in a hospitable manner."

Tom rounded the corner, Browning pistol in hand, and came face to face with three persons. Or at least that is what he thought at first. But studying one of the three, he saw what could only be called anomalies. Extra fingers, various growths from different parts of the body, and a lack of apparel, other than a pair of shorts. Of the other two, one was a hired thug, tall, bald, and well-muscled, holding a submachine gun. The other, short and chubby with a head of thick curly hair, was the brains of the three. Outgunned as he was, Tom lowered his weapon and then put it on a nearby shelf.

"You were not exactly what I expected," quipped Tom. "I asked for a lady, not three men. I don't exactly lean that way, so I'm afraid you guys will have to leave. My date should be here any minute."

"Oh, we have us a comedian, do we? Well, for your information, your lady friend won't be able to make it. Let's say she's tied up at the moment. But we'll be sure to take good care of her for you once we are finished taking care of you. Now my boss would like to know who you are, a cop or what? And no bullshit about not knowing what I'm talking about. You and your fake boob bimbo friend were too obvious about making sure you met each other. We also have cameras set up outside our offices, so we saw her get out of your car."

"I gather you didn't tell her to her face that she had fake boobs, otherwise you wouldn't be talking to me right now. Okay, this is the scoop. If you guys give me your guns right now and leave, the guy who hired me might be gracious enough to let you live for the moment, thereby giving you a chance to save your souls. Otherwise, not even your boss will be able to protect you."

"I think you're forgetting one thing here, Mac. We're the ones with the firepower right about now. Besides that, my ugly friend over there doesn't even need a gun to tear you to pieces. Now you start answering my questions, or I'll tell him to start pulling you apart one limb at a time. Maybe starting with your fingers, or better yet, we can make sure you never get a chance to reproduce. So, what'll it be, answers or body parts?"

Trying to buy time, Tom tossed around different ideas on what to tell them. Figuring the truth to a point might work, he said, "Choices, choices. Well, I can start by telling you I am not a cop. I'm a private detective hired to find a missing person. We thought that this person might be here. Do you know of any missing persons working for this escort agency?"

Unfortunately, this hired help was not as stupid as most of his genre. "You must be looking for my master, then. He said someone might come looking for him, but he figured it would be someone slightly more abnormal, like my friend with the extra body parts. You gave yourself away by not being surprised at the sight of him. You obviously know about demons. Still, I am surprised that two humans would be stupid enough to go looking for a major demon."

Tom realized then that they did not know Laura-Luss was a demoness. They probably just locked her up somewhere, maybe having used chloroform or something. If that was the case, then she might be able to break free and get here to help him. If it wasn't for the demon, he would probably get out of this situation without a problem. The demon complicated matters because Tom had not had the chance to reload his guns with the bullets his brother had given him. An oversight he would correct immediately after he got out of this bind—providing he survived it.

Weighing his chances, Tom decided to go for the guy with the machine gun first. The head guy might be packing, but had nothing at hand. Hopefully, the demon would be slow enough that Tom could knock off the other two, put a couple of rounds in the demon to slow him down, and then try to quickly load his Browning with the bullets his brother had given him that were inconveniently in his pocket. Since his legs were hidden from the view of his assailants by a couch, Tom slowly raised his left leg until he was able to reach his Smith and Wesson, all the while maintaining eye contact with the head honcho.

Just as the guy with the machine gun turned to say something to his partner, Tom quickly pulled out the pistol and fired, catching Baldy in the shoulder and knocking him backward into the wall, where he dropped his gun and then his heavy body to the floor, out cold. Not taking the time to see if that one got back up, Tom turned immediately to the demon and emptied the rest of the clip into its head, then reached for his Browning

sitting on the shelf. Just as his hand clasped onto the gun, the demon was on him. The

demon knocked Tom to the floor and with one hand only on Tom's throat, it was slowly

squeezing the life out of him.

CHAPTER 7

Laura-Luss was working up to quite the temper tantrum. This time, however, it was directed at herself. She could not believe that she'd been stupid enough to allow herself to be imprisoned like this. A simple puff of gas from a pen, and this from a guy that she should have known was trouble. For sure, he did not know she was a demon, or he would have made sure to finish her off rather than just locking her up. Now she kept playing in her mind what she was going to do to this puny human once she got her hands on him. Castration to start with, and then she would get vicious.

Even though there was no light in the room, Laura-Luss' demon eyes allowed her to see perfectly in the dark. There was not much to see. The room was entirely made of concrete with only a heavy wooden door to break the monotony of the walls. There was no furniture, no boxes, not even a carpet anywhere in this place. Probably a storage room of some sort was her thought, one that was seldom used.

Checking her own internal clock, she realized that almost two hours had passed. It was almost time for her supposed tryst with Tom. If they knew she was an impostor, they knew that Tom was also, which meant he was in trouble. Although she felt that Tom could handle just about anything human, her guts told her that there was a demon involved somewhere. She was sure she remembered the slight smell of demon when she entered the place, but it had been so faint, she wasn't sure at the time whether it had just been a passing creature or one who worked here. Now she was pretty sure it was the latter. She had to get to Tom before anything happened to him, or her boss would kill her. Besides, Tom was cute for a human.

Now to figure a way out of here. She could always pop herself back to Hell, but occasionally the time differential between Earth and Hell was all mixed up, and she could end up arriving too late. Anyway, going back to Hell would announce her presence there to those she might not want to have that kind of information. No, it had to be out of this room and building while staying on this level of existence.

If she tried to blast down the door, her cover would be exposed, as well as announcing to every demon within a hundred miles that she was there. Phasing through the door presented its own set of problems. How far to phase through, how thick was the door, and exactly what was on the other side? If only the door had a window. Or even a peephole like Tom's apartment. Then she could see where to shift to. Then it hit her. She only had to use a bit of her powers to cut a small hole in the door. Then she could teleport herself to the other side.

Looking around, she located a section of the concrete wall that was loose. Pulling on it with only the minimum of demon strength, she was able to get a section of the concrete that was sharp and long enough to do the job. Returning to the door, she drove it through the panel and did a lateral cut before removing it. Looking through the small hole, she was able to see to the opposite wall. More than enough to teleport. Using her senses, she could detect no trace of life around or near the door. However, being afraid there might be cameras or motion detectors, she only partially phased herself. That way she could check around without having her full physical presence in a detectable position. A quick scan assured her that all was clear, and she completed her teleportation. So far, so good. Still, she could not leave this building until she knew exactly where she was. That meant using normal human methods of subterfuge and mobility. How mundane.

Sensing outwards, Laura-Luss realized that she was in the basement, probably two levels below the reception area, assuming she was in the same building. Still taking a chance with slight use of demon powers, she located the stairway behind a steel door at the end of the corridor. Thankfully, this door had a glass mesh window, and Laura-Luss was able to check for detectors and cameras before proceeding. Apparently, the owners here only worried about the upper levels when it came to security. Sure enough, after climbing two floors, she came to the main level and, looking through the door's window, was able to see enough of the lobby to confirm that she was indeed still in the same building.

Figuring that surprise was the best course, Laura-Luss opened the door, entered the lobby area, and walked out the front doors without so much as a word to the receptionist. Let them puzzle out how she'd escaped. By the time they could conclude that she was anything but a human female, the case would long be wrapped up—she hoped.

Now, what was the fastest way to get to the rendezvous hotel without telegraphing her arrival to every demon in town? Any type of human transport would take too long. Teleporting from corner to corner would run the risk of exposure; besides which, continuous use of her powers, even the smaller amounts used for teleporting, would give away her presence to most demons, and definitely would be something that Asmodeus would sense. Just then, she spotted a crow. There was the answer. Talking to a crow only used minimal power. Calling the crow to her, Laura-Luss allowed her body to shrink to thumb size, again small use of her powers, made the crow grab her in its claws, and directed it to where she needed to be. As the crow flies, she thought, allowing herself to enjoy the little joke, it was only a short trip.

"This trying to hide my powers is surely causing me to be imaginative," she said aloud. "The next thing you know, I'll be stooping to take a bus." The crow turned its head slightly in Laura-Luss' direction and gave her a wink. Damn those crows, she forgot they could understand demon talk.

It was an enjoyable flight with the wind rushing through her hair and the last traces of the sunset casting a red glow, making it almost feel like home. Except, of course, the flying part. You couldn't fly well in Hell.

Ten minutes later found them slowly spiraling downwards towards the hotel where Tom should be. Checking her internal clock, she realized that about now, Tom should be entering the hotel. But knowing Tom, he was probably early, so she had better not waste any time. Laura-Luss extended her senses as far as she could, trying to feel for Asmodeus. If he were here, she wanted to be prepared. She did not sense him but did feel that there was a lesser demon nearby. Being careful not to call attention to herself, she worked her senses around this demon's emotional field to see if she could find a trace of Asmodeus on him. Sure enough, she could feel Asmodeus' presence linked to this demon. This greatly complicated things. Now she had to try to disable the demon without attracting Asmodeus' attention. She did not want Asmodeus to know that a demon was on his trail this early in the search. Even though he would be alert to the possibility, one of the advantages they felt they had now was that he did not know how close they were.

Laura-Luss had the crow drop her on the ledge outside of a fourth-floor hall window. Because of the wind, it took more strength than she had expected to hold on to the ledge without being blown off. She did not want to lose time by having to re-climb the wall. If she had known exactly where room 425 was from the outside, she would have landed on that balcony and could have entered the room right away. Instead, she phased through the window and walked the halls until she found the right room.

"Damn, no peephole," she muttered to herself. However, looking up, she saw a small vent well above the door. Crawling up the wall, another demon trait that used little or no power, she reached the vent and was able to get a good look at what was going on inside.

What she saw was Tom facing three figures. At first, she could not make them all out. She saw what appeared to be the leader of the group, talking easily and with no weapon in his hand. Next to him was a regular hired thug, holding a machine gun of some sort. Nothing that Tom could not handle, she felt. Then her attention shifted to the third figure standing in the shadows. Before she could study this one, she saw Tom act, pulling a pistol out of his pant leg and shooting the thug in the shoulder. Movement from the shadowy part of the room brought her gaze back that way as the third figure launched itself at Tom with the speed that only a demon could have.

Not taking the time to think, Laura-Luss phased into the room and, with an almost primitive roar, grabbed the demon just as it was landing on Tom, pulling it away before it could use its claws to eviscerate him, and swinging it against the wall over and over until there was nothing left but a bloody pulp.

Tom was lying on the floor watching in amazement, but not so the last human standing. He had pulled out a gun and was aiming at Laura-Luss' head. Seeing the motion out of the corner of his eye, Tom raised the Browning still in his hand and shot the thug in the knee, the only part of his body he could count on hitting from this angle. Thankfully, it was enough as it caused the man to collapse just as he got his shot off. The bullet passed by Laura-Luss with only inches to spare. Tom wasn't sure if it would have killed her or not, but with her attention on the demon and not on her phasing abilities, he had no way of knowing what the result would be.

The bullet smashing into the wall near her head caused Laura-Luss to turn, where she saw their assailant collapsing to the ground and smoke coming from Tom's gun. That bullet entering her head, with her attention on the demon, could have been quite disconcerting, as it probably would have sent her back to Hell, a failure that would have been worse than death. Returning her attention to the demon at hand, she saw that there was very little left of it. Being a minor demon, she couldn't be sure whether it had returned to Hell or been destroyed permanently. Either one had its own set of consequences. Still, the satisfaction she got from pummelling it to oblivion was worth whatever price she would have to pay. Besides, he was serving Asmodeus, and the devil should not punish her for doing her job.

"Took you long enough to get here," were the first words out of Tom's mouth, and he immediately regretted them. She had, after all, just saved his life.

"Well, if you weren't always in such an all-fired rush to be early, we would have arrived at the same time," Laura-Luss snapped back. "Anyway, I was too busy escaping from a concrete room and trying to get over here as fast as possible to save your sorry ass, and all this while trying not to overly use my powers and call attention to us. Protecting you is going to be the end of me, I am sure. Don't you know that demons can kill you?"

Looking up into her face and seeing some caring in it made him forget for a moment that she, too, was a demon. "I am sorry, Laura-Luss, you are right. Thanks for saving my bacon there. I guess the surprise of almost getting ripped to pieces got the better of me."

"And I guess I should thank you, too. A shot in the head at that point would have messed up my stay on Earth, and that would have been quite the pain, in many ways."

"Well, anyway, good job, Laura-Luss. Maybe having you on this case will have some advantages after all."

Being complimented like this made her feel good inside, but realizing that she was blushing from it, and not liking the feeling, she decided to turn the tables on Tom. As she reached over to help him up, she changed her attire to something more befitting what she was supposed to be here, and a sleek suit became fishnet stockings and a diaphanous black bra and panties.

"Since we're already here, and you did pay for my services after all, why should we let such an opportunity pass?"

Pushing her hand away, Tom jumped up and turned his back. "Why must you act this way all the time? Just as I start to think of you as a partner, you have to pull this demon nymphet shit. I have told you before that if you need to satisfy yourself, there are plenty of men, I am sure, who would line up for it. I am not one of them!"

Turning even redder, this time in anger, Laura-Luss softly said, "This is the thanks I get for offering you the time of your life. I guess you must truly be asexual or maybe just self-sexual."

Before Tom could answer to this, there was a loud moan from the guy with the shattered kneecap, followed by pain-ridden words, "Could you guys have your lovers' quarrel some other time? I'm in agony here. Get me an ambulance or something."

"Do you truly think we have any intention of helping you vermin, or of even letting you live?" said Laura-Luss as she made her way over to the injured guy.

Seeing an opportunity to exploit the good guy/bad guy scenario and hoping that Laura-Luss would pick up on it, Tom said, "Back off, demoness, and let Curly alone. I prefer not to have a human hurt by one of you hellspawn."

Turning back to Tom, Laura-Luss was about to give him a piece of her mind when she caught his wink. One thing the demoness wasn't was stupid. She immediately grasped Tom's intentions and thought it might be just the way to play it out.

"You humans. Just because he is of the same existence as you doesn't mean he deserves your protection. He works for a demon. That makes him vermin and part of my domain. And I have some pretty powerful desires right now, desires along the lines of what I just did to that demon over there. Only much slower so he can feel the agony for a long time until I finally decide to send him on his way to hell."

"Well, your desires are not an issue here, and just remember that your orders are to obey me. Now, be a good demoness and go sit down while I tend to Curly."

Turning to Tom with steam coming out of her ears, Laura-Luss said, "My orders are only to obey you as to matters with this case and only for as long as this case goes on. Remember, at the end of this, your flesh might become my possession." But before turning away from Tom, she gave him a wink and proceeded into the larger part of the room, where she sat on the end of the bed.

Breathing a large internal sigh of relief, Tom walked over to their prisoner and knelt beside him.

"Okay, instead of me calling you Curly all the time, why don't you start by telling me your name?"

Through pain-clenched teeth, Curly responded by saying, "Why don't I start by telling you to fuck off?"

"Alas, I am trying to be friendly to you, and you act like this. Maybe my demoness friend has the right idea. Maybe you have already sold your soul and truly belong in her domain. Maybe I should just let her have you."

Tom stood and managed to take one step before the guy, in a tremulous voice, said, "Please no, for the love of God, you can't possibly do that. I have seen what these creatures can do to us. How can you allow something like that to happen to a fellow man?"

"Well, wasn't that what you planned on doing to me?" Tom demanded.

"Look, I'm sorry. It wasn't supposed to come to this. My name is Dick Payton. Please, can you get me something for this pain?"

"I tell you what. You give me the answers I want, and I will see to it that you are taken care of. Now, does that sound like a good deal or what?"

"And if I say no?"

Tom just turned his head to look at Laura-Luss, and the prisoner turned even paler than he'd been.

"Okay, I get the message. But please do something for the pain. I can hardly think."

Walking over to the bed, Tom spotted what he expected: a small bar where the booze was automatically added to your credit card. Pouring a large shot of the cheapest whiskey there, Tom brought it over to Dick and watched as he downed it in a single gulp. After a few moments, he visibly relaxed. Taking a look at the other thug and seeing him still motionless, Tom signalled for Laura-Luss to keep an eye on him so he could devote his full attention to the matter at hand.

"Now, Dick, I have helped you, and I am protecting you. What are you going to offer me in return? It had better be worth me putting my neck on the line with a demoness, or I just might let her have you after all."

"Look, the truth is I don't know much. Wait, don't get up, please. I will tell you what I do know. I started working for this guy about three months ago. His name is Vince Faustelli. He is a local crime lord or something. Runs a lot of the prostitution and gambling that goes on around here. Supposedly, he came out of nowhere about a year ago. Nobody seems to know where from, only that he came with lots of money and some special muscle. It didn't take him long to take charge. One or two demonstrations of what his muscle could do to a person were enough to convince anyone not to cross him. I just decided to work the lucrative side of the street.

"A couple of hours ago, I got a call. Some fuzz had decided to investigate one of his establishments. Since the girl was already in one of our places, it was easy to get her out of the way with a bit of spray chloroform. God had I known she was a demon, I would have let the muscle handle her. As it was, they had planned on keeping her around for a while to offer to some of their clientele. Boy, would they have been surprised.

"Anyway, we set up the room for you here, and my job was to find out what you knew and either buy you or, if that didn't work, get rid of you. The muscle was not my idea. I prefer something clean and simple. A bullet to the head if you don't accept the deal, a wad of cash if you do. Honestly, that is all I know. I never had intentions of letting the demon have you. It all just happened so fast. Damn, you were quick with that gun. And all those shots to the demon's head—and it did not even affect it. God, I must have been dumb, after seeing that, to think that my lone bullet could have stopped your demoness."

"What does this Vince Faustelli look like?"

"I never met the head honcho. I was always hired by phone or through the brothel. But gossip says he has a large manor up in Montreal, Canada, and only visits here occasionally. I can tell you, though, that Madame Vanessa, who oversees the particular brothel that you visited today, has met him and might be able to tell you more."

Getting up and walking towards Laura-Luss, Tom was trying to figure out a way to manage the situation without allowing the two thugs to die while not letting them get information to their boss and eventually to Asmodeus, when he heard the prisoner gasp in fright. In the blink of an eye, Laura-Luss was standing over Curly, demon eyes flashing bright green.

"Laura-Luss, no, I gave my word."

"But I didn't," was the response as she bent over the prisoner and seemed to kiss him. His body went limp like a piece of spaghetti.

"What have you done to him?" shouted Tom.

"Oh, no need to worry, I didn't kill this human, as much as he deserves it. What I did do, though, works better if they are pretty well scared shitless. He will probably regain consciousness in a couple of hours, still in pain but with no memory of what happened from about the time you shot the other thug. He won't remember me, and he won't remember that he squealed like a pig. The amount of demon power I had to use was minimal, so by the time he's discovered, it should have dissipated. It's a bit of a chance, but less risky than hoping he doesn't talk. Of course, killing him would have been easier, but then I would not have heard the end of your harping about it."

Not exactly mollified by her last sentence, but still pleased with the outcome, Tom asked the question foremost in his mind. "What about the demon you killed? Won't they find it strange that a human was able to handle a demon like that?"

Laura-Luss pointed to the wall where the demon had been destroyed, and all Tom could see was a hole. There was no trace of the demon.

"As you can see, there are no demon remains here. About now, his demon essence is somewhere in the lower levels of Hell. The odds of Asmodeus learning about this are slim to none, as I am sure my boss will not release that kind of information. And the lesser demons are notorious for wandering off in the middle of a job if something else catches their attention. No, I doubt that Asmodeus will find anything here to alarm him."

"Well, thank God for small blessings. Now I think it is time for us to pay a little visit to Madame Vanessa. I've always wanted to meet a real madame."

CHAPTER 8

Tracing down the whereabouts of Madame Vanessa was easier than Tom would have thought. One call to the office provided all the information he needed. The madame had used the services of P.I. International on several occasions. Mostly, it was to find various employees who had run off with money from the till, but once she had used the agency to track down a client who had kidnapped one of her girls. The police had not been much help. Since it was only a prostitute that had been kidnapped, they did not want to waste their resources on such as that. It did appear that Madame Vanessa cared about her girls. Unfortunately, the girl was dead when the P.I. detective found her, but her murderer was brought to justice because of his work, and the madame had been pleased with the results, even paying a bonus.

Her business may have been centered in New York, but the madame preferred to reside away from the hustle and bustle of the big city. Their trip took them to Rockaway, New Jersey, an area of larger homes and estates, where very few properties sold under the three-million-dollar range. The madame's house proved to be no exception, except maybe it could be called one of the more prestigious residences.

Nestled at the back of a two-acre lot, the home looked more like a manor from *Gone with the Wind*. The landscaping was marvellous with a variety of rose bushes, sycamores, and various other flowering bushes, as well as a large fountain that fed a fishpond. As they passed the water, Tom could see large goldfish as well as a few other types, which he could not quite make out. Already parked in the grand circular driveway were a couple of limousines, a Ferrari, an Acura, and, of all things, a Volkswagen Beetle.

Discussing how to approach Madame Vanessa, the pitch they decided on was simplistic and something that would appeal to the madame's caring side. Laura-Luss would play the part of a former call girl looking for the guy who had beaten her up and left her for dead. Using her shape-shifting ability, she even made a scar appear on her throat as though the assailant had slit her open in the final coup de grâce. Tom, of course, would just be himself, a detective from P.I. International, the firm that Madame Vanessa herself used.

Arranging the appointment had been a simple matter, and when they rang the doorbell, the butler had been told to expect them, as they did not even have to introduce themselves. He greeted them by name and led them into a den-slash-studio-slash-library. If they'd been in awe at the splendor of the entrance with its high ceiling, cathedral chandelier, and circular staircase, then the room they now found themselves in knocked their socks off.

The size of a small public library, almost every bit of wall space was occupied by shelves full of books. Anything from encyclopedias to romance novels, from science journals to best sellers, lined the shelves. The front of the room was a solarium, allowing plenty of the afternoon sunshine to brighten the place, as well as several plants to give the room atmosphere. With its back to the solarium was an imposing, solid walnut desk that must have weighed a few hundred pounds, with a high-back beige leather armchair currently facing outwards, and in front of the desk, two smaller beige armchairs. As they entered the room, the main chair swiveled around, and the room's only occupant stood to greet them.

Madame Vanessa was not in the least what Tom had expected. Very tall and elegant, she could easily have been on the cover of any high-fashion magazine. She had a model's beauty and carriage, and had Tom not been told ahead of time, there was no way he would have thought of her as being fifty years old. He also would never have pictured her as the head of one of the largest brothels in the state.

"Please come in and be seated. Gaston will be here shortly with some refreshments." Her voice was melodious and quite easy to listen to, almost hypnotic. Seeing the effect it had on Tom, Laura-Luss gave him a not-very-discreet poke in the ribs, being a little upset that this woman could have more of an effect on him than she could.

Trying to hide that her jolt to his ribs had been quite painful, Tom walked over to Madame Vanessa and shook her hand, introducing himself, and of course, his client, Tess Watson.

"We're sorry to disturb you with this type of situation, Madame Vanessa, especially on such a lovely day. I would have gone into detail on the phone, but felt this is the sort of thing that should be discussed in person."

"Nonsense. Whenever the P.I. firm wants my help, I am glad to be of assistance. It has mostly been the opposite, with my coming to you. Now, no further business until the drinks have arrived. I was not sure what your preference would be, but Gaston is coming with tea, coffee, soft drinks, and juice if that is more to your taste. You will not find any alcoholic beverages here. It is one vice I frown upon, I'm afraid.

This statement startled Tom. Who would have thought that the person who was the head of one of the largest prostitution rings in the state would find the consumption of alcohol to be such a moral issue? Still, she was a client of his firm, and he had a case to work on, so such things just had to be accepted and passed over.

"You have a marvelous place here, Madame Vanessa," commented Laura-Luss. "The grounds are absolutely beautiful. And the décor is marvelous. I bet you picked it all out yourself."

Once again, Laura-Luss startled Tom with her ability to come out with the one thing that would turn the client's attention favorably towards her. Then again, demons had to learn more than one way to ensnare a human. It was obvious that this was working on the madame.

"Please just call me Vanessa, both of you. And I will call you Tom and you Tess. I find that calling people by their first name makes things more intimate and tends to allow people to be more honest with each other and with themselves. I like this Tom and Tess thing. It has symmetry to it. I love it when there is that cosmic connection.

Yes, I did do all the decorating myself. Most decorators just don't seem to see the flow of things. They have to have vivid contrasts and splashes of this and flares of that. Everything seems to collide together in a chaotic mess with them. I like things to come together as if they were meant to be that way, with shapes, colors, and even aromas blending in harmony. But alas, it is not easy to achieve the right atmosphere. I have had to travel to many different parts of the world to find all the items I needed to arrive at what I now have."

"I did notice, though, that your choice of books happens to be of a more eclectic mix."

"How very observant of you, Tom. That is the one part of life where chaos must rule, because literature contains all the real truth of man, and mankind is chaos personified. We love, we hate, we glorify, we vilify, we build, and we destroy, sometimes all in the same five-minute span. These books hold all of man's emotions, desires, successes, and failures within their covered jackets. I feel that if one could come to read every book ever written, one would come to truly know human nature, and maybe even the secret of life itself."

"That is quite the contention, Vanessa. How close are you to achieving it?"

Her light laugh was like the tinkling of a wind chime. "Come now, dear Tess, do you believe that it is possible to read every book ever written in one lifetime? That is the beauty of it. No matter how hard we would strive to do just that, we could never catch up to what is written in one year, let alone all of history. No, life will remain a secret to man. I just try to catch a glimpse of it now and then."

Before either could respond to this, Gaston entered the room with another servant in tow, both carrying large trays. Gaston's tray contained a pot of tea, a pot of coffee, cups, sweeteners, and cream. The other tray contained glasses, soda, and fruit juices as well as various pastries. Pulling out some stands from behind one of the shelves, the servants placed their trays next to Vanessa's desk and left the room as silently as they had entered it.

"I do prefer to personally serve my guest their beverages. Now, what would you two like?"

Tom chose coffee, and Laura-Luss and Vanessa both had tea. For the moment, the pastries were left aside. Taking in the rest of the room as the madame poured the drinks, Tom noticed a few objects he had missed at first glance. Hanging above a few of the shelving units were various objets d'arts from different parts of the world. He saw Egyptian sculptures, African carvings, Mexican masks, and even a couple of paintings that were definitely from the Renaissance Period, whether originals or copies, Tom was not enough of an art connoisseur to tell.

"Now that we are comfortable, we can discuss what you came here for. I am assuming that what I can help you with has to do with my profession. Which, of course, is making people happy."

"Yes, Madame, sorry, Vanessa. My client had worked in a similar profession for several years. She did quite well and had a thriving business out west. Like you, she kept her staff happy and protected them well. In the last couple of years, she rarely did any servicing herself and never took on any new clients personally. She made one exception and well—"

"The son of a bitch cut me up good and left me for dead," interrupted Laura-Luss. "It is the only time I so misjudged an individual, and it cost me. Two months in intensive care, five different plastic surgery operations, and many months later, it took before I could even show my face in public again. I kept one scar that I would not let the doctors cover up. Call it a mark of war to remind me what can happen when you let your guard down, as well as a reminder to keep me on the hunt until I catch this guy and make him pay for what he did." Laura-Luss then removed the scarf, hiding the supposed scars left when her make-believe assailant had slit her throat.

"I know to what extent you have gone in the past to bring to justice those who assaulted your girls, Vanessa. All my client wants is the same type of justice for her."

"I can well understand how you feel, and of course, I would be glad to oblige, but I just don't see how I can be of help."

"We had traced the assailant to New York a few weeks ago and then caught a break. His name came up in a routine police investigation. Of course, you know the availability we have to those files. Even though we were not directly connected to the case, the police allowed us to interrogate the prisoner. Although he said he had never met the guy, he was hired by phone, he was told the guy's name, and it came up in conversation that he was associated with you."

"Well, unfortunately, a name can be changed. Tell me what the gentleman looks like, and I will be glad to tell you if I know him."

"As funny as it may sound, I never saw him directly," Laura-Luss interrupted. "He had set up the appointment by phone after mentioning the name of someone I knew well. When I arrived at the hotel room, he grabbed me from behind, tied and blindfolded me, and after taping my mouth shut, proceeded to rape and torture me. He ended by slitting my throat. The only reason I am alive is because of an accident I had many years ago that required surgery on my neck. When he cut through that old scar tissue, it bled profusely for a few minutes. He thought he had cut through the main artery and just left me to bleed to death. No, I never saw his face, but he was arrogant enough to tell me his name. I guess he figured I would not live to tell anyone. His name is Vince Faustelli."

"Oh damn!" The first time Vanessa had said anything that was not elegant was a profanity that seemed exceedingly strange coming from that persona.

"I gather you know him?" prompted Tom.

"Yes, I do—or rather did. Shit, I should have gone with my original gut feelings." Standing, turning away, and taking a deep breath, Vanessa stayed facing out the window for a few moments. Tom and Laura-Luss kept their silence.

Finally, she returned to her chair, the cool and elegant lady once again.

"He first came to New York about a year ago. Supposedly from the West Coast. Said he wanted to open a small operation, mostly massage parlors and gambling halls, and wanted to work with me rather than against me. The deal he offered was that he would stay away from the type of clientele that I normally handle, and in return, I would introduce him to some of my, shall we say, legal contacts. I went along with the deal, provided that there would be no drugs and no killing involved. Overall, the deal worked out well. Until recently. Suddenly, he had a new partner. I met this new partner once. There was something there that I just could not put my finger on, but he felt, I don't know, evil. Yes, that would be the word. Evil with a capital E.

"Well, I called Vince the other night and told him the deal was off. He just laughed and said he no longer needed me. He then said he was heading back to his home in Montreal for a few weeks, but when he returned, he would be making a new deal with me, and if I did not accept it, he had some new friends who would help persuade me that it would be in my best interests to accept. That is why all the extra security. You probably didn't notice, but there are about fifty security officers on the premises at any one time. I don't think he would dare to try anything now."

"To tell you the truth, Vanessa, I would highly recommend you take a leave of absence for the next while," Tom responded. "This extra help he has is, shall we say, highly specialized and could probably take out most of your security force without much problem. Still, we may be able to prevent that. I have hired a few specialized individuals myself and hope to put a stop to Mr. Faustelli's activities. What I need from you is an address where to find him, and a physical description."

"That is simple enough. He owns a small manor on the waterfront in Montreal. Technically, it is just off Montreal Island, but still part of the city. A small island called Île Bizard. Here is his address," she added, handing Tom a piece of paper. "Also, I have here a glass which Mr. Faustelli drank from. I had planned on running it for fingerprints to find out more about him, but I never got around to hiring you guys to check him out. A bad decision in hindsight. He stands about five nine, weighs, I guess, about one-seventy-five, has jet black hair, quite greasy looking, eyes so dark they appear almost black, a cleft chin, a pointy nose, and must wear a gallon of Aqua Velva cologne or something like it. Are you serious about my taking a vacation at this time?"

"Vanessa, our company has never steered you wrong before. This partner of Faustelli is bad news if it is who I think it is."

"And that is—?"

"Someone you are better off not knowing about," said Laura-Luss. "He is a distant relative of mine and would stop at nothing to get what he wants."

"So, what does he want?"

"Absolute power," Laura-Luss answered, causing Tom to snap his eyes in her direction.

CHAPTER 9

"Okay, all the arrangements are made," Amy told Tom as he walked into the office. Your flight leaves just after midnight tonight. You will arrive at Pierre Elliot Trudeau Airport in Montreal at about 1:30. I have the two of you booked into the Airport Hilton hotel for the night, separate rooms, of course, and a rental car will be ready first thing in the morning. In this file is the address of our local office on Sherbrooke Street, along with the phone number and contact person, should you need it. Remember, it is a different culture there. I am not sure of our office's relationship with the local law, but should you get into any trouble, you would be better off having one of our local people handle it, as a basic working knowledge of French might be required.

"Also note that in the file I have included maps and points of interest. Just in case you have a few hours to kill between appointments. Montreal is a beautiful city, and it would be a shame to let the opportunity pass."

"Thank you, Amy, this will do fine. Have you come up with anything on Vince Faustelli?"

"No, it is almost like this guy doesn't exist. Not even so much as a driver's license. We even Googled him and found nothing. Are you sure this is a real name?"

"I'm not sure of anything, Amy. Most likely, it's an alias. Since the guy tosses around the name like he were Donald Trump or something, he's not worried about anyone tracking him down. I assume that you checked all records for a Faustelli in Canada. Did anything come back for that property in Île Bizard?"

"Yes, it is registered to Ms. Pauline Welsley. Again, other than the registration of the house, there is no other record for her. Not even a driver's license. She bought the house a year ago and paid cash. Well, it was a bank draft drawn from a bank here in New York. Money had been transferred there from offshore just before the transaction. And that is where the trail dies."

"I can't say that I'm surprised. Any other messages by the way?"

"Yes. Your client said to pass on to you something you would find of interest. Here it is, and I quote 'One of my little helpers just showed up. Apparently, you sent him home. I will see to it that he remains occupied and unavailable for the duration.' Mean anything to you?"

"Yes, it does, and don't bother asking for an explanation. I don't think I could give you one if I tried."

"Very well. Mr. Potenkins wishes to inform you that all company resources are at your disposal. The Montreal office has been ordered to cooperate with you in any way you require. Quite the open checkbook, I must say."

"Well, knowing who the client is, I can just assume what the penalty would be if there was any effort lacking in this case."

"Tom, you could not even begin to imagine."

"Well, thanks again, Amy, and thanks for coming in early to take care of this stuff. Now I'd better get my temporary sidekick and get going. Have things to do before we board that flight."

"You are quite welcome, Mr. Wilkins."

Picking up the change in the tone of the conversation, he turned to see Laura-Luss walking towards him.

"Oh, speak of the devil, and who appears."

"You are quite the comedian, Tom, but if only speaking about him were enough to call him, then he would be everywhere, now wouldn't he? As you are quite aware, to make him appear, you must call him by his true name and truly want him to come. Now I would suggest we leave here. You had said you have a couple of stops to make before we head to the airport. I assume one is your apartment to pack, but you have not yet told me the other."

"No, I haven't, now have I," said Tom as he picked up the file and walked to the front door.

Tom refused to say anything further after they got into the car, other than telling Laura-Luss, when she pushed to know where they were going, that she would see. Once she realized Tom was not going to answer her, she sat silently and pouted. A short while later they neared a church.

When Tom pulled up in front of the stone structure, Laura-Luss started laughing.

"Do you think anyone here can be of assistance to us?"

"Yes, actually, I do. My brother happens to be the parish priest. He's been quite helpful till now, and I think it's time for him to meet you."

"Then you had better have him come to the car, and maybe we can go for a coffee somewhere. In case you forgot, I am a demon. I can't even step on church property without feeling great discomfort, and should I try to enter a church, well, there would be hell and heaven to pay for that, besides which I could quite possibly be destroyed."

"Trust me, my dear, we have all this covered. Here's my brother now."

Watching the priest come down the walk, Laura-Luss could see the distinct family resemblance. Although Tom was taller and spent more time in the gym, the priest walking towards them was not a slovenly man. He moved with the grace and ease of an athlete. His brown hair was much lighter than Tom's black, and his face was slightly rounder, less chiseled. As well, he had dark brown eyes compared to Tom's blue-green. Still, having met Tom, it was easy to place John as his brother.

"You can get out of the car, Laura-Luss. He won't hurt you."

"No, but I might cause him harm just by my presence. I don't think my master would be pleased if I hurt the brother of the detective he hired."

"There is no need to fear that," said the priest as he opened her door. "Precautions have been taken." Then looking over her at his brother, John added, "It is as I said, Tom. She has human and demon blood."

Feeling unusually comforted by this priest, Laura-Luss was not even able to come up with one of her normally sarcastic and caustic remarks. However, she did take a step back when he offered to shake her hand.

"It's okay, Ms. Laura-Luss. My touch at this time won't harm either of us. I did make special preparations to allow this meeting. Now, if you can find it in you to trust a priest, or at least to take my word at face value, then start by taking my hand, and we can go on from there."

Tentatively at first, then with determination not to look like she was fearful, Laura-Luss reached for John's hand and clasped it in a firm handshake. To her surprise, nothing happened, other than a comforting feeling of meeting someone interesting for the first time.

"How …?"

"It turned out to be easier than I had originally thought it would be. First, I had to prepare myself. Now you must remember that Jesus met with sinners all the time, and as well, what is not mentioned in the Bible, he met with the occasional demon that he was not trying to exorcise. Also, as you are most likely aware, there have been high-level meetings between representatives of your boss and people from the Vatican many times over the centuries. They did have to make sure that everyone was protected.

"I started by going through a ritual of self-cleansing. Then there is a ceremony that allows me to put a sort of barrier, whereby I can touch a demon, or a person of extreme evil origins, without the taint of his evil passing to me, nor my godliness affecting him, her, or it adversely. After all, we had to be able to walk amongst the pagans and unbelievers without harming them; at least that was what was believed in the early and mid centuries of Christianity. That has been the problem of all religions: what becomes strongly believed in eventually becomes fact. In this case, it does allow us to do good work in difficult situations."

"That answers the physical contact, but how is it going to get me into your church?"

"Because I was able to shake your hand without any discomfort whatsoever, it tells me that you are not here to harm any of my brethren. It makes it possible to do a small ceremony that once again erects a barrier, call it maybe a neutral zone, where good and evil can intermingle, just so long as neither party intends harm to the other at that time."

"How long is this going to take, brother? We must be at the airport in a few hours," Tom asked from the other side of the car.

"I knew that before I invited you over. The ceremony is very quick and easy. Do you recognize this?" asked John, turning to Laura-Luss and producing a cross.

"Isn't that a cross of the convention? But how did you get one?"

"Very good. Yes, that is exactly what it is. You see, I worked in the Vatican for several years and was privy to a lot that transpired there. Knowing my brother's penchant for getting into trouble, and seeing a side of the church that few get to see, I decided to stock up, with permission of the church, of course, on several items that were available to me."

Turning to his brother, he said, "Let me explain this item to you, Tom."

Tom nodded. Eying the item with interest.

"Because of the need to meet from time to time," John began, "the bureaucracies of Heaven and Hell had to devise a way to do this. Again, lore comes into play. We all know that a properly blessed cross affects demons in unpleasant ways. Eventually, an upside-down cross came to represent the Anti-Christ, or devil if you will. One day, a clerk in the Vatican concluded that for evil and good to meet halfway, the main symbol of the two should also meet halfway. Once a proper blessing and anti-blessing could be devised, it was bestowed upon a number of these crosses at a special convention held in the late 5th century. That is why," he concluded, holding the item up between them, "it came to be called the Convention Cross."

Tom considered for a moment, then asked, "If you know all this, maybe you can tell me the true name of the devil so I can call him when I need him to pick up the package?"

"Sorry Tom, no can do. You cannot be told the name; you have to discover it on your own for it to work. I can give you one little hint, though. Go back to reading your Bible, especially the Old Testament. Then think of how Jesus came to us. That is all I can tell you."

Tom sighed but said nothing more as John redirected his attention to the demoness.

"Now, Laura-Luss, do you know how the ritual goes with this?"

"For the most part. I believe I must swear on all that is good and evil not to break the codes of the convention with the pain of ultimate sacrifice should I cause any harm under this roof, nor use access to this place to plot future harm. Then you must do the same, but about me instead of the place. Oh, and we must both do it simultaneously while holding the Convention Cross. Is that correct?"

"You were right, brother, she is smart and well-versed."

"You said that?" asked Laura-Luss, turning to Tom.

"Well, not exactly," he replied. "I added onto that—when you want to be."

"Now, Tom, there's no need for that," said John. "We must all work together here, so at least let us do it in a civilized manner. After all, if a demoness can be civilized, the least my brother can do is act the same way. Let us proceed," he said, turning to Laura-Luss and offering her his arm, leaving Tom standing there with his mouth open, staring at his brother.

John led them to a small gate on the side grounds of the church, where visibility from the street was limited. Here, they were able to conduct the ritual quickly and in privacy. They then proceeded onto church grounds, Laura-Luss with some trepidation. However, since she felt no discomfort on the church grounds, she continued with more confidence to the side entrance of the church itself, usually reserved for members of the clergy when they wanted to leave for a few hours of relaxation.

A matter of moments later found them all seated in the same room and at the same set of chairs where John and Tom had first discussed this case, such a short time earlier. If Laura-Luss was at all discomfited by being in the church, she wasn't showing it. Nor did John seem the least bit unnerved by having a demon under the same roof where he gave communion. They gave the appearance of being former opponents who had eventually become good friends.

"It is not often I come across a priest who is as well-informed in worldly matters as you are, Father John. It is a pleasure to make your acquaintance. Still, I do not see the need for this meeting in the first place."

"Ms. Laura-Luss, please call me John. The actual reason is twofold. First, I want to do what I can to protect my baby brother. Knowing what I know about our planes of existence, and knowing how easily my brother attracts trouble, I wanted to meet with you and make sure the whole thing was not just some elaborate plot by your master to trick or trap my brother's soul.

"Secondly, I wanted to make you feel comfortable with me, as I do intend to help my brother with this case. Since that also means working with you, I think we must somehow come to a working relationship with a certain degree of trust. There have been times in the past when the Church and the minions of the Underworld had to work together for a common goal. This is one of those times. I would also like to know, of course, what your intentions are with my brother. He is a pain in the ass at times, I know, but he is the only brother I have, and I would like to keep him around for a while longer, thank you."

"Well, thank you, brother, for those heartwarming words and desire to protect me, but I do quite a good job of taking care of myself," Tom declared, with some heat.

"He is kind of cute when he gets angry, isn't he?" said Laura-Luss, facing John. "If he weren't so human, I might even become attached to him. No, John, as long as your brother can learn to behave himself, I have no plans to harm him in any way. However, you should try to teach him some manners and keep his hormones in check. And also explain to him that it is not wise to try to get a demon mad."

"Listen, demoness, it is you who keeps coming on to me, not the other way around. I would sooner sleep with a rattlesnake."

"That could quite easily be arranged."

"Now, now, Tom, remember I told you to be civilized," interrupted John before this could turn into a shouting match. "Don't worry, Laura-Luss, I will teach my brother the proper way to treat those from your world, and you can rest assured that from now on, he will treat you with the respect you deserve."

John looked from one to the other, confirming acceptance of the truce.

"Okay, now that that's all settled, maybe you two can fill me in on the case to date. Since my point of view is different from both of yours, I might be able to add something, or catch onto something you two missed."

The next fifteen minutes were spent discussing the case over coffee. John was particularly interested in the confrontation in the motel room with the demon and the human helpers. He had both of them relate the incident from their perspective, all the while studying them closely. He picked up on something that worried him, but felt it was not the time or place to discuss it openly.

"What can you tell me about Vince Faustelli?"

"Not much really, Tom replied. "I did a background check on him using both regular computer searches and even obtaining access to FBI and NSA files. He appeared out of nowhere about a year ago, leaves no fingerprints, and seems to hate physical contact. Oh yeah, and apparently, he wears a lot of cheap cologne. Average build, black hair, and eyes. That's the basics."

After a few moments' consideration, John said, "I would venture a guess that you are dealing with a golem."

"Damn," cursed Laura-Luss. "It all makes sense now. I don't know why I didn't see that."

"What in hell is a golem? And don't tell me it is a character from Lord of the Rings."

"No, brother, it is not. The original golem is from Judaic history. Or legends or myths, if you prefer. It is the story of a rabbi who watched the people of his city work hard all day and into the evening with little time for rest or play. He decided to do something to help. Finding an ancient holy book, the Cabbala, he discovered how to create a creature out of mud. This creature could be trained to do all human jobs. This rabbi had him guarding the city, working farms, even playing with and watching the children. The golem became so human-like that he decided one day he wanted to be just like a human. When his advances in this way were rebuffed, he took his revenge, throwing bricks at people and breaking things. Unfortunately, one of the bricks he threw struck a child and killed her. The golem was so horrified by what he had done that he ran away from the village and was never seen again. It was believed that he tried to create more of these creatures himself. These creatures, though, were far from the perfection he tried for, and most were destroyed. Some did survive, though. Most shunned humans, but a few have been known to live amongst us from time to time, some of whom have sworn themselves to different masters. This one probably swore himself to Asmodeus."

Tom looked stunned. "How dangerous is he, and how do we handle him?"

"I can answer that better than your brother, Tom, since I had the misfortune to clash with one once. Golems are very hard to kill. Since they are made of mud, you can cut them, shoot them, try and poison them, even blow them apart, and they can always reform and come back at you. They are nasty creatures with a sense of purpose that they won't turn aside from. If they are following a master and he orders them to kill someone, then they will pursue that person to the depths of Hell, if need be, to fulfill their mission. Believe me, when it happened to me, it almost killed me, permanently. They are stronger than humans by at least tenfold, and they can do seemingly impossible feats, like jump off or onto, ten-story buildings."

"Then how do we kill it?"

This time, the explanation came from John. "To create a golem, the word of life, also known as the Hebrew word for truth, 'emet', must be stamped on its forehead. If you can manage to change that word to death, the Hebrew word being 'met', it will die. This is not as easy as it sounds since this word is invisible under normal conditions. Other than that, the best you can hope to do is slow it down. I've managed to come up with a few more holy weapons for you that might be of assistance."

Pulling out a small cloth bag, John dumped the contents into his hand. What landed there appeared to be three small grenades.

"Inside of these is a small amount of a special explosive. It is almost untraceable and undetectable, so it should pass through security in your luggage. The main component is a new type of holy water. It is a mix of water and nitro, blessed by the Pope, and will only explode if you say, 'in Jesus' name.' Although it won't permanently destroy a golem, it will incapacitate it for a while, allowing you to get away."

"I assume this was originally meant to be used against us demons?" said Laura-Luss. "Well, I guess you were looking out for your brother's interest after all."

"Yes, Laura-Luss. However, now that I've met you, I seriously doubt he will need these when dealing with you. For a demon, I find you quite honorable."

"And for a priest, I find you quite comfortable to be around. But I do believe we should be getting underway. I have enjoyed our visit, but it is time to head for the airport. I will go and wait in the car so you two can have a few minutes on your own." And with that, Laura-Luss stood and left the room.

"You are not worried she will do something to your church while not in your sight, brother?"

"She cannot, Tom. The convention is too strong. The minute she tries, or even thinks of trying anything, the convention protection is removed, and she will suffer horrible pain. Besides, I kind of like her, for a demoness that is. You could have done much worse for a partner, you know."

"Whose side are you on, John? From the moment you met her, it's like she's captivated you or something."

"It's more you being captivated that I am worried about, Tom."

"Don't worry, I have no intention of letting her seduce me, no matter how many times she tries, and believe me, she has tried often enough."

"I am sure she has, after all, she is a succubus, and it is in their nature to do just that. However, I am not concerned about your nether regions, brother."

"Don't worry, I plan on keeping my soul to myself."

He gave his brother a strange look as if to say, you just missed my point entirely but decided not to pursue this course any longer. What will happen will be the Lord's will.

"Please be very careful, brother," John said, his tone relaying an undeniable sense of urgency. "Now you're dealing not only with the toughest demon from hell, but also a supra-human golem. Still, I truly believe you can trust Laura-Luss, at least for now. When it comes down to it, depend on her rather than trust a human. It's her mission and goal to succeed here, and from what I can judge, part of her goal is to bring you back alive. And remember, it is not wise to anger a demon or demoness, even in jest. They might forget themselves in a moment of anger."

"Thanks, John, I will seriously consider your words."

"Also, there may be some help available for you once you get to Montreal. About a forty-five-minute drive from the airport is the Oka Abbey. It is a large monastery, home to many monks, amongst which is our cousin, Dom Dominic Sicone. I had the chance to work with him during my years at the Vatican. He is, like myself, privy to several church secrets. You can talk with him. I'll apprise him of the situation and let him know that you may be calling on him."

"How did he come to serve at a monastery in Quebec?"

"That is a long story, and one better told by him should you get the chance to meet. I will also inform him of your traveling companion. He will probably have to meet you somewhere, or alone, since he can't take the same precautions for the entire abbey as I was able to take for a small church during off hours."

They stood and walked to the door. The two brothers hugged, and Tom followed the trail of Laura-Luss to the car.

CHAPTER 10

"So, what gives with you and your brother?" asked Laura-Luss once they were in the car. "It would seem that the supernatural doesn't bother either of you in any way. Like you have been dealing with it all your life."

"We both go back a long way with unusual things happening in our lives. We've had some strange things happen to us."

"Yet you became a detective and a nonpracticing Catholic, and your brother became a priest. Is there any particular reason for this?"

"It goes back to a certain incident that happened when we were kids. At least I think that was the turning point." Tom sat back in his seat and reminisced about that faithful day.

****

"If you don't let me go, I am going to tell Mom." Tom's whining voice was beginning to bother John.

"I told you, little brother, this is not the place for someone your size. Only big boys like us can climb up and down the ladders and ropes. You can not do it."

"I can too do it. I'm big enough, and I can climb ropes better and faster than Jimmy. He's so fat he can't even climb a step stool."

"Look, Tom, it's a little dangerous too. If something were to happen to you, Mom and Dad would never let me hear the end of it. I would be grounded forever. Jimmy may be fat, but he's strong and also, he's also fourteen years old like Derek, Matthew, and me. You're only eleven. Anyway, the mine shaft is dark and deep and scary, even for me, so you would only freeze up, and then we'd have to come out without seeing if it's true about the gold."

"I'm not afraid. I've been in scary places before." Tom was about to tell John about the haunted house, but remembered that he had promised his friends he would tell no one.

"If we let you come, you have to do everything we tell you to do, no questions asked. If you get scared and make us come home, we will never take you anywhere again. And you must promise not to tell anyone, especially Mom and Dad."

"I promise, John. And I'll be so good and helpful, you'll be happy to have me with you." For a chance like this, Tom would have promised anything.

"Don't try to help or anything, Tom, just do as we tell you and behave yourself, okay?"

Tom and John met up with the other three boys in front of Jimmy's place, since the mineshaft was in an area behind where he lived. After a few minutes of arguing, mostly about Tom tagging along, they set off on bicycles, first taking the small residential road for ten minutes, then turning onto a dirt truck trail, long since abandoned. The warning signs and concrete barriers did nothing to deter the boys.

The Old Mill Mine had long since been mined out of gold. It had never really been a productive operation, having been in use for less than ten years, the last two of which were years of losses for the owners. After several geological studies came to the same conclusion that this area had very little gold to begin with, the company closed the mine and boarded it up. The original plan had been to blast the entrance shut so no one could enter it again. No company wanted a lawsuit because someone had trespassed on their property and had an accident. However, the so-called dynamite expert had underestimated what he needed, and the front entrance had not been completely sealed. Rather than bring in more explosives, the company had used a bulldozer to push dirt against the small opening left, assuming that that would be more than enough. Of course, they never counted on boys' ingenuity and determination.

Recently, a group of older teenagers had used an ATV with a tow cable to pull away some of the larger rocks on the bottom, thus shifting all the pile and creating a small opening that, with a few shovels and some hard work, created a hole large enough for them to crawl through. Word had not gotten back to any of the parents yet, or something would have been done to close it.

So far, a few groups of boys had been inside, one of which had claimed to have found gold. But if that were the truth, you'd have expected that same group to have gone back several times to try to get it. Yet the truth was none of those who had entered the mine had ever gone near it again.

Still, no thoughts like that would interfere with the plans of these boys when they got something into their heads. Locking their bikes against trees, the five prepared themselves with flashlights and lanterns, rope, shovels, and picks, all the while pretending they were brave miners ready to do their day of work and bring out a ton of gold.

Jimmy went first, with the twins Matthew and Derek next, followed by Tom, with John bringing up the rear. Getting in had been easier than they thought. Jimmy was standing before a split entrance area, just a dozen feet from the outside opening, waiting for everyone to get together. Here was where they had to make a decision, just like the other boys had told them. Pulling out a large ball of thin string, Jimmy tied one end to an outcrop of rock and put the ball itself in a pouch on his belt, leaving space for the string to play out.

"Terry warned me that it would be easy to get lost down here. He went in only partway and got mixed up. He was lucky that Johnny found him when he did, or he might have been in here forever. This way, that can't happen to us as long as we all stick together. Is that understood, everyone? We all stick together no matter what."

After making sure that all the boys had nodded yes, especially Tom, Jimmy led the way down the left shaft. Normally, teenage boys hated having one of the younger brothers tagging along, but in Tom's case, everyone liked him. Even at eleven, he was almost as tall as the rest of them and never seemed to be afraid of anything. Also, he wasn't a nag like most kids his age, and he never ever tattled.

"You know, Tom, I hear there have been Tommy-knockers seen in here," said Derek with a wink to his twin. "I certainly hope we don't see any."

"Cut out the nonsense, Derek," snapped Jimmy.

"What are Tommy-knockers?" asked Matthew right back, ignoring Jimmy and playing along with his brother.

"Oh, you know, like the book by Stephen King. Only the ones here only chase after someone with a name like theirs," responded Derek, this time with a direct look at Tom.

"Okay enough," said John and Jimmy at the same time. Jimmy continued by saying, "Stop scaring Tom. We don't need anyone to panic now."

"That's okay, Jimmy," Tom piped up. "Tommy-knockers don't scare me at all."

"They don't?" said Derek and Matthew in unison. "How could they not?" followed up Derek.

"That's because I know what Tommy-knockers are."

"And that is …?" asked John.

"They're mining spirits, supposed to be the ghosts of dead miners. They were first discovered in Staffordshire, England, and only came to be found in North America less than fifty years ago. As long as you respect them, they won't hurt you. They can be really helpful as they have been known to show miners where to mine to get the best ores. They hate to be seen by anyone but the one or two they decide to help, so if you accidentally see one, pretend you didn't. If you get them mad, they can be very bad, making things disappear, taking things, and even leading people to their deaths."

"Where did you learn all this, Tom?" asked Jimmy.

"I read a whole book on monsters, spirits, demons, and so on. I wanted to buy a copy, but Mom and Dad wouldn't let me."

"You know they don't believe in this hogwash, and neither do I," said John. "The priest says it's all nonsense, and I believe him."

"What do they look like?" asked Derek.

"Well, they're hard to see, mostly invisible to people, but those few who have seen them say they are about two feet tall, have big heads, long beards, wrinkled faces, and long arms that almost drag along the ground. And they are always wearing their mining outfits, with hats, and carrying their mining equipment like picks and so on. Mostly, you can only tell they're nearby by the sound of their knocking and banging as they continue to mine even after death. As I said, just don't get them mad, and we'll be okay."

Now Derek and Matthew were looking at each other nervously, and Tom was the one with a smile on his face. Jimmy was going to ask Tom if he was kidding about the Tommy-knockers, but the fact that the twins had shut up made him decide that not knowing was best if it would keep those two quiet.

The shaft continued slightly downwards, their flashlights making patterns and shadows against the mine walls as they walked it. Jimmy kept playing out the rope as they slowly made their way, and the silence of the twins continued as they appeared to be getting a little unnerved. They walked this way for almost fifteen minutes before Derek asked, "How much further do we have to go? That ball of string you have won't go on forever."

"We should be there soon. I was told that it was only a short way in. Just keep shining your lights on the walls and looking for the glitter of gold." However, another ten minutes brought them to the end of the ball of string, and still no one had seen even the slightest bit of shine anywhere.

"I think those guys were lying, Jimmy," said John. "They probably got scared and ran out of here and made up the story about finding gold."

"I saw the gold dust with my own eyes," said Derek. "And I touched it," said Matthew.

"Who had the gold?" asked John.

"It was Terry. It looked like he had a whole bag full," answered Matthew.

They heard laughing and turned to see Tom lying on the ground, grabbing his stomach, loud bellows of laughter coming from him.

'What's so funny, Tom?" asked Jimmy.

Between fits of laughter, Tom finally managed to say, "Didn't you guys know that Terry's uncle works for the special effects department at Universal Studios in Hollywood? He gave Terry a bag of 'gold dust' for Christmas. All it is is sand that was colored gold. They use it in lots of movies."

"What?!" Yelled Derek and Mathew together. When we get out of here, I am going to bash Terry's head in," said Derek. Meanwhile, Jimmy and John had joined in Tom's laughter.

"Come on, guys, it was a good joke, one worthy of you two," said Jimmy to the twins. "It was a fun adventure, but let's just head back now."

"I still say that I am going to get my revenge," said Derek, "but beating his brains in may be a little extreme. Maybe setting his pants on fire would be better. But I agree with you about getting out of here. This place is starting to give me the creeps."

Heading back, they came to a junction they had not realized was there on the trip in. That should not have been a problem except that at that point, their rope had been cut, and the trail ended. Now the twins were starting to panic. Derek wanted to have Tom and John go up one tunnel, and he, Matthew, and Jimmy go up the other one, but Jimmy refused to have the group broken up.

"Look, guys, this is probably only a joke by some of the guys from school, but we can't take a chance. If we all stick together, we'll be safer. I know that from about this point, it was fifteen minutes at a slow walk to the entrance. We'll go down the left tunnel, and once we get to that time, if we have not found the entrance, we'll come back here and take the other tunnel. I'll use the rope that's left to make sure we can retrace to here. We'll just have to be careful that there are no other branches along the way."

"Wait, I just saw something," said Matthew, who had been watching down the other tunnel the whole time. "Down there to the right. I think it may have been a Tommy-knocker."

"Stop with the games, this is not the time for it." The anger in John's voice was unmistakable.

"I'm not kidding. There was something there. I saw it. Really!"

"What did it look like?" asked Derek, voice trembling with fear. By this time, the others realized that this was not one of the twins' pranks.

"It was a little like Tom said before, but with a shorter beard, little horns coming from its head, hoofs for feet, and a little tail. And it had no clothes."

"Oh no!" said Tom aloud.

"What? What's wrong, Tom?" asked Jimmy.

"That's a satyr that Matthew described."

"What is a satyr?" asked John.

"Will it hurt us?" asked Derek.

"I only know what I read. A satyr likes causing trouble. I don't think he can directly hurt people, but if his little pranks get people hurt, he doesn't care. It was probably him who cut the rope. I think wherever he goes, we should go in the opposite direction."

"Wait, I think I see the rope down there where it went," and with that, Matthew rushed down the right tunnel, forcing the others to follow him.

When they finally caught up to him a few minutes later, it was only to see him standing there with a small piece of the rope in his hand and no sign of the rest of the rope or the satyr. Turning around, the boys saw that they had entered a room with several entrances and exits, and no way to figure out which one they had come from.

"This is a fine mess we are in now, Matthew," yelled Jimmy, his voice a mixture of anger and fear. "We told you to stay with us."

"I'm sorry, but I was sure I saw the rope."

"That was the intention of the satyr," said Tom. "They like to cause trouble for people, and getting us lost is trouble. I just don't understand what one is doing here in the mineshaft."

"The question is, how are we going to get out of here?" said John.

"We could always just wait here. Someone will eventually come looking for us," was Derek's idea.

"Even if they do come, it may take days before they find us. I don't know about you guys, but I don't like the idea of spending a day or two here in the dark with some type of magical creature trying to do who knows what to us." They all looked at Jimmy when he said this, but it was John who said, "What do you mean in the dark?"

"How long do you think these batteries will last? Even if we keep only one lit at a time, they'll be out within twenty-four hours. With it totally dark, what's to stop that creature from coming and taking us away one at a time and leaving us all in separate places? No, I think we have to try to retrace our steps and find our way back unless anyone else has another idea."

"Yes, I do," said John. "Let us pray."

"Oh, come on, John, you know I don't believe in that." Jimmy gave John a look meant to say, why did you have to start that now. "You know I'm an atheist."

"Look, what have we got to lose? If nothing else, it will help clear our heads and calm us all down. And if it is a satyr like my brother says, then who better to protect us and save us than Jesus?"

"I'm ready to try," piped up Matthew.

"Me too," from Derek.

"Oh, okay. But don't think you'll get me to convert. I am just doing this for everyone else."

"Everyone, come over here and stand in a circle. Hold hands. You too, Tom. That's it."

For the next few minutes, John led them in prayer, asking to be delivered from there and asking to be protected and given courage. It was while this was going on that Tom spotted the Tommy-knocker. It was standing at the entrance to one of the tunnels and pointing at Tom, indicating that they should follow him. Then he took out his pick and banged it against the wall before disappearing.

"What was that?" asked Derek, voice quivering.

"It came from over there, where that tunnel entrance is," responded Tom.

"That must have been God answering our prayers and showing us the way!" This from Jimmy the atheist.

"Well, what are we waiting for? Let's go," said Derek.

"What if it's the satyr?" asked Matthew.

"Trust me, it wasn't," answered Tom. On his word, they all piled into the tunnel Tom had pointed to, no one even asking how he could be so sure. Tom was thankful for that because he was afraid that if he told them about the Tommy-knocker, it would not help them anymore.

They came across two more junctions after that, and at each one, there was a banging to indicate which way they should go, and each time, Tom was able to see the little creature for just a moment before it disappeared. The boys became more confident by the moment that they were going the right way, and sure enough, they soon could see the literal light at the end of the tunnel. As soon as they got to the mine entrance, or in this case, exit, the boys plowed their way over the debris and out into the light of day, yelling and cheering as the sun touched their faces.

"You know you were right to pray," said Jimmy as he turned to face John. "Maybe we all do need something to believe in. Do you think maybe I could go to church with you tomorrow?"

The next day found five young boys sitting together near the front of the church; however, one still had doubts in his head. Tom knew that it was the Tommy-knocker that had led them out of the mine, not an angel from God. But from that day on, his brother's future was decided. John entered into training for the priesthood that year.

****

Hearing the story from Tom's point of view gave Laura-Luss a special insight into the type of person Tom was and his relationship with his brother. Part of her was analyzing this and trying to see how best she could use it, yet another part of her, a part she never suspected, had softened towards Tom. Not wanting to show this, or even feel this, Laura-Luss covered it up in her usual way, with her acerbic tongue.

"Well, it is obvious that you took the wrong path. At least as a priest, you would have a reason for your lack of sexual appetite, other than just not being able to perform."

"I guess it just shows it doesn't pay to tell a demoness anything about your private life. They are just not capable of any sense of humanity and caring," was Tom's quick response. He started the car and turned to look at the oncoming traffic, missing the flash of pain that crossed Laura-Luss' face.

CHAPTER 11

It was a quick stop at Tom's apartment and a quiet ride to the airport. Thankfully, John had been right about the new weapons passing through the detectors. Though Tom had to check his guns in as usual. The flight was non-eventful, and the hotel was a short shuttle ride from the airport terminal. Check-in was quick with all having been prearranged, and the suite was quite adequate. In the end, they had adjoining rooms with a lounge room dividing them. Amy had chosen well.

Tom was quite thankful that room service was still delivered at these hours. Laura-Luss had been right about the eating. He tried not to attract too much attention and therefore ordered only four sandwiches, three bags of chips, and three cans of Pepsi, figuring that he could have a big breakfast in a few hours. Consuming these in short order, Tom retired to his room and tried to get some sleep, leaving Laura-Luss sitting on the couch.

The sun shone on Tom's face a couple of hours later, rousing him from a fitful sleep. Fortunately, the demoness had also been right about not needing much sleep. After a shower and shave, Tom felt his normal self once again and was ready to take on the challenges this new city had to offer.

As he went into the living room, he heard Laura-Luss talking on the phone but could not understand much of what she was saying until he realized that she was

speaking French. He walked over to the small fridge and grabbed a bottle of water.

"Oui. Oui, monsieur. Okay, ça va. Dans cinq minutes? Okay, c'est parfait.

Merci." Laura-Luss hung up the phone and turned to Tom.

"I have just ordered you breakfast. A six-egg smoked meat omelet with bacon,

sausage, hash browns, and baked beans. A local favorite. The beans are cooked in maple

syrup. You will love it. Oh, and don't worry, the desk clerk thinks it is for two. I also

asked for extra toast. I told him I was pregnant and needed a lot of food."

Tom spat out a mouthful of water upon hearing that. Looking over at Laura-Luss,

and seeing the self-satisfied grin on her face, he could not resist asking, "You mean

demons can use sex for something other than corrupting innocents?"

"Tom, you do not know the half of it," she responded and quickly turned away,

but not before Tom noticed a wistfully sad smile appear, putting an abrupt end to the next

caustic remark he was going to make. To cover up his lack of reply, Tom pulled out his

laptop and checked for messages.

Other than the usual emails trying to sell him Viagra, giving him stock tips, or

offering him a diploma, there were only two messages of any import. One from Amy,

with contact information at their Montreal office, and the other, a more interesting one,

from his brother.

Tom. I am currently on a flight to Rome. I have called for an emergency meeting

with the Pope. Something that Laura-Luss mentioned got me thinking. She said

that her boss wanted this wrapped up without Church intervention. It got me thinking that maybe there was more to the demon's departure from Hell than he had told us. Although I don't believe that he sent or aided the demon in his escape, I do believe he may have left a back door open to his realm. This could allow our fugitive demon to get Hell-borne help. So, keep an eye out for that. It could also mean boss man has ulterior motives. I hope to get some extra help in determining this and will keep you informed.

One last thing. A hint, shall we say. The devil came physically to earth before God did. And when you call the devil to get his demon, you can make use of this to protect yourself.

Tom quickly closed his message center before Laura-Luss could see what was there. Although his brother seemed to trust the demoness, he still had his doubts. Would not her first loyalty still be towards the master of the nether worlds?

"Any Earth-shattering news?" she asked as Tom closed his laptop,

"Not really. My brother is trying to get more information for us through his sources," said Tom, glossing over the full import of the message. "And my office with the contact information for our local office. We have an appointment there in about an hour. A car will be here soon to pick us up. Someone here doesn't like the idea that a case is under investigation touching his jurisdiction, and he isn't allowed to have any information whatsoever. However, we do have a cover story worked out. We're investigating something the Church wants to be kept hushed. The Church here still has a lot of influence, and that will keep them from being too pushy. By the way, you'll be happy to hear that for the moment, your cover is as a mother superior."

This time, it was the demoness's turn to splutter.

****

"You look very much the part and much improved in that outfit," said Tom to Laura-Luss in the back of the Limo. "I'm glad Amy chose this cover for you. It suits you. Makes you easier to be with."

"It makes me look like a frumpy spinster," replied a disgruntled Laura-Luss. "And I bet you are enjoying every minute of this, aren't you, Mr. Wilkins?"

Tom put on the best "mister innocent" look he could, but could not keep the humor out of his voice as he responded, "Whatever do you mean, Ms. Luss?"

"I must remind you of something your brother told you. It is not wise to anger demons. We tend to respond in a manner you would find most disconcerting."

Before Tom could answer, the car pulled up in front of the old greystone building.

"What is it with your company? You only rent offices in older types of buildings?"

"I guess the owners are into historical-type properties. Come to think of it, our offices in London, Paris, Berlin, Moscow, Peking, and Cairo are all in buildings of this design."

"You have been to a lot of places in your short time with the company."

Tom laughed. "I've only visited one of those. But I remember looking at the company website before I agreed to join and seeing pictures of their offices."

The short walk from the limo to the front door of the building was blessedly mild. Tom wore only a light overcoat on top of his suit and had expected the weather here to be more severe than in New York at this time of the year. But late March in Quebec this year was proving to be a record breaker, with only a little amount of snow on the ground and temperatures in the sixties.

The front reception area was a twin of the one in his office in New York. The receptionist who greeted them, however, was a bit too effervescent to ever be confused with someone in a similar position in any major office back home. Putting her over-bubbly personality behind her, the young brunette was efficient and informed, and when she spoke, her slight French accent was pleasant to listen to and did not take away from her excellent command of the English language.

"It is a real pleasure to have someone from our New York office stop by for a visit, Mr. Wilkins. The office manager has made it quite clear that we are to assist you in any way that we can. An office has been prepared for your use while you are here. If you need any translation work, I will be more than happy to assist you."

While talking, the receptionist had stood and come around from her desk to welcome Tom in the typical Quebec fashion with a two-cheek kiss. Looking at her, Tom began to see why some claimed that Montreal's women were boasted to be amongst the world's best looking, none of which escaped the notice of Laura-Luss.

Knowing that she could never compete dressed as she was, the demoness decided it was time to get Tom away from this vixen so they could get to work. "I am sure that Mr. Wilkins is just as pleased to make your acquaintance, Miss, but we are here to do a job and do not have time for chit-chat and kisses. As for your offer, I am fluent in French and will handle anything of that nature that is required. Could you please show us to our office and tell your boss we are here so we can get down to business."

Glancing at Laura-Luss and realizing exactly why she was all of a sudden very business-like, Tom decided not to push his luck with an inappropriate comment at this point. He nodded deferentially to the "Mother Superior" and followed the two women to the back office they were assigned.

When they were finally alone, the demoness commented that she hoped most of the people in this city were not as cutesy and happy as this girl seemed to be. Other than a comment that he thought it made for a refreshing change, which got him a dirty look from Laura-Luss, Tom decided it would be best at this time not to do anything to further upset the demoness. After all, it must be tough for her to hide her true nature behind this cover.

The white-haired man who entered the office a few minutes later was not at all like what Tom expected. He must have been close to eighty years old, yet was spry and moved with the ease of a man forty years his junior. His ice-blue eyes held an obvious intelligence that seemed to hint at a level of awareness beyond what one would expect in someone of his employ.

"Good day, Mr. Wilkins, Mother Superior." his voice was soft, yet strong, with a slight melodiousness to it, but without a trace of an accent. "I am Benoît Côté, office manager here. Is there any way I can be of assistance?"

Tom came over to shake his hand and was surprised at the strength in the man's grip. The bigger surprise was realizing that this person appeared to recognize Laura-Luss for what she was. That made Tom wonder even more than in times past about the nature of this company's ownership. Surely only someone accustomed to meeting demons would recognize one right off the bat. However, Laura-Luss did not seem to recognize that her cover was, well, uncovered, as she kept on with her persona. Tom stored this bit of information with other bits he had come across in this case. A pattern was beginning to emerge that, if he could discover what it was, might be useful, maybe even of paramount importance to his continued existence.

"What we need is access to police records going back about a year, I would say," answered Tom after the greetings were complete. "As well, ownership records for properties. Do you have direct access to the land transfer office?"

"Indeed, we do, and here it is called the registry office. I will have Tammy, our receptionist and junior researcher, assist you with this. Even though the Mother Superior is fluent in French, she is not trained in the use of the computer access to this program. As for police records, if you could narrow down what you are looking for, it would make things much quicker. Our records are sorted by date, name, criminal offense, and more. With the proper input, our search program can find what you want in seconds."

"That is fine, Mr. Côté, just send in this Tammy girl and she can show us how to work the program," answered Laura-Luss briskly. "I am sure we will be able to proceed on our own after that."

Taking this as a dismissal, Benoît Côté excused himself after once again assuring Tom that the full resources of his office were at Tom's disposal. A few minutes later, a much-subdued Tammy entered the office. Her boss must have informed her not to act overly friendly. She was quite businesslike and had shown Laura-Luss the workings of the program in just a few minutes, then vacated the office as quickly as decorum would allow.

"Making friends is not one of your specialties, I see," said Tom after the door closed.

"We are here to do a job and not socialize, and I suggest you keep that in mind, Mr. Wilkins. We have no time for idle chit-chat or love-struck young puppies. Had that little girl gushed over you any more, I would have puked."

"Jealousy does not become a demoness," responded Tom, but he quickly bent his head back down to the papers he was looking at so as not to see the reaction this caused. It was one thing to tease a demoness; it was another to look her in the eye while doing it. For her part, Laura-Luss ignored the comment and continued to run the search program on the computer.

"Here may be something," she said after a few moments. "These police records show a pattern of violent sexual assaults on prostitutes at various times over the last year. Look here, Tom. If you compare this to the reports of the New York police department, the times show that when there is activity in New York, there is none in Montreal, and the converse is true for Montreal. It looks like Asmodeus has been planning this for a while and making periodic stops in these two cities to set this up. What I don't understand is why here and in New York. What is distinct about these two cities?"

"Let me see these. Okay, see here the dates. Do you notice another pattern? Look carefully. Focus on the amount of time between assaults in the two cities. There is exactly a three-week difference if you factor out the slight splattering that could be explained by human infractions. Look just at the groupings. There are two days of heavy activity in one city, then nothing for three weeks, then two days of heavy activity in the other city, and the cycle repeats itself."

"Oh, my devil, I think I see something of even greater significance," Laura-Luss exclaimed. "I would have to verify it with my sources down below, but if memory serves me correctly, I am sure these periods coincide with those times that my boss sent Asmodeus on supposedly information-gathering missions. He has been setting this up for a long while."

"You mean that Asmodeus somehow set it up so that all these missions were necessary? I can't believe that Satan is that naïve."

"No, Tom, it is not Satan that has been naïve. It is you and me."

"What are you talking about?"

"Tom, I must leave you for a while to confirm this. If my suspicions are correct, we are both in a lot more danger than we could possibly imagine."

"What could be more dangerous than trying to capture the most dangerous demon in the nether regions?"

"Don't ask me now, for I will not say anything until I can verify certain things."

"If you're going wandering, I suggest we have a less conspicuous method of communication than just popping up or whatever you do. Here's a cell phone. Programmed into it is my cell number as well as the office numbers. Tom handed the

Samsung model phone to Lara-Luss, who surprised Tom by grabbing his hand and saying, "Tom, this is important. I want you to go and see your cousin at Oka Abbey while I am gone. You will be safe there. Just don't do any more investigative work until I am back."

"But—" Was all Tom got out before Laura-Luss disappeared, leaving him with a lot of unanswered questions and an empty nun's habit that he would have a hard time trying to explain.

CHAPTER 12

The trick to traveling back and forth between Hell and Earth, when not directly summoned, was to know the secret gateways. The knowledge of the various entry points was usually reserved for the greater demons, and since they were not allowed by covenant to enter the realms of normal Earth, with all its checks and balances to prevent their departure without the powers that be knowing of it, it was usually enough to keep the demons in Hell. Occasionally, a minor demon stumbled across one of these and came to Earth to cause a bit of a scene. The Devil allowed this, as it gave him indirect access to the realms of the Earth by seeing through the lesser demons' eyes when he wished. Heaven allowed it as it was good training for the priests in how to deal with their ilk, and also strengthened the belief of those Christians who encountered them.

Not being considered one of the greater demons, Laura-Luss was never given knowledge of these gateways. But bored out of her skull one day, she had done a little exploring in parts of Hell she technically was not normally allowed to access. When she came across the core of an extinct volcano and was able to follow it to the surface, she discovered herself in the realms of Earth, a place she had never been before.

Realizing that information like this could be valuable, she kept her discovery to herself. She spent several days that time observing humans while keeping hidden. Knowing that she should not be absent from Hell for too long, she returned with a thirst for more knowledge, both of this gateway and human culture. The question was how to get this information without other demons knowing about it.

Getting access to Hell's computers was the first step. Demons were encouraged to learn the use and advantages of these computers, but access was strictly monitored. Laura-Luss' one advantage was her standing in the demon hierarchy. While not considered one of the greater demons, she stood well above most of the lesser demons, which gave her access to more of Hell. That, combined with her human blood, prevented the devil from being able to see through her eyes like he could with all the lesser demons and even some of the greater ones.

She kept it simple at first. She started by researching human cultures and religions, something that the Devil approved of his demons knowing, and something that had never interested her before. One trip topside was enough for her to want to know everything about her human side. She drank up every bit of knowledge in the computer's database but knew that this was only the tip of what there was to know. It took longer to get access to the World Wide Web, as that was usually considered dangerous material for the average demon. But again, because of her human blood, permission was granted, as it did not seem out of the ordinary for a demon with human blood to want to know more of that part of their being.

The tricky part was to research where to find the various gateways. She wanted to visit all the different parts of the Earth, but if she only used one tunnel to travel, eventually her excursions would become known. If a demon uses his or her powers on Earth's plain, the Devil can easily become aware of it. And to travel from place to place on Earth within the time limits she would have would not be possible without using her demon abilities.

She started by researching areas she would like to visit first checking out the usual things that demons should check, local religions, the closest church, areas of evil according to local legends, and so on. Then she varied the search to look at local points of interest both historically and geographically. Invariably, if there was an extinct volcano anywhere nearby, it was mentioned. She developed a map of these areas and then, one by one, explored the adjacent areas in Hell. Sure enough, when she went to see these places, they were all in areas where lesser demons were not generally allowed.

For Laura-Luss, access to most of these was not a problem, but she still had to take care that her movements were not being monitored. She was careful to take only a passing interest in most of these places, but did explore a couple of them more extensively. Each one she explored had access to Earth! Her research did point out to her that Hell was not located at the center of the Earth. It was more like an alternate plane of existence, which, because of man's belief, had access directly through the crust of the Earth itself. This was a case of myth becoming fact due to belief.

One thing she did discover was that the island of Montreal was originally the site of a volcano eons ago. Mount Royal, sitting in the center of the island and overlooking the downtown core, was the extinct volcano itself, and sitting atop this was a large cross that, when lit at night, shone for miles around. Laura-Luss had researched this site particularly well, as the idea of the cross on top of a gateway to hell fascinated her. Did some past missionaries suspect the possibility of the gateway, or was it entirely coincidental? Not being a big believer in coincidences, knowing as she did that most of these so-called coincidences were usually the mechanisms of her boss or the boss up above, Laura-Luss tried to get to the bottom of the mystery.

Through her searches, she found that a cross was first erected there in 1643 by Paul de Chomedey, just ninety-five years after the discovery of Mt. Royal, to give thanks to God for saving the colony from a flood. In 1924, the current cross was built. Standing over a hundred feet tall and thirty feet wide, it was first illuminated on December 24, 1924, with the use of two hundred and fifty fifty-watt bulbs. The incandescent lights on the cross were replaced by a fiber-optic system in 1992, allowing the use of colored filters placed before thirty-two projectors.

The Catholic Church has also played a critical role in the history of the cross. Three times in the course of the last eighty-one years, the lights had been changed to purple to signal the death of a Pope—Pope Pius XII, Pope Paul VI, and Pope John Paul II. As well in 1960, they were turned yellow to celebrate the Great Mission, an event organized by the Diocese of Montreal.

None of this was lost on Laura-Luss. She had no doubt whatsoever that the planting of the cross was a manipulation of him upstairs. Which made it quite obvious that the entry point must be near the cross. So, how was she to get to the entry point without falling within the shadow of the cross?

Normally, a cross that was not in the hands of a true believer, strong in the faith, would not discomfort her in any way. However, such a storied cross, that was placed through the machinations of Him upstairs, would be something entirely different. Nighttime would, of course, be the worst idea as the light of the cross would shine for miles around. Scouting from a distance, Laura-Luss noticed that there was one approach, not accessible to the public, that might allow her to do this. It meant climbing over the balcony from the observation deck without being noticed, and clinging to the side of the mountain, making her way around. Slightly modifying her physical form allowed her to do this with ease.

As she had thought, when she had scaled down enough, the dark spot she had seen from below was a cave. Entering the dark recess, her demon eyes quickly adjusted, allowing her to see what humans could not: the access entry port. To humans, it was just a stone wall; to Laura-Luss, it was the outline of the face of Satan. By kissing his mouth, the wall faded away, and access was granted. Her one concern was that her master could discover her entry. If he were not paying attention to this portal, she would probably pass unnoticed. She chuckled to herself as the brief thought passed through her mind that she could only "pray" it was so. But praying for her was praying to the devil, and that would only draw the attention of the one she did not want to notice her.

Had a human happened to be standing nearby as she passed in this light, he would only have seen two red spots floating by; the red of her demon eyes that allowed her to see in these tunnels to Hell. Soon enough, her eyes spotted the second gateway, twin pillars supporting two large gargoyles, the first of the guardians of Hell. If by chance any humans somehow managed to get this far and tried to pass these pillars, the gargoyles would rip them to pieces. Laura-Luss passed these with some trepidation, not knowing if they had been programmed to watch for her. She passed through without event and with some relief realized that her master was probably unaware of her presence.

Eventually, she spotted the telltale signs that she was approaching her master's domain. Phosphorescence covered the walls, allowing illumination so the lesser demons could work more easily. Hell's ever-present smell of brimstone now surrounded her. Knowing that there were usually guards near these entry points, she proceeded carefully, but as usual, the guards were lax and either dozing or out looking for something to eat, so she easily slipped by their post and entered Hell proper.

What she needed most was information. In Hell, information was a commodity. It was something you traded for, and you had to know who to go to for accurate and difficult-to-get information. Laura-Luss knew there was only one she could go to who would be in a position to know what she needed and with whom she might have some leverage to get that information. Could she trust him? Probably not, but it was a chance she would have to take.

Finding the Fox Fairy was quite simple. Just go to the local gathering place. Wherever a large group could be found, that was where the Fox Fairy would be. A lot of myths surrounded him. He was considered highly dangerous by some, and even many of the demons held him in awe. He was thought to originally be one of the "Shen"—a spirit of the dead rising from the grave. In his younger days, he liked shape-shifting into a wicked young lady, but now, when he traveled on Earth, he preferred his persona of an older man or scholar. Often called the trickster, he could take on the appearance of someone recently deceased and approach their loved ones. Many felt that this was how he got most of his information. Laura-Luss knew differently. She was one of the few who know of the Shadow.

No one knows for sure exactly how the Shadow came to be. Originally of Chinese lore, the shadow was thought to be the dark part of a human's psyche. When humans, even those considered good or even angelic, had bad thoughts about others, or thoughts of doing evil to others, these thoughts or feelings rested in a dark corner of the mind or Ego, if you will. At times when a human looks at someone and becomes suspicious, it is the dark part of their psyche leaving their mind and superimposing over that of the one they are suspicious of. This became known as the Shadow. Still, a relatively harmless and minor character in the scheme of things in Hell until, it is suspected, a mid-level demon possessed a human that had a particularly strong Shadow also residing there. Exactly what happened may never be known, but somehow these two fought, merged, and then permanently separated from the human host, cursed to wander forever, neither demon nor full shadow but part of both.

Due to this merging, the Shadow could move easily from human host to demon host and depart without any being the wiser. While in the host, it could read his/her/its thoughts and feelings. It would know all that the host knew.

Laura-Luss had discovered, quite by accident, the existence of the Shadow and the Fox Fairy's control over it, while doing the Fox Fairy a favor one day. Seeing the advantage of having others in the demon realms owe her, she was quick to help all who needed it. The Fox Fairy, who wanted to make a deal with a particular demon named Jesses, who had refused to meet with him, asked Laura-Luss to act as an intermediary, knowing that she and this demon were acquaintances. She had made the arrangements and then left as requested by both the other parties. But not fully trusting the Fox Fairy, she had decided to keep an eye on things.

She had prepared a little hiding spot earlier and was easily able to slip into position without the others realizing she had never left. She had just settled in when she saw it happen. From out of nowhere, a Shadow appeared behind Jesses. Then it slowly merged into him. All the while Jesses seemed completely unaware of what was happening. A short while later, the Shadow left Jesses and disappeared. The meeting finished a short while later, and although Jesses seemed pleased with whatever arrangement they had made, it was the Fox Fairly who had the bigger smile. Laura-Luss soon discovered why that was so.

She heard the Fairy Fox call for someone, and then the Shadow reappeared. They had come closer to her hiding spot, so she heard what they were talking about. It appeared that the Shadow had left Jesses' body with something after all—everything that Jesses knew, it knew.

That night, Laura-Luss had done some hard research and discovered what the Shadow was, and that he may be the only one of his kind in existence. The how or why he had come to work for the Fox Fairy was still a mystery, but the fact that she knew about him, and the Fox Fairy did not know she knew, was something she was about to make use of here in the present.

Sure enough, The Devil's Horns, a popular drinking place amongst the lesser and mid-level demons, proved to be a lucky first guess on her current mission to track down the Fox Fairy. Although humans thought of Hell as a place of pain and suffering for all, it was mainly the human souls that had the pain and suffering. The workers in Hell—

demons, sprites, and so on—had to have a place to go and wind down after a hard day's work. Not needing regular food, since demons usually survived on human emotions, they still enjoyed the human vice of drinking. Hence, the many drinking establishments located in Hell.

As usual, the Fox Fairy was sitting amongst a group of drinkers, draining them of information simply by knowing what questions to ask and, of course, providing the liquid sustenance. It only took her a moment to catch his eye and signal him, then she made her way to a vacant table near the rear of the place. She did not doubt that the Fox Fairy would come to see her as soon as he could make his excuses to his current drinking companions. He owed Laura-Luss too much not to. Besides, she was one of the few whom he trusted enough to talk with and who did not ask something from him first. Today, of course, would be different.

It took him a good fifteen minutes to extricate himself from the group of now obviously drunk demons, but he arrived with two drinks and a large smile.

"As always, it is a pleasure to see your beautiful face, my dear," his raspy voice not hiding the genuine warmth of his greeting. "You are truly one of the few I am always glad to see."

"The charmer, as always, Foxy. And up to your usual tricks I see, getting them drunk and gaining their information for next to nothing," said Laura-Luss as she nodded towards the table the Fairy Fox had just vacated.

"You have always known my ways and still accepted me, my sweet Laura-Luss, and for that, I am thankful and will do something I rarely do, give information for nothing." Now the smile was gone from his face, and Laura-Luss saw a seriousness she had never seen on his face before.

"It must be something of great import for your ever-present smile has left your presence," Laura-Luss replied with a slight laugh in her voice, only to see the Fairly Fox become even more uptight.

"Laura-Luss, I can only tell you one thing. Whatever you are in the middle of, get out of it now, your very existence depends on it."

"Most things I do are risky; that is why I enjoy doing them."

"This is not a laughing matter, Laura-Luss. Something really big is going down, and you are but a pawn in the middle of it. Get out while you can."

"You'll have to tell me more than vague threats to get me to act differently than my usual self, Foxy."

"It is all I can say. Information of that sort is hard to come by. I only heard some references to a major event and you being in the middle of it, and the feeling that you are not expected to come out of it alive."

"Look, Foxy, it is not as easy as that. What I am doing is something for the Master himself. Besides, there is a human involved, and if I leave him now, he would probably be destroyed. Surely there is more you can tell me that might help me in this."

The Fairy Fox looked sharply at this comment. "Look, Laura-Luss, this is not exactly the kind of information that people are free about. No one is going to tell me exactly what is going on."

Looking him directly in the eye, Laura-Luss played her main card. "I am sure The

Shadow has already told you everything I need to know."

For the first time, Laura-Luss saw the Fox Fairy completely stunned and at a loss for words. She waited for him to respond. After many long seconds, he finally did.

"I won't ask you how you know about him, as you are smart enough to keep information like that to yourself. Still, you must care for this human to divulge your knowledge of this to me here and now. Okay, here is what I have learned. If you ever tell anyone that you know this, it will probably cost both of us our lives.

"So here goes. Asmodeus being on earth was not an accident, nor was this just his own doing. I don't know all the whys and hows, as that is probably information known only by the top dogs themselves, but this is the gist of it. Our master arranged for Asmodeus to be on Earth. It is dog breath's job to arrange for a cult mass suicide or something to open a small area on Earth where our master can take physical presence permanently. He needed to make it look like it was strictly Asmodeus' idea, hence the hiring of a human and demon team to hunt him down. Once he has some dominion on Earth, he feels that he can slowly spread it until he has taken over a sizable chunk. As long as he doesn't try to bite off too much at once, he feels our adversary won't do much to stop him, leaving choice as always up to the humans."

"That explains a lot. But it makes my choices tougher. Going against our master would be out-and-out idiocy, but letting my human counterpart be destroyed goes against my demon ethics. I am supposed to be his protector."

"Look, Laura-Luss, forget the human and get out. It is your only real option."

"You know me well enough, Foxy, to know I could not do that."

"Then I had better tell you the rest of what I have learned. Your life will depend on it. I just learned today from one of Asmodeus' local assistants about a plot within a plot. He did not know any real details or even what the plot was, only that there was a plot. So, what I am going to tell you is strictly supposition. I think that Asmodeus plans on somehow either trapping or even destroying Satan himself."

"What! How could that be possible?"

"I don't know Laura-Luss, but I am willing to bet on it. You are going to be caught in the middle of a battle between the two greatest powers in Hell, and no matter who the winner is, you will not survive it. I am asking, no begging you, as the only friend I can say I have, to let the human go and stay out of it."

Seeing the genuine caring in his eyes, Laura-Luss softened her response. "I truly thank you for caring. I never would have suspected it of one of our kind, and I will be very careful, but Foxy, this is something I must do."

"So, it can happen; a demoness can truly fall in love with a human. Don't let anyone know, Laura-Luss. You know the penalty for that."

"Oh, hogwash, I am not in love, just not ready to fail in my job, so forget that nonsense. I will have to leave here for a time. Believe me, Foxy, I will be very careful. One last thing. Have any of your 'sources' mentioned the golem and how he fits in all this? It is unusual for a golem to get involved in politics."

"That was easy to piece together, even before my sources told me. The one thing a golem truly wants is to be human. That is what Asmodeus promised him. Satan is unaware of the deal and of golem's involvement. I think Asmodeus plans to use the golem in his plan to trap our master. That will probably result in the golem's destruction, but that is of no matter to Asmodeus. Besides, if the golem gained his humanity by dealing with evil, well then, he would gain a soul only to lose it right away, either to Satan or Asmodeus, whoever won the day."

"Thanks for everything, Foxy. Keep me informed when you can if you hear of anything that could be useful, and in return, I will pass on to you information I learn about what is happening up top. Deal?"

"Of course, my dear. And one more thing. Please keep the information about my source to yourself."

"My lips are sealed," responded Laura-Luss as she got up from the table and left the room. The smile on her face was from knowing she still had something to hold over the Fairy Fox should she ever need to.

Laura-Luss knew as she left The Devils Horns that she had to get this information to Tom as soon as possible, but still, there was one more thing she had to do before she left for the surface. She somehow had to get access to Hell's computers and see if she could trace who were Asmodeus' most trusted servants and which ones were located on Earth. By running a program tracing minor demons' paths over the last two years, and from that deducing who they served, she might be able to use this to find out what she needed. She knew she could not possibly spend the time required here to run the program, but she could start it and have the computer automatically forward it to Tom's email address, then she could finish the program on Tom's laptop. The trick would be to start the program here without anyone knowing.

Laura-Luss knew just who to turn to for this. Ilyish the Imp. A small blob of a creature he just happened to run in the same circle as many bogies, smoky, amorphous creatures that liked to live in cupboards and the like. There just happened to be a bogie, Barttle was his name, who lived in the cupboard in the computer room. Ilyish also happened to have his own computer and was sweet on Laura-Luss. The fact that she treated him kindly helped, of course, and she was smart enough to know it.

Finding Ilyish was another problem. For hours, Laura-Luss walked through the corridors of Hell asking after him and calling out his name. Finally, she remembered he liked hanging around the library. A cursory check there proved unsuccessful until she thought to check the cupboards. Sure enough, at the back of one of the rear storage cupboards, she found him conversing with a rather dark-colored bogie. In his delight at seeing Laura-Luss, he ran through the bogie, causing a loud popping sound as the bogie disappeared.

"So sorry, Larry did not mean to dissipate you like that," said the imp over his shoulder as he rushed over to Laura-Luss. "Laura-Luss, I am so happy to see you. It has been so long. What brings you here now? You must be looking for me. Why else would you be looking in closets in the library? I am sure you did not leave a coat here. And the Librarian would not have told you to go find something in this closet, as the only thing in here is Larry the Bogie. I mean, why—"

"Slow down, Ilyias. I know you are excited to see me, but you must learn to curb your enthusiasm." An imp's tendency to yak on and on without pause has caused many to ignore them as being the safest way not to get caught in a two-hour conversation over nothing.

"I am sorry, but I can't stay here for long. I need your help with something, and then I have to rush and help a client. You know I hate to ask and run, but this is very important."

With a big sigh, Ilyias answered with a patience seldom seen in an imp, "I understand, Laura-Luss. You are one of the few who take time to listen, so if you are in a hurry, it must be important. What can I do for you?"

"Thank you very much for understanding, Ilyias. You are a gem amongst imps. I need to run a program from Hell's computers, but at this time, I can't be seen to be here. I would need your computer to prepare the program and then the help of the computer room bogie to run it for me. Do you think you can do this?"

"This sounds highly intriguing and dangerous to me. Could the bogie get hurt doing this?"

Trust Ilyias to think of the bogie and not himself. If humans only knew what happens amongst Hell's lesser creatures, Laura-Luss thought to herself.

"There is a small chance, but if we do not tell him what it is about and lead him to believe he is only doing as his master says, then it would be minimal. If all else fails, you can blame it all on me, saying I forced him."

"Won't that get you in big trouble with our boss?"

"Probably, but it is also quite possible that he will reward me greatly instead."

"Okay, then we had better get to work."

Turning back to the cupboard, Ilyias said, "Larry, do you think you could carry a parcel and some instructions to Barttle for me later?" There was a slight coalescence in the cupboard and then nothing again. "Thanks, Larry, I appreciate it. I will bring it to you in about an hour."

Turning to Laura-Luss, he asked, "Will that give you enough time to prepare the program?"

"Yes, it should. I have already thought out the parameters in my head, so it should be quick. Just lead me to your computer."

Less than forty-five minutes had passed when they returned. Explaining what to do took a good fifteen minutes, but Larry seemed finally to understand that all Barttle had to do was put the disc in the CD-ROM and it would start automatically. Although Laura-Luss was a little concerned about his grasp of what a CD-ROM was, Ilyias told her not to worry as bogies tended to learn a lot about their immediate surroundings and little about anything else. Once Barttle had it in his hands, he explained, the bogie would know what to do with it. Fortunately, Hell had not progressed quite as far as humans in their technology. Explaining how to use a CD-ROM was easy. Trying to explain ports and programming would be quite another.

Laura-Luss and Ilyias waited impatiently for Larry's return. It was almost another hour before he coalesced in the cupboard and made some noises to Ilyias, who then turned to Laura-Luss with a big smile on his face.

"Barttle told Larry to tell you that your program is running fine, and he set the computer to erase the disc and the info on the hard drive once it had emailed all the information to the address you had preset. See, I told you Barttle knows what he is doing."

"Thanks, Ilyias. I guess it takes someone like you to take the time to learn about others. I appreciate this and won't forget it."

"I guess this means that you are leaving now?"

"Yes, I am. Sorry, Ilyias, but I must leave now. It would be better if you did not tell anyone you saw me. Things could get uncomfortable for anyone who appears to be my friend for a while. Keep low and be careful, okay?"

"You too, Laura-Luss. I hope this human is worth all you are doing for him. You must care for him."

"Why does everyone think I could care less about a human? He is only an assignment. And anyway, how did you know my client was a human?"

"Just the way you are acting. Goodbye, LL," and with that, the imp disappeared.

CHAPTER 13

"Hello, could I speak with Dom Dominic Sicone, please?" Tom asked the fellow who answered the Abbey's phone. Finding the number had proved quite simple. A visit to their website provided all the information Tom needed.

"I am sorry, but he is currently working in the fields. I do expect him in shortly. Can I have him call you back?"

"Yes, please, it is his cousin Tom. I am currently in Montreal on business and would like to see him if he is available." Tom then gave the clerk, or brother, or whatever he was, his cell phone number and closed the connection. He then did a quick MapQuest search on how to get to the Abbey, closed his laptop, and left the hotel. He knew he could have just programmed the Waze on his phone, but did not want to eat up data unnecessarily. Realizing it was a good hour's drive, Tom figured he would head that way and hope his cousin could see him.

Tom was thankful that the rental car came with a cell phone rest and Bluetooth so he could drive along while waiting for his cousin to call. He didn't need to add a traffic violation to his expense account if a cop spotted him talking on his phone. He had been informed that they were quite strict in Quebec about that. The mild weather allowed Tom to lower his window and take in the fresh air. The sun continued to shine brightly, and Tom could almost forget the case he was working on and just enjoy the drive.

He had just crossed the bridge into Laval on the 13 Highway when his phone rang.

"Tom, is that really you?" came the baritone voice of his cousin Dominic.

"Hi, cuz, how are you doing?" Tom responded with genuine enthusiasm. It had been years since he spoke to his cousin.

"What in heaven's name are you doing in this neck of the woods?"

"Working on a case and thought since I was nearby, I would drop over and have a coffee with you. That is, of course, if you can see me at this time."

"Of course, I can see you. The Order doesn't keep us locked up in little cells where we're forced to take an oath of silence, like some seem to think. When do you think you could come over?"

"I am already on my way. Probably arrive in thirty or forty minutes."

"That would be wonderful. I just came in from clearing some of the fields and could use a shower first. With these unseasonably warm temperatures, we decided to prep the fields ahead of time for spring planting. Just come through the main gates, and I'll meet you there."

"Okay, Dom, see you soon." Tom closed the phone.

The drive over was quite peaceful, and the countryside was beautiful. There were still traces of snow on the sides of the highway, but for the most part, the area seemed to be in spring thaw. Like New York, the Montreal area appeared to have had an unusual winter with frequent warm spells.

Pulling up in front of the Abbey was an experience. The mostly stone building itself was large and well-maintained, and the grounds were quite extensive. His cousin was standing at the front entrance, waiting for him.

Dom Dominic was a large, imposing figure; however, not much of his size had to do with fat. His brown hair was thinning but still covered his large ears well. As kids, they used to call him Dumbo since he sported a crew cut back then. His face was all angles with a sharply cut, squared-off chin, almost like the old G.I. Joe army figures. But when he smiled, his entire face lit up, including his deep brown eyes.

"Tom Tom, you are looking well as always. I'm so glad you stopped by while in Quebec. It's been way too long."

"Monastic life seems to agree with you, Dom. Or maybe I should call you Dom Dom. You're as fit as I remember you were when you were a Marine, those many years ago. How we all envied you, in that uniform, the older cousin going off to fight the bad guys."

"We keep busy here and work hard, but it is worth it. Brings us closer to God, I believe. As for my old Marine days, well, suffice it to say the things I saw are what led me to this life, I think. And if you call me Dom Dom again, I will show you how fit I am. Let me give you a tour of the grounds and then we can grab a coffee, park ourselves on one of the outdoor benches, and you can tell me what brings you here, okay?"

"I would love that. The place here is quite impressive. Also, any time you call me Tom Tom, I will call you Dom Dom, and risk the beating."

"Point taken. As for this place, Tom, you don't begin to know the least of it. I've been here for five years now, and still, it amazes me. I seem to discover something new all the time. For instance, this building we are facing. Originally built in the early 1890s it has twice been destroyed by fire, the first time in July 1902 and the second time in December 1916. It seems this place was plagued by fires, losing various other structures in 1895 and, of course, during the fire of 1916. This main building underwent major renovations in the early 1970s.

"Over there, you can see the barns, the fields, and so on. Attached to the main building is the store where we sell a lot of what we produce. We're famous for our cheese, amongst other produce. We have honey bees, maple syrup, chocolates, jellies, and so on. We're pretty well self-sufficient."

Dominic showed Tom through the buildings, going into places that the general public usually did not get to see, and finished in the main lobby, which included aerial views of the property.

"This actual order began in 1881 when eight Trappists left the Abbey of Bellefontaine in France to begin a new foundation in Canada. However, if you check the origins of our order, we are part of the Cistercian order, which goes back over nine centuries. The order now has a hundred and sixty-two monasteries, some sixty-six of which are for nuns.

"As for me, this is the life I prefer. I feel close to God every time I work the orchards, touch the soil, or pray and worship with my fellow brethren. Your brother chose his way to be close to God, and I chose this way. In both cases, we are serving and worshiping the Lord. However, enough about me. I would like to hear what brings you to me on this beautiful day. Let us grab a coffee from the store and take a seat over by the main building."

A few minutes later, they had settled on a bench facing the sun where they could soak in its warmth. Tom was just considering how much to tell his cousin when Dominic spoke up.

"I received a brief call from John just before you arrived here. We could not talk for long, but he did tell me that your case was of a religious nature and that some of the special information of which I have been privy may be of use to you. But before I can know what could be of help, maybe you can fill me in on what this is all about."

"Trust my brother to be one step ahead of me as always. Okay, I was trying to figure out how much to tell you and what you would accept about it, but if John thinks it is all right to tell you, then I will trust his judgment. I assume you are more aware of the actual dichotomy between the Church and God and the servants of Evil than the average lay Christian? Just by your expression, I see you are. So then here it is."

Tom proceeded to outline the case to his cousin, leaving out few details, except maybe the actual dynamics between himself and Laura-Luss. His cousin's facial expression hardly changed throughout his discourse, and he remained silent the whole time, so when Tom finally wrapped it up with Laura-Luss' sudden departure, he had no idea whether his cousin even believed a word he'd said.

After several minutes, Dom Dominic finally broke the silence.

"Tom, Tom, Tom, you were always the one of us who knew how to get into the deepest pile of manure, weren't you? Here, there are probably a dozen members of our large family deeply involved in the Church, and you, the hold-out, happen to be the one who gets to go head-to-head with old twin horns himself. I tell you, if not for what I personally have seen and read, I would not believe a word that you have said."

Tom was about to respond when Dom held up his hand to stop him.

"I will tell you something that happened to me several years ago that I have only told your brother, John, and no one else, not even my confessor. Get ready to hear a hair-raising tale, one that you would never have believed before you started this case.

"I was nearing the end of my term as a Marine. I had already decided to resign from the forces and follow a religious path. But what happened to me then just confirmed that my decision was the proper one.

"My last year as a marine proved to be a busy one. My contract was to expire in 2010, but was extended unilaterally by the government. This was towards the end of the Anbar campaign. In theory, our role as Marines was finished; however, we were still running black ops that the public did not know about.

"Iraq was a hellhole, not because of the country itself but because of what the Iraqi army itself did to it. As they retreated, they destroyed many of their historical monuments, as well as the homes of any groups that did not support them. Walking through some of those areas, we even needed masks to allow us to breathe because of the carnage.

"But it wasn't only the destruction of buildings that made Iraq a hell. It was also the human tragedy. Besides the thousands of displaced, there were many hundreds of dead, sometimes just lying on the side of the road, sometimes in shallow graves, but often in makeshift torture chambers. Some of these places were truly evil. Liberating one small town, one of its former councilors led us to a particularly horrible place. The building was not very noteworthy in itself. A small brick structure located off the main square. Even entering what proved to be a former dentist's office, there was nothing in view that would have led anyone to believe it was anything more than it seemed, a small office building. But as soon as I walked in, I could feel the evil of the place.

"The city councilor would not go any further than the front door, but he kept pointing towards the back of the place and saying, 'really bad down there, really bad'. There were five in my immediate squad with me, as I had the rest of my troop watching the front of the building. We took up positions to cover each other and made our way to the back. Just down the hall and around the corner, we came to a door that was partly ajar and led to a flight of steps. Standing at the top of the steps, the stench that came from the lower level was unbelievable.

"We slowly made our way down, but arriving at the bottom landing, we realized that we would not find anything living here. Strung along the walls were manacles bolted to the bricks themselves, as well as some hanging from the ceilings and the floors. Still attached to many of these were people, men, women, and even a couple of children, probably a couple of dozen in all. Some appeared to have been dead for days, some for only hours, but all had been brutally tortured.

"I set my men about the task of finding the keys so we could remove the bodies from here, as no one deserved to be left like that, at the same time as seeing if there were any still alive. I hoped that none were, because of the horrendous things that had been done to them. I walked around the room checking for doors or hallways. At the far right rear, I saw what appeared to be an opening, and sure enough, there was a hallway there.

Since the lighting did not extend back that far, I took out my flashlight and shone it down that corridor. I walked a little way down when I heard a noise. Calling for one of my troops to follow me, I continued. Just as I got to where the way seemed to turn, I came across a sight I wish to this day God would burn out of my head forever.

"Lying on the ground was a man, by his uniform, an Iraqi soldier. His stomach was ripped open, and some creature, a demon from hell, was standing over him and devouring his intestines. Tom, the man, was still alive while this was going on!

"I raised my gun to shoot the creature, but it just looked up at me with these evil red eyes, and I could not do a thing. Then it spoke. To this day, I remember every word it said. It is burned into my brain; it was so shocking to me. I quote: 'Put down your weapon, Dominic. This one belongs to me. He has tortured and killed with relish, enjoying the suffering of all his victims. Now it is his turn to suffer, but his will be for eternity. And yet you can pity him if you wish. For he was only following in the steps he chose when he decided to worship my master.' Then he picked up the still squirming body, waved at me, and disappeared.

"Tom, for all that I have always believed in God and the ways of the Church, nothing confirmed it more than seeing that. I had already decided months before to leave the Marines and take the vows of a religious life, but that helped me to decide how."

Dom Dominic went silent for a while, sipping his coffee and staring at nothing. Tom was afraid to disturb the moment, realizing that his cousin still had more to tell him, but he had to focus his thoughts.

After several minutes, Tom felt compelled to say something.

"I had not realized that such travesties of humanity had taken place in Iraq, but to see a demon, well, if I had not experienced these last few days myself, I would not have believed your story."

"Tom, it goes much deeper than that. The other Marine with me who saw this, well, to this day, he is still in a psychiatric hospital. No one believed his story, except me, and those I came to work with after.

"When I resigned from the Marines a few months later, I knew what I wanted to do. I wanted to become a demon hunter. However, I did not begin to know where to start. It was your brother who guided me in that. He had just taken his vows in the priesthood, and well, he was knowledgeable in ways that surprised me. I confided in him about what happened and what I wanted to do about it. He was quite reticent about helping me, and I was so sure it was because he did not believe a thing I told him. I expected him to tell me that it was all a delusion, something my mind did to me to account for the horror of what I had seen. I could not have been more wrong.

"He was trying to protect me. It was only after he realized that I was determined to do this with or without his help that he agreed to set me on the right track. He knew that if I succeeded in confronting even a single demon without the right tools, my fate would have been even worse than death.

"There is a group within the Catholic Church that does what I wanted to do, tracks down and destroys demons that have made an unwelcome presence on Earth. I will not tell you who they are or what they are called, as I have been sworn to secrecy. I spent three hair-raising years with them, battling not only demons but other supernatural creatures. I watched a couple of my teammates die, usually in horrible ways, and fought and destroyed various evil creatures. When I got to the point that I was beginning to enjoy doing it, I realized it was time to get out, before I started to become as evil as the creatures I fought. When I was offered the chance to come here and live a life of peace and closeness to God, I jumped at it. It was probably the best thing I have ever done.

"Still with all that I have done, I never came close to tackling one of the major demons, let alone old horned toad himself. Do you have a plan of action?"

"I guess the next step will depend on what Laura-Luss has to say when she returns. Probably confront the golem. He is nearby, accessible, and has knowledge we can use."

"I might be able to help with that. The funny thing is that golems are not evil creatures. They are kind of one-tracked in that once they are set on something, they are almost impossible to turn away from their goal. But they aren't stupid. Try talking to him first. I am sure John must have told you how difficult they are to kill. There is one tiny trick to slow them down, though. A cross, of course, means nothing to them, but the Star of David is another thing. It won't physically harm them, but it sort of puts them in a trance, long enough to either escape, reason with them, or maybe kill them in the way John must have told you."

Reaching into his vest pocket, Dominic pulled out a velvet pouch and handed it to Tom.

"I took the liberty of bringing this when John mentioned to me that there was a golem involved. Inside the pouch is a Star of David made of pure silver. I still have several souvenirs from my demon-fighting days, and this is one that I kept and could never figure out why. I guess the Lord provides when it is needed."

"Thanks, Dom, I appreciate this. I tell you, I never realized what the Church went through until I started on this case. Those old Hollywood movies about demons and fighting the Devil barely touched on the reality of the situation. I understand why the Church doesn't fully disclose what is going on, but don't you think they should do something more to prepare the public?"

"It is never simple. The Church does a balancing act and must be very careful about what it says and recommends. The witch hunts of the 17th, 18th, and 19th centuries show what can happen when good intentions are left to run their course with the wrong people in charge. That started as a plan to wipe out demon presence from the face of the earth. It started well, but then the devil had some of his followers within the Church, and yes, there probably still are some there to this day, who start to shift the hunt from just devil worshipers to all who showed any type of magical powers at all, even some that were truly blessed by God. Then, of course, man's normal greed took over from there, just as Satan had planned.

"There have also been other attempts. Hollywood itself played a role in that with movies like *The Exorcist*. What we don't want to do is cause panic. At the same time, if we come on too strong, people will just laugh at us and say we're using scare tactics to get people to go to church. The best we can do at present is to fight those demons as they appear and try to get people to act morally. God's edict of allowing humans the right to choose their destiny also makes it difficult to get people to follow a more righteous path.

Free will or dictatorship. Damned if you do or damned if you don't. Like I said, a difficult balancing act."

"I see what you mean. I guess all you can do is try to have the right people in the right place at the right time and pray all falls into place. Let me ask you something, Dom. With all the experience you've had fighting demons, have you ever come across any that are not evil, that have some goodness in them?"

"That is a tough question since I mostly fought the ones that were doing harm. Several supernatural creatures are neither good nor evil but can do either. But I know that is not what you are asking. Let me put it this way. If it has one hundred percent demon blood, I would find it highly unlikely that there is any capacity whatsoever to do good or to care about a fellow creature at all. However, if there is human blood in its ancestry, well, that can change everything. The human capacity to overcome any difficulties seems to be able to overcome even bloodline disadvantages.

"So yes, your demoness is probably capable of thinking and even doing good deeds. And many demons do act in an honorable way, at least by their standards. However, should one ever happen to fall in love, well, that is an emotion they are not allowed to feel by the Devil's edict. Should a demon, even one that is more human than demon, fall in love, well, they would end up being sent to the deepest pits. Even demons can be made to suffer in Hell."

"I already heard that one from Laura-Luss. It seems a lot of what she has told me has been confirmed by other sources. Any other advice for me then?"

"Yes, don't fall in love with a demon! Seriously, though, keep your wits about you. Generally, we humans have only two real weapons against evil. Our wits and our beliefs. Don't be afraid to turn to prayer if you find yourself in a tough situation. God often provides in ways we can never fathom and often only realize in hindsight, if at all."

"Thanks for everything, Dom. I guess I should head back to town and see if the demoness has returned. We have a lot to do and little time to do it in."

"Listen, Tom, pay careful attention to what the demoness tells you. She seems to be acting honorably, but remember who her master is. Still, you are better off with her at your side when you are fighting supernatural creatures like the golem than being on your own. So don't try to tackle him until she is back, okay?"

"I will heed your words, cousin," Tom replied as he stood to leave. He hugged his cousin and walked back to his car. He was just getting ready to put it in gear when he saw that his cell phone had a message on it. He did not remember hearing it ring, but that was the way with cell phones sometimes. It was a text message from Laura-Luss asking him to meet her at Mt Royal Park, up near the observation deck. It seemed a strange place to meet, but then again, demons were strange creatures. Tom backed his car out of the parking place, eased into the traffic on Oka Street, and headed back towards Montreal.

CHAPTER 14

The trip to the surface took longer than Laura-Luss would have liked, but she had to make sure she was not seen. Knowing that her master had his eyes elsewhere at the moment was a bit of a relief; however, there were still enough spies around to make things uncomfortable. Climbing through the cave's mouth and into the light of day gave her a moment of hesitation due to the presence of the cross. Still, she was out of sight of it and should be able to climb around the side again without falling under its shadow and without being seen.

Sure enough, she reached one of the lookout rails and was able to climb over in a moment when no one else was present. Pulling out her cell phone, she entered Tom's preprogrammed number.

"Hello, Ms. Laura-Luss," Tom's voice was crisp and clear, almost as if he were beside her.

"Tom, we have no time to chit-chat. Things are moving faster and are much bigger than we originally thought. I am currently on Mt. Royal. How soon can you be here to pick me up?"

"I am already here. As per your message, I headed here right after I met with my cousin, Dom Dominic. I'm currently on the path to the observation deck about two-thirds of the way."

"Tom, I never sent you a message. I just got back from my trip a few minutes ago.

Someone is obviously on to us. Keep heading to the observation deck, but I suggest you pick up the pace, even run if you can. I will meet you there in a few minutes. Maybe in public, we will be safe. Don't close the line, though, so I can hear if you get into trouble."

"I'm assuming we are expecting trouble of the kind from your world, not just regular ruffians like back in New York."

"We can probably count on this being completely otherworldly this time. How close are you now?"

"I can see it from where I am now." Tom's breath was becoming a little ragged. "However, now I think I'm being shadowed by something in the woods."

"Just stay on the path and keep surrounded by people."

"Only as long as they stay in the woods. If they come after me on the path, I will not endanger innocents."

"I understand your compassion, Tom, but if we fail in what we have to do, thousands of innocents may perish."

"I will not allow any to die if I can help it. So far, they are remaining in the woods, and I am now entering the observation deck area. I do suggest you hurry, though."

"I see you now, Tom, do you see me? Good, then make your way over here."

In a few moments, the two stood side by side with Tom gulping in air.

"I thought I was in shape," he said between breaths," but running half a mile straight uphill at full speed in a suit is not the easiest thing to do. Thank God it's almost spring. Doing this with temperatures well below freezing would have been damn near impossible. What type of creature do you think is out there?"

"I was able to catch a glimpse of one as you entered the observation deck. It looked like a hellhound, which means trouble. They usually hunt in packs of eight. By the way, congratulations for using God and damn at nearly the same time. You are getting into the spirit of the hunt now, so to speak."

Ignoring her comment, Tom asked, "Exactly what is a hellhound? Is that something like the hounds of the wild hunt, and can we expect the huntsman to be with them?"

"I am assuming that these are just the minor hellhounds because the two major ones, Cerberus and Orthrus, are currently guarding the gates to Hell. Most of the hellhounds are direct descendants of these two. Also, the hounds of the wild hunt and the huntsman only hunt at night and are much more intelligent than these probably are. They are what they sound like, dogs from hell. They stand about five and a half feet at the shoulder, weigh about three hundred pounds, have vicious fangs, can breathe fire somewhat, and smell of brimstone, Hell's trademark aroma. Usually, they are a brownish-red color, their teeth are black, and their eyes are a fiery red. Once they have their prey's scent, they follow it until either their prey is dead, they are dead, or they are called back. I am sure we can assume they will not be called back. So, either we have to kill them or let them kill us. Which do you prefer, Mr. Detective?"

"Oh, I am all for killing them. Any special tricks for doing that?"

"Well, first off, don't let them breathe on you, and of course, don't let them bite you. Even a small nip is deadly for a human. Poisonous, you know."

"I kind of figured that would be the case. How easy or difficult is it to kill one?"

"Silver bullet through the heart or the brain should do the job. Also, ripping their heads off their body tends to stop them cold. I do hope that the gun you have under your jacket has more than just regular bullets in it."

"My brother has me covered. What we need to do now is find a place where they can only come at us one or two at a time, and where there are not any people around. Besides not wanting to hurt anyone, we would have a hard time explaining to local authorities what happened, and I'm sure neither your boss nor the one upstairs wants something like this to become too public. And since your boss happens to be my client, I don't think my boss would like me to blow this case wide open in this way."

"More than you know, Tom, more than you know. You are right about not staying in public. For now, they are holding back, but eventually, their bloodlust will overcome the little intelligence they have. They will attack soon. Since they already know where we are, and have obviously been tracking our moves for a while, or at the very least anticipating well, then it will probably be safe if I use a bit of my demon power.

"What I am going to do now, Tom, will drain me so I will be literally at your mercy for a few minutes. I guess there comes a time when even demons must learn to trust a little, huh? Follow me over to that rock there so we can be out of sight of the general public. What I am about to do would be a little hard to explain to the common person."

"And that is?" asked Tom.

"I am going to phase us to another location."

"What? But I thought you said you could not do that?"

"Well, I was not entirely truthful. I can move us, but only a short distance, and I will be totally without strength for several minutes after that. I won't even be able to walk on my own."

"How far is a short distance?"

"Probably not much further than a half a mile, maybe three-quarters of a mile if we are really lucky."

"And what will that accomplish?"

"It will get us away from public eyes and into a place we can defend, I hope. As well, it is easier than trying to run in the snow that is remaining. But it won't take long for the hounds to pick up our scent again, so we will have maybe two or three minutes at most to get into position. Once I get us there, it will be up to you to defend us until I can recover. I spotted a place back in the woods near an embankment that should be easy to defend if I can get us that far. Pray that I can."

"To whom do you prefer, your master or my God?"

"About now, we may only have your God to depend on." Seeing Tom about to speak again, Laura-Luss continued. "I'll explain it all later. Let's do this now while we have a chance and while I still have the nerve."

Seeing how nervous she was about putting herself into a vulnerable position in his hands, Tom decided now was not the time to crack a joke about being in a position to finally take advantage of her. Instead, he watched with Laura-Luss until there was no one nearby and ducked behind the rock with her. She put her arm around his waist, and the whole world seemed to fade away. They reappeared a moment later in a different place, but from what Tom could see, they were at least a few hundred yards from a defensible position, and Laura-Luss had just passed out in his arms.

Tom knew he had little time. Throwing Laura-Luss over his shoulder in a fireman's carry, Tom settled into a run that he hoped he could sustain long enough to reach the spot Laura-Luss had picked out. Sure enough, he had no sooner set out than he could hear the howling of the hounds as they picked up their scent. Hearing their howls was enough to give Tom that extra burst of adrenaline to get him there.

What Laura-Luss had picked out was a small U-shaped outcropping of rocks where they could set their backs against something and would not permit the hounds to come at them from more than one direction. At most two hounds could come at a time.

Gently laying Laura-Luss on the ground, Tom pulled out his Smith and Wesson 357 and picked up a large stick lying nearby. He had just gotten himself into a defensible position when the first of the hounds made its appearance.

It was easily as large as the demoness had told him. Steam was coming out of its nostrils as it ran towards him, its fiery red eyes blazing in hatred. Now Tom could see the others coming behind, but this lead one was not waiting for the others. All it saw was a helpless human holding a gun whose bullets should not have been able to hurt it. Tom was quite thankful he had thought to load it with the special bullets given to him by his brother as he watched the lead hound's head blow apart from impact with his first shot.

Seeing the lead hound fall, the others slowed their pace, holding back to let one of the others go first. They may not have been very intelligent, but they were not stupid enough to just throw away their lives. Even though Tom was a good shot, trying to hit a moving target from two hundred yards with a pistol was not a sound strategy. Especially since he only had seven rounds left in the pistol, and as the demoness had told him, there were a total of eight hounds in the pack.

"Seven rounds and seven pups. Guess I can't afford to miss." Tom thought his voice sounded quite steady considering what he was facing. Taking a glance behind him, he saw that the demoness was still in the same position he had left her. No help from there for now.

The hell hounds were showing more caution now with one of their number lying dead on the ground in front of them. Tom knew this would not last for long. Laura-Luss seemed quite sure they would not leave unless their job was accomplished, or they had died in the attempt, and Tom and no reason to doubt what she said. Now he was to put all those extra days at the firing range to the test.

The woods were darkening as the sun began to set, and now Tom began to see that time might not be on his side either. The hellhound's night vision was probably far superior to Tom's. Also, the cross was now lit up and would soon dominate the area, and Tom had no idea how this would affect Laura-Luss once they left the cover of the woods, that is, of course, if they managed to defeat the hounds so that they could leave.

Tom was just beginning to prepare a desperate plan in his mind, one that had him rushing the hounds to draw them to him and then trying to get back to the shelter before they did, when the hounds took the option out of his hands. As a pack racing two by two, they suddenly charged.

Resting the stick against a rock, Tom took a two-handed stance with the pistol and faced the charging hounds. Waiting until they were less than a hundred yards away, Tom fired two shots in quick succession, dropping the two lead hounds. The ones behind them leaped over their fallen brethren and continued. At fifty yards, Tom fired off two more rounds, both making contact, and two more hounds hit the dirt.

Quickly, the hounds adjusted, now running single file. Thirty yards. Twenty yards. Fifteen yards as Tom fired a single shot. Down went the lead hound again, but now there was not enough time to fire another as both hounds leaped at him. Tom hit the ground, grabbed the stick, and simultaneously fired off the two shots. One hit one of the hounds in the hind quarters as it flew over him, the other missed completely as the rear hound grabbed his stick-bearing arm, ripping the sleeve and pulling Tom back to the ground.

Desperately, Tom hit the hound in the head with the empty pistol, smacking the creature over and over again with all his strength until it finally released its grip. Rolling away from the creature, Tom got only to his knees before the creature leaped at him once again. With no time to spare, Tom pulled the stick in front of him and braced himself as the hound hit him full force, impaling itself on the stick.

Tom pushed the creature away with the stick still lodged in its chest and backed up, preparing to continue to fight bare-handed should the hound try to rise again. However, that hound would never rise again as the wooden stake passed right through its heart.

He was just breathing a sigh of relief when he heard a crunching on the ground behind him, and as he turned saw the hound he had wounded in the air and almost on him. Realizing he had no time to react and no hope of killing this last hound, Tom faced his death.

Tonight, however, was not the night he was destined to die. From seemingly out of thin air, two huge hands grabbed the hound by the throat, snapped its neck, and sent the creature flying onto the rocks with a sickeningly final crunch. Facing his rescuer, Tom only saw the ever-bodacious Laura-Luss standing in front of him, hands as feminine-looking as always.

"That was some fine shooting, Mr. Wilkins. I guess your brother did prepare you. Normal bullets would not have even slowed a hellhound, let alone killed it. What are you packing?"

Taking her nonchalant attitude in stride, Tom responded just as flippantly, "Oh, just a few silver bullets packed with gunpowder mixed a little differently than the norm. However, those beefsteak mittens of yours sure came in handy. How did you manage that?"

"Just a trick I picked up at demon school."

"What, you go to school to learn demon tricks?!" exclaimed Tom.

Seeing the expression on his face, Laura-Luss couldn't help but laugh. "Tom, Tom, just a little joke. Most demons, mid-level and higher, are capable of a little shape-shifting. I just felt it would be easier to ring that loathsome creature's neck if I had hands to wrap around it."

Tom chuckled a little at himself as he pictured in his mind demons of all shapes and sizes sitting in a classroom. Crazy idea!

"I gather from the way you referred to the hound that you are not overjoyed with these creatures?"

"They are the lowest scum from the depths of the pits of the deepest tar sands in Hell. They stink, they slink, and they serve no purpose but to kill, and they will even kill demons if they can get away with it, just for the pleasure of killing. The fact that these were set upon us means that someone is afraid of us."

"Why do you say that?"

"Because hellhounds are just as likely to turn on the one who sends them as they are to kill their prey. Only top-level demons would even attempt to use them."

"Which means either Asmodeus is on to us or your master has decided we are getting too close to his plans."

This time, it was Laura-Luss' turn to be surprised. Looking him right in the eye, she asked, "Do you have new information I am not aware of?"

"Just being logical. Everything here points to major demon activity. If not Asmodeus, who else but the head honcho himself?"

"Well, Tom, you may be closer to the mark than you realize. What I have learned is that my boss and Asmodeus had made a plan together to give my boss a little more power on this plane of existence. That is the real reason Asmodeus was allowed by you know who to come here. However, now I feel Asmodeus is setting a trap for my overlord."

"A trap? For what purpose?"

"To rule Hell, of course."

"I don't see that it makes a difference to us humans who rules Hell. Maybe if they are allowed to fight it out, both will be weakened, and God will just step in and mop up the remains."

"It's not as easy as that, Tom, and yes, it makes a hell of a difference who rules Hell."

"Why is that?"

"Satan understands that there must be a balance between Heaven and Hell. Also, he wants to rule on Earth, and to do that, he needs humans to populate it. For Earth to remain Earthlike and not just become a reflection of Hell, humans still have to have free choice, to still be able to do good. Satan wants to be stronger on Earth, not to wipe it out. If Asmodeus takes over, he will make Earth Hell-incarnate. In essence, he would want to tip the balance in his favor and eventually rule all. In that world, there would remain no humans with the capacity to do good."

"Okay, I get the point. The Devil is bad, Asmodeus even worse. So, how does Asmodeus plan on trapping your boss? How do we stop him, and at the same time send everyone back to where they belong so the balance remains as is with no net gain for Hell? I do mean that, Laura-Luss. If the plan is to help Satan succeed in establishing a toe hold on Earth, I will not be a party to that."

"Good, I am glad that is out in the open. It allows me to make a deal with you. You help me stop Asmodeus from completing his plans, and I will do all in my power to ensure that Satan departs without that toe hold on your Earth. Deal?" asked Laura-Luss, holding out her hand.

Looking her in the eyes, Tom felt with all his soul that she meant what she said. He shook her hand firmly and said, "Now I think we'd better get out of here before anything else comes at us. Besides, I'm sure you can't be too comfortable with the cross shining on you as it is."

Looking up to where Tom was facing, Laura-Luss realized that the lights from the Mt. Royal cross were shining right on her, and yet she felt no discomfort. Afraid of what that could mean, she turned away and quickly marched back into the woods and towards the main paths. Tom followed right behind her, knowing that something profound had just happened but not understanding what it could be.

CHAPTER 15

"So let me get this straight. Your plan is to go and ring the golem's doorbell, tell him who we are, and try to negotiate with him. That type of fool plan is liable to get us killed!"

Laura-Luss was back in her fiery form, eyes blazing as she faced Tom. Sitting in the passenger seat, car idling, the discussion went on as to how best to handle the golem.

"Look, what you have told me gives me every reason to believe that he's being used and that we can make use of that ourselves by turning him on Asmodeus. My cousin is quite sure we can talk with him, although he did say we should take precautions. This Star of David should help equalize things a little."

"That will give us what, a minute or two?"

"More like fifteen or twenty seconds."

"Tom, there is no way you have that much of a silver tongue that you can convince him in that amount of time, and being a golem, my type of feminine persuasions would not move him in the least. No, I still say we sneak into his house later tonight, jump him, and after I have torn him apart a little, you do that little thing about stamping whatever on his forehead, and we will be done with him. No more worrying about him coming up behind us."

"And no information that might help us. Remember, golems are just as powerful as demons, if not more so. If you don't hold him long enough, he would probably finish us both off very quickly, and anything I tried to say to dissuade him would be ignored at that point. Besides what we've learned about this particular golem, he would probably be amused at us just walking up to his door, knocking, and asking to talk with him. He might not necessarily believe us right away, but I have a good feeling that he would listen to everything we had to say."

"So now we are going to trust this entire mission on a … feeling? You are not playing with a full deck, Mr. Tom Wilkins."

"Right now, gut feelings may be all we have to go on, Ms. Laura-Luss," returned Tom just as formally. "Humans rely on it. You demons should try it sometime. It just might bring you a step closer to us humans."

"Perish the thought!"

"Okay, maybe I am pushing it a little. Still, I do feel that we have a chance that way, and my 'feelings' have paid off for me many times in the past."

"Well, if we are going to do this, then let's get it over with. I do reserve my right to rip him limb from limb if he tries anything against us."

"Laura-Luss, if at any time I get the impression he is about to attack, I will be right there with you. But let's just hope it doesn't come to that. I don't like the odds of completing our mission if we are killed by a golem."

Laura-Luss looked strangely at Tom, decided he was trying to be funny, not stupid, then faced forward again and said, "Well, put this car in gear and let's get going. I would like to know if I am going to live or die before midnight, if you don't mind."

This time, it was Tom's turn to cast a side glance at Laura-Luss. Seeing no smile on her face, he decided to ignore the comment, shifted the car into reverse, backed out of the spot, and drove towards the parking lot exit. Merging into the circle and heading back towards Côte-des-Neiges Boulevard brought them alongside a large cemetery. Looking over at all the tombstones made Tom realize something. Possibly, after all these years of mock human existence, what the golem might want was true death; maybe that was why he wanted to become human so that he could die someday. It might be something to keep in mind in their talks with him. Especially if he was given the chance to do good in his life and avoid the grasp of the Devil in death.

Had this been a couple of hours earlier, the traffic on the Decarie Expressway would have kept them tied up for quite a while. But with the time pushing 9:00 in the evening, traffic was flowing well, and within minutes they had left the lower expressway and entered onto the 40 westbound. Passing along the highway, Tom saw that Montreal Island had been booming over the past few years since he had last visited. New office buildings and industrial complexes had popped up on both sides of the highway from Decarie into the area of Montreal referred to as the West Island. The western part of Montreal was home to several municipalities and a population of about a quarter of a million people. The home of the golem was located on a small island called Île Bizard, linked to the main island by one bridge and a ferry, and was still considered to be part of the city of Montreal. It was also home to several celebrities.

Tom took the exit for St. John's Road, now referred to as Boulevard St. Jean since the language reforms, and headed north. There was still some traffic here, as two major shopping complexes were located just at the exit, one of which still had stores open. Still, the late evening hour assured that the traffic was not overly heavy, and soon they were on Pierrefonds Boulevard and then turning on Jacques Bizard Street and crossing over the bridge onto the island of Île Bizard itself.

The house they were looking for was a large manor home on the waterfront at the far end of the island. Pulling up in front of the address Tom's office had given him, the first thing they noted was that the property was gated and required either a passkey, or remote, or to be let in by someone from the residence. They could not see the structure itself as it was set back from the road and on a wooded lot. Although the darkness did not help, Tom was sure that even in the daytime, they would have had difficulty making it out.

"Do you want to do the honors or shall I?" said Tom, pointing at an intercom on a post to the side of the gate. Its positioning required whoever came to exit his car to call the house. There was a camera above the post, assuring that no one would be let in who was not welcome.

"Since this is your foolish plan, I suggest you do it," Laura-Luss shot back.

"Well, just to let you know, your plan would not have worked anyway," said Tom, pointing to a sign warning of guard dogs. "I am reasonably sure that sign is not just for show."

"And why is that, Mr. Wilkins?"

"Look carefully under the tree over there. They're well trained, obviously, since they don't come barking at us while we're outside the gate, but I'm sure they would give off quite a brouhaha if we entered without permission."

Seeing what she had originally taken as a rock move, Laura-Luss was inclined to agree with Tom.

"Okay, you don't have to brag about it. Let's just call him now and march to our deaths so I can go home and get some sleep."

"I thought you told me demons don't need much sleep?"

"Not that kind of sleep, wonder boy."

"Oh yeah. Okay, here goes."

Tom exited the car and walked over to the intercom, but never had a chance to make the call. While he was standing there, the gates started to open. Tom noticed that standing just on the other side of the gates were three Dobermans. He was easing his way back to the car when the intercom spoke.

"The dogs have their instructions and will not harm you. Please leave your car there and follow the path to the house. I have been expecting the two of you for quite some time."

"I guess we don't have to announce ourselves," said Tom, turning to Laura-Luss as she got out of the car. "Unless, of course, you're in the mood for fighting three Dobermans and then a fully prepared golem?"

"Has anyone told you you have a dry sense of humor, Mr. Wilkins? However, there is a third alternative. You could go play with the puppies while I entertain our friend up there."

"If that was supposed to be a joke, your sense of humor is even worse than mine.

And if you're serious, you're suicidal."

"Well, since I do not have a death wish, why don't you lead the way?"

"That would be my pleasure, Ms. Laura-Luss."

"I am assuming you have some type of plan or at least an idea of what to say when we get there?

"Not a clue, my dear. I am just going to wing it."

"I sure hope your God protects you because otherwise, if we have to depend on your wit, we are in deep shit."

"Very funny. Have you considered going on stage with that routine?"

"Why don't you just shut up and pick up the pace a little? The suspense is killing me," said Laura-Luss, completely pan-faced.

Tom took a quick look at his companion and decided it wasn't worth pursuing this line any further. They remained silent throughout the good five minutes it took to walk to the front of the manor. Facing the imposing structure, Tom counted dozens of windows and realized this house had to have at least fifteen to twenty good-sized rooms. From where they stood, they could see a significant part of the lot, flood lights playing over a large in-ground pool, a spacious gazebo, and an expansive patio.

"I guess if you're going to have supernatural powers and an extremely long life span, you might as well live in luxury," said Tom, staring at the imposing structure.

"You could have a similar lifestyle if you sell your soul to my master, but it won't be a long one," replied Laura-Luss.

"I'll pass on that one if you don't mind. Meanwhile, do you want to ring the doorbell or should I do the honors?"

"Either you two can stand there yapping at each other, or you can allow me to show you into the study where the master of this house awaits you." The voice came from a tall and cultured butler standing in the now-open doorway. Trying not to show how startled he had been, Tom bowed to Laura-Luss and waved her on with the usual, "After you, my lady."

Laura-Luss gave him a 'stop your silliness' look and proceeded into the manor. Tom followed in her trail and, once the door was shut, the butler led them to the study.

The first thing Tom noticed as he entered the room was the walls lined with full bookshelves, every volume hard-covered. There were thousands of different titles, some leather-bound and quite old. The next object he noticed was a big globe of the Earth, beautifully rendered in crystal, sitting on the large oak desk. Behind the desk was the golem, rising from his chair as the two came into the room. The butler remained outside.

The golem was just as Madame Vanessa had described him. Even from where he stood, Tom could smell the cologne. Now, of course, he knew why the golem wore it.

"Ah, Mr. Wilkins … and I presume this here assistant is the demoness Ms. Laura-Luss? It is a pleasure to finally meet you two," he said, extending his hand to shake theirs.

Tom took the golem's hand and said, "I hope this meeting can have results that are satisfactory for all concerned." Laura-Luss refused to shake the golem's hand.

"No need to be like that, Ms. Laura-Luss. We are all civilized folk here. Even if there is only one human among us. And no, I do not intend on killing you two, at least not at this time."

"And later?" asked Tom.

"Well, later will bring what it will bring. A lot will depend on how this meeting goes. I also hope that this meeting can bring satisfactory results for all parties. Please be seated," he continued, pointing to the two large leather chairs facing his desk. He returned to his chair as Laura-Luss and Tom took theirs. "My butler will be bringing drinks shortly. I believe you prefer cognac, Mr. Wilkins. And for you, Ms. Laura-Luss, I have managed to import some Jalava juice. Straight from Hell central. I know it is a favorite of most demons. My local 'partner' prefers the local alcohol, so I was able to save some for you."

Laura-Luss was surprised that the golem was able to get his hands on Jalava juice. Made from a type of vine grape that can only grow in the sulfur pits of Hell, it is very hard to get, even there.

The butler arrived shortly with the refreshments, resting the tray on the desk, and departing in silence. Seeing Laura-Luss hesitate, the golem hurried to reassure her.

"Please, Laura-Luss, if I had wanted you dead, I would have eliminated the two of you before you even entered my house. The refreshments are safe. You have my word on it. You know it is hard for golems to lie."

Realizing the golem was right, she took a tentative first sip, then a larger one, the pleasure evident on her face.

"This is good, a particularly fine vintage."

"I live to please, Laura-Luss."

Tom raised his glass of cognac and said, "A toast. To a mutually acceptable resolution to our conflict."

"Amen to that," said the golem, raising his glass of cognac.

Even Laura-Luss raised her glass to that. However, her suspicion did not ease.

"Let us put the pleasantries aside for now and get right to business, shall we? My partner and I have certain goals we are trying to achieve, and you two, for some reason, are here to stop us. My partner is ready to offer you a lot to just back off and leave here in peace. Absolutely no effort on your part is required, but the rewards for your cooperation will be beyond your wildest dreams. For you, Laura-Luss, you could stand amongst the highest demons in Hell. For you, Tom Wilkins, riches far more than you could ever imagine. Your every hope and desire could be yours. All for just going home and doing nothing. How is that for an offer that is impossible to refuse?"

"And if we do refuse?" asked Laura-Luss. "We don't leave here alive, right?"

"Wrong. I gave you my word, you will not come to harm tonight. But should you refuse this extremely generous offer and get in our way, then our next meeting will be your last."

"We might happen to have a counteroffer for you, Vince Faustelli, or is that your real name?"

"My proper name is lost in antiquity and of no real matter. I have gone by Vince Faustelli for many centuries. It is a name I am comfortable with. As for a counterproposal, I don't see that you could have anything to offer that my current partner has not already guaranteed me. I am sure you can't begin to offer me what he has."

"And you think that he will live up to anything he has offered you?" asked Tom.

"He is probably the only one who can," was the answer.

"And did you stop to think what will happen to you if and when you are given your humanity?" Laura-Luss looked the golem directly in the eyes, capturing his attention as she asked the question.

"So, you know what it is I seek. Not surprising since you read up on my kind before seeking me out. Yes, I did think about it. For many centuries. To feel, to hunger, to desire, and so much more. That is what will happen."

"And to die. Asmodeus is using you, and when he is finished, you will die."

"Your point is?"

"Laura-Luss, after many centuries of half-life, I think now that the golem would prefer death to continue as he is. Especially if he gets to feel humanity, even if only for a few minutes."

"You have had time to figure that out, have you, my friend Tom? Yes, death is much preferable to this type of immortality. And to feel and die as a human. That would be wonderful."

"Wonderful enough to suffer for all eternity?" asked Laura-Luss.

"Pardon me?"

Taking a deep sigh, Laura-Luss continued, but with much more empathy for this creature. "If your last act alive is the result of a deal with evil, and you have become human, that will mean you have a mortal soul, one that will be claimed by the victor of the battle between Satan and Asmodeus. If Satan wins, well, you know how he will treat one who tried to destroy him, and if Asmodeus wins, well, let's just say he has a peculiar way of rewarding his allies, especially if he believes his purposes would be better served with you out of the way because you know too much."

"Look, Vince, we are here to offer you another deal," continued Tom. "Work with us, and Laura-Luss will speak to Satan on your behalf. At the same time, I will speak to certain contacts in the Catholic Church and see what I can do to help you obtain your humanity. I know I can't promise I can deliver it for you, but I am sure that hope is more positive than an eternity in Hell, with Asmodeus' demons having their fun with you. Or maybe Asmodeus will get more pleasure out of giving you your humanity for moments only than taking it away. Your own personal version of Hell, shall we say."

"What would you expect of me if I did decide yours was the better offer?"

"We need to know what Asmodeus' plan is for starters. From there, we would know how you could help."

"Alas, I am not in a position to reveal that to you. I am bound by certain restraints for the moment. Besides, I am not in the least convinced that my purposes would be best served working with you. However, I will do this. I will let you leave here tonight with no strings. I will consider what you have said. Then I will contact you, either to tell you I am of a mind to assist you or to give you one last chance to accept my offer before I come after you. Is that not a fair compromise for the time being?"

Laura-Luss was about to say something further, but Tom forestalled her with a wave of his hand. Standing, he leaned over the desk and shook the golem's hand. "A fair compromise for now. I will give you my card with my numbers on it."

"That will not be necessary, Mr. Tom Wilkins. I know how to reach you when I need to. It has been an absolute pleasure meeting with you two tonight. If nothing else, your company has enriched my life. Now I suggest you get on your way before my partner decides to make one of his infrequent yet unexpected visits. We all would find that uncomfortable at this time."

Laura-Luss reached over the desk and shook the golem's hand, surprising him. "You are more honorable than other golems I have met, Vince Faustelli. You may already be on your way to achieving humanity even without demonic help. Consider that."

"I will, Ms. Laura-Luss, I will."

The golem remained sitting behind his desk long after the departure of his two guests, waiting for the next arrival. Sure enough, an hour later, there was a dip in the air pressure around him, like air being sucked out of a tube, and before him stood Asmodeus.

"I sense that you had visitors, and I do not see any dead bodies. Are you forgetting our deal already?"

"Not at all, Oh powerful demon. Now was just not the time to do them in."

"And why is that?"

"They have knowledge that we can use. What you plan is dangerous for all of us, but the rewards will be great. To obtain this, we must use every available source. These two could become excellent sources of information if played right."

"Just remember that rewards part golem. If you fail me, I can guarantee you will not achieve your desire. Plus, my minions will see that you spend the rest of eternity regretting that failure, no matter what becomes of me."

"I forget nothing, demon. That is why I desire mortality, so I can have the power to forget. However, your threats don't mean anything to me. I do what I do for my own sake. You would be well to remember that."

Asmodeus gave the golem one last look of fury and contempt and then disappeared once again. The golem sat back in his chair, took a long sip from his cognac glass, grimaced a little as it went down, and then set his glass back on the desk. He switched off the lights and remained sitting like that for many hours, deciding his future.

CHAPTER 16

"So, where to now?" asked Laura-Luss of Tom as they drove off the golem's property.

"Back to the hotel for some rest and food. I'm starving."

"Why the hotel? Montreal is world-famous for its restaurants and its late-night nightlife. I am sure we will find a quality place open now."

"And you don't think someone will think it is funny if I order four steaks with all the trimmings? Because I feel hungry enough to eat at least that."

"Well, we'll stop and order a couple of steaks to eat there, and then a couple to go. I suggest going to either Gibbys or the Rib'N Reef."

"Where did you learn about Montreal's fine restaurants? I thought demons did not eat?"

"Demons don't need food, but that does not mean we don't enjoy it occasionally. Most of us don't do it often, as it does cause some discomfort since our digestive system is somewhat different for the most part. Still, I am sure you have heard that one of the deadly sins is gluttony. I do love a good meal once in a while, and this is not the first visit of mine to this fair city."

"Ms. Laura-Luss, you continue to surprise me. Okay then, let's hit the Rib'N Reef. By the name, they must also have seafood. I could use a good surf and turf about now. With what I am feeling now, I'm more than up to the task. Add on a few appetizers and a great dessert or two, and even in my current condition, I will feel satisfied. While eating, we can discuss our next step."

With traffic being light, they found themselves seated in the restaurant within fifteen minutes. Even for Montreal, though, it was getting late for restaurants, and the staff hurried to take their order so as not to be working beyond the usual closing hour. Tom decided to order three appetizers, the seventeen-ounce roast beef, with all the trimmings, lobster tails, and a Coors Lite Beer. Even Laura-Luss ordered a full meal, albeit with only one appetizer and a glass of water.

"You can't mean to tell me that demons don't consume alcohol?" asked Tom jokingly.

"That is one taste I never really acquired. And since alcohol does not affect me, it seems like a waste to order any."

"What about wine? There are some really enjoyable ones out there."

"Sorry, but I have only tried a couple of different ones and did not enjoy them, so I never drank it again. Maybe one day I will try another type, but not tonight."

"Who knows, maybe when all this is over, I will take you to a place that serves some really good wines, and you can sample some."

"Are you asking me out on a date, Mr. Wilkins?" asked Laura-Luss with a bit of a laugh.

"I guess the adventures of the night have made me forget what you are for a moment. Just forget I said anything."

"Oh, but Tom, demons never forget things. I might just hold you to that offer."

Looking her in the eyes, Tom was not sure whether she was playing with him, joking with him, or serious. Rather than allow himself to think about the possibilities, he decided to change the subject.

"Okay, we know there is a planned double cross. If we just went to your boss and told him, would that not solve the issue?"

"Two drawbacks to that. One, my boss might not necessarily believe us, as most of this is supposition and rumor. Then we would be tipping him off that we knew his plan, which would be quite dangerous, especially for you. And two, even if he does believe us, he would take this into account and modify his plans. Either way would still lead to your elimination. I am sure you would not like that to happen."

"Point taken. Then that leaves us with figuring out Asmodeus' plan and then a way to counter it. To do that, we need to find out what cult they plan on using for their cult suicide. If we can stop the cult, maybe we can nip this in the bud."

"Even if we do find the cult, I would not suggest you use the same plan with them that you used with the golem. Cult leaders are notorious for being suicidal, especially if they can take many with them. It is easier to convince them to do it than not to. I am sure they have planned this for a while and have the cult leader well primed for it."

"Having had some dealings with cults in the past, I could not agree with you more. Still, I'm not ready to sacrifice lives just to foil the plan. We'll have to find a way to stop them from killing themselves. Of course, we have to find them first."

"Since you are not intending to rush in and converse with a cult leader, I can tell you that I have a theory on how to find them. To set this up, there had to be a lot of trips topside for several demons, especially for ones loyal to Asmodeus. Most comings and goings are monitored in Hell and then stored in a massive data bank. Being who he is, Satan is somewhat paranoid, so he likes to know what is going on at all times.

I happen to have a few friends who have access to Hell's computers and had them run a program for me. It is a search over the last ten years of all the movements of Asmodeus' followers to Earth. Once it is complete, I have set it up for the results to be emailed directly to your address. I figure by the time we are back at the hotel, we should have something. Then we can use the internet to cross-reference the areas of most activity with known cult sites. Knowing, though, that the golem has had his residence here for a while would lead me to believe that the cult is located in either Eastern Canada or the Northeastern States, so he could keep an eye on them."

"All this gets me thinking of something, Laura-Luss. There have been several cult mass suicides. I can think of Jonestown in the late '70s, where over 900 died. Then there were the Branch Davidians in Waco, Texas, in the early '90s, and more recently the Order of the Solar Temple, and others I could name. Were these failed attempts by your boss to empower himself here on earth?"

"I would think not. You could ask your brother about that, as I am sure the Catholic Church investigated these thoroughly for signs of hellish evil. Had there been anything tangible, they would have been more ready for something like this. No, I think those were just my boss taking advantage of man's tendency towards evil."

"Yeah, you're probably right. Sometimes I think our species as a whole doesn't deserve to have God's eyes on us at all. Maybe we all just belong in Hell anyway."

"I don't think you truly believe that, Tom. Besides, man has also shown and done great good. Haven't you learned anything from this case yet?"

"I think I have truly learned irony. Here I am talking about how evil men can be and that we belong in Hell, and there you are, a demon, talking about man's capacity for doing good. If that's not ironic, I don't know what is."

"Well said, Tom."

They finished their meal in relative silence, paid the bill with Tom's company card, and headed back to the hotel.

Entering the room, Tom sensed immediately that all was not as it should be. It was not as if anything was out of place, nor was anything different from when they had left earlier. It was more of a feeling. As Tom had learned over his time as a detective, trust your feelings. This would be especially so in a case involving the supernatural. Pulling his recently heavenly reloaded pistol, Tom faced the direction where his gut told him something was wrong and prepared to fire. But Laura-Luss grabbed his arm and pushed it down before he could. Tom turned, ready to fight her if need be, when he saw her put her finger to her lips, telling him to be quiet.

Moving away from Tom, Laura-Luss circled to the back of the couch, reached over, and grabbed something. As she did, Tom switched on the lights and saw Laura-Luss holding a pint-sized demon by the ears. This particular demon looked very similar to the caricature in the stop-smoking commercials.

"Okay, Lupus, what are you doing here? demanded Laura-Luss.

"Easy on the ears, LL. It takes me months to get them straight and pointy again once they have been ripped off."

"Then you had better start talking, or you will have to get to work growing them right away."

"Anything you say, LL, just let go of my ears."

Laura-Luss dropped the demon unceremoniously onto the couch, rounded it to face the little demon, pushed him back into the couch, and with anger in her voice said, "Then you had better start talking quick or I might just arrange some other of your body parts to match your soon-to-be missing ears. Start with how you knew how to find us."

Tom watched the entire scene with bemusement.

"All right already. Easy on the flesh. Growing it back is a real pain. I was sent here by the head boss. He wants to know if you have made any progress."

Laura-Luss took a quick look at Tom, winked, then turned back to the demon, grabbed his ear once again, giving it a good twist, and asked, "So which boss do you serve, Satan or Asmodeus?"

"Ouch, ouch!! That smarts, LL. You know I only serve the prince himself. Please let go of the ear!"

"That's enough, Laura-Luss. There's no need to abuse my client's messengers," said Tom abruptly. "He's only here to deliver information and bring a report back. Isn't that right, little guy?"

Looking back and forth from the demoness to Tom, the little imp watched the contest going on between the two and decided his chances were best if he answered Tom.

"Yes, yes, that is true, good sir. Please tell the demoness to let me go."

"You heard him, demoness. He is here to help. Let him go."

Turning furiously towards Tom, Laura-Luss tossed the demon back onto the couch and walked away muttering, "Stupid humans think they know how to handle demons. I will show him how to handle little imps like this." But as she passed Tom, with her back to the imp, she gave Tom a big smile.

Tom walked towards the now very nervous demon and said, "Look, Lupus, you don't mind if I call you by your name, do you?" Seeing the imp shake his head, Tom continued. "Good, then let me start by saying that as long as I feel you're telling the truth, and not holding anything back, I'll make sure that yonder demoness keeps her claws off you. Is that fair enough?"

The imp quickly nodded his head up and down.

"Well then, we can get started. First off, what news do you have for us?"

Glancing once again at Laura-Luss, the demon started talking like his very life depended on giving these two what they wanted. Of course, the fact that that was the case helped inspire him.

"Look, I am only a lower-level imp and not much in the know about what is going on. Our boss sent me to ask you what progress you have made to date. It was he who told me where to wait for you. He seemed puzzled that he was not able to follow your movements and sent me to find out why. And to get a complete report on the case to date."

"How would he be able to follow our movements in the first place?" Tom asked.

"You know when he did that thing to you to allow you to recognize Asmodeus? It also allows him to track your movements.

Tom shot a glance at Laura-Luss, who shrugged as if to say she knew nothing about it, then turned his attention back to the imp.

"Did he give you any news to pass on to us?"

"Not really. He just said to tell you that he thinks Asmodeus is stepping up his plans, whatever they are, and that you should track him down quickly before he becomes too powerful on this plane."

"Forgetting whatever message he gave you, what aren't you telling us?"

"Why nothing. I don't know anything," the creature whined.

Heaving a big sigh, Tom stood and turned to Laura-Luss.

"I guess you are right. You know how to handle these better than I do."

Seeing that things were about to get nasty, the imp quickly backtracked.

"Wait, there might be something. Please don't let the demoness have me."

"So, talk. My patience is not infinite."

Looking into Tom's steel gaze, the imp swallowed once and started talking.

"There is a lot of talk going on in Hell. A lot of action and undercurrents. We all know something big is going down. Asmodeus has something up his sleeve that even the head guy doesn't know. He has found something in Hell that he can use to neutralize some of the boss man's power. But no one can figure out how there could be something down in Hell that the Devil would not know about."

"Have you mentioned this to Satan?" asked Tom.

"Of course, but he only laughed and said there is nothing on Hell's plane that could harm him in any way. Then he smiled and added that there is more than one level of planes, whatever that meant."

"I believe you have told us what you know," said Tom. "Go back and tell your boss that we are hard on the trail, are making progress, and should have news for him in a couple of days. Now go."

With relief etched on his face, the demon popped out, leaving Tom and Laura-Luss alone.

"What do you think of this news, Laura-Luss?" asked Tom. "Is there some secret weapon or something in Hell that can be used against your boss?"

"Nothing that I have ever heard of. It is funny, though, that he said in Hell's plane and not in Hell."

"Probably just semantics. Let me check my computer and see if there's anything in yet."

Hooking up to the internet via the hotel's wireless, Tom was soon downloading all his messages, thirty-five in total. After sifting through the junk and stock market tips that somehow still got through despite his spam filters, Tom finally got to an email from his brother. After reading it through, Tom called Laura-Luss over to see.

"What do you make of that?" he asked.

"We know in Hell that the Vatican has many secret files on our activities going back to the beginning of the Vatican's existence, so yes, it is possible there is something there."

"But a way to destroy Satan? Don't you think they would have used it a long time ago if it worked?"

"Tom, I could think of several reasons why they would not, many of them good reasons on their own, and probably supported by different factions within the Church. First, depending on how far back this goes, the Church, through a lot of its history, ruled in many countries by fear. Fear of evil, fear of witches and spells, and so on. If the Church managed to destroy Satan, and word got out, they would have lost a lot of their base power.

"Then there would be the knowledge that some demon or other would be ready to take Satan's place. Who would it be? At least with Satan, they have a foe they know and understand somewhat. Also, one they can communicate with from time to time to prevent a world crisis from getting out of hand. Even Satan doesn't want the world destroyed; he wants a world full of humans that he can rule. Another demon may not have the same desires or the brains to realize that ruling a barren world is not something worth working for.

"And one more point. There have always been, and still are, those in the Church who make deals with my boss. Yes, Tom, don't look so surprised. I am sure you have heard of the various scandals, some sexual, some monetary, that have rocked the Church from time to time. What the Church doesn't tell the public is that often there was a connection with Hell involved."

"Okay, I guess I can buy that. Still, would not some Church member full of righteousness and feeling Holy come across this and use it, thinking he was saving the world or something?"

"That is why it is hidden in the secret archives that your brother mentions in his message. Only the top officials have access to these. I am quite surprised your brother even knows about them, never mind asking you to join him there to look through them."

"Well, I guess I had better make a call and book us a flight to Rome right away."

"No, Tom. It is a trip I can't make. Yes, your brother could get me into a neighborhood church, but into the Vatican itself? Never!"

"Oh well, I guess it's one ticket then," Tom answered as he reached over to delete yet another junk mail, trying to sell him a cruise.

"Wait, what is that message?!" exclaimed Laura-Luss.

"Just an ad for a cruise. I get them all the time. Why do you want to go on a cruise now or something?"

"No, Tom, look where it goes. Read the list."

"So, we have Jamaica, Panama, Cozumel, Mexico, and …"

"Grand Cayman. Look at the name of one of the towns that they recommend on one of their shore trips."

"I see. Hell, Grand Cayman. So?"

"Remember what Satan said to the imp? Not on Hell's plane. But what about Hell on Earth? Tom, my demontuition has just sent warning bells through my entire body. Something there is what we could be looking for!"

"Normally, I would say you are chasing a wild goose, but I have learned always to trust my intuition, so how could I tell you to doubt yours? Do you plan on leaving right away?"

Surprised that Tom accepted her feeling so casually, Laura-Luss nodded and said, "Yes, but I think you should book me a flight. Using my powers to go there may tip someone off."

"One thing, though, that I find may be just too much of a coincidence, and something we need to consider," said Tom.

"What's that?"

"Don't you find it strange that almost at the same time that an imp from Hell mentions there is a way to neutralize your boss's power, I get a message from John that there may be a secret, hidden in the Vatican, about a way to destroy him?"

"What are you thinking, Tom?"

"Divide and conquer. So far, our enemies have not been able to stop us as long as we are working together. Now comes this information that separates us. It just feels like the timing goes far beyond coincidental."

"Maybe you are just being paranoid," replied Laura-Luss. "But when dealing with minions from Hell, paranoia can be a good thing," she continued before Tom could respond.

"The question becomes, what do we do about it? Both these trips could be fruitful, or either one could be a death trap."

"What if it appeared like we were sticking together?" suggested Laura-Luss.

Tom gave her a quizzical look.

"Book two tickets to Rome. Have another detective, preferably a female, from your office, go with you. She doesn't have to go into the Vatican, just get on the plane to Rome with you. She can stay at the hotel. That would look more realistic anyway. Since I can modify my appearance, anyone watching would think it was me. Then I can use the identification of that detective to travel to Grand Cayman."

"Wouldn't any demon know it wasn't you on the flight with me?"

"Not if I give a piece of myself for her to carry, kind of a spell. Not to worry, it would not harm her in any way, nor taint her soul. You have my word."

"I think that would work; however, there will be one minor change. A detective from my office will go with you. He only has to be told that he is to protect you while you are working undercover. He will be told the same as everyone in the office, that you work for my client. I don't want you going without some type of backup."

Laura-Luss was going to comment on Tom caring, but seeing his face, she felt it was best not to push him away like that. It might make him careless.

"Agreed. You make the arrangements with your office. But keep it low-key. My boss knows a lot about what happens at your agency. It might not be a good idea for him to know what we are doing, as he may be behind a lot of this. Do you have someone you can trust to arrange it?"

"There may be one person. At least I hope I can trust her." Tom picked up his phone and made a call to Amy.

CHAPTER 17

Tom sat in the lounge of the airport, awaiting the arrival of the detective Amy had arranged. Laura-Luss and a second detective would be leaving in a couple of hours for Grand Cayman, but it was decided not to have them leave at the same time, so as not to tip off whoever was watching. The demoness was waiting outside the airport and would give her "piece" to the detective who would be accompanying Tom.

A few minutes later, Tom saw Laura-Luss walk into the lounge.

"I thought we should not be together right now," he complained.

"And I thought you wanted to go on a trip with me," was the answer, but the voice was that of Amy.

"What are you doing here?" exclaimed Tom.

"You said you needed someone who could be trusted. Of all the female detectives at the agency, the only one that I could trust was me."

"But you're a receptionist. You have no experience, and this could be dangerous."

"You think I have only ever been a receptionist? I worked as an investigator when you were still in high school. After I had a child, I decided I no longer wanted the danger, so I agreed to a change of position. Now that my child is almost an adult, I decided I missed the action and wanted one more case. As for the investigator with Laura-Luss, he happens to be my brother and is someone I can trust completely."

"I didn't realize this company was a family affair," joked Tom.

"There is a lot about this company you don't know," replied Amy with a wistful look on her face.

Before Tom could respond, his cell phone rang.

"Hi, Mom. Didn't expect to hear from you while you were at the seminary. How are the courses going?"

"Oh, Tom, you know all about religious training. I'm sure your brother told you about what he went through to become a priest. Well, it is not a lot different from becoming a nun. Just lots of praying, meditation, and reading scripture. After your father passed, it was all I could think about, so for me, this was just the next natural step. When do you plan on taking your training?" his mother asked, although Tom could almost see her smile through the phone.

"To tell you the truth, Mom, these last few days I have been thinking more and more about the need for some good Catholic scripture."

His mother gasped at first and then heard the hint of laughter in his voice.

"You almost had me, Tom. You know it's not nice to lie to your mother, especially when she's about to become your sister."

"Oh, I am being completely truthful. But nothing to do with me wanting to join the priesthood. More to do with the case I am working on. Just a lot of deviltries involved."

"You know, joking about the Devil is not appropriate when talking to a sister."

"But, mother, you're not a sister yet. However, I'm not joking. I can't tell you much about this case, but just to mention it, I happen to be about to board a plane to Rome to meet John and visit the Vatican."

"That's strange, John didn't mention to me that he was heading for Rome when he stopped by this morning."

"Probably didn't want to get your hopes up," laughed Tom. "Well, they just announced the boarding for my flight, so I have to say bye for now. Love you, Mom."

"Love you, son. Take care of yourself. This case you're on sounds like it might be a little hellish." With that, the line went dead.

"Is something wrong?" asked Amy as they walked towards the boarding ramp.

"I don't think so. It's just that I'm surprised John didn't mention to my mom that he was headed for Rome. He usually tells her every time he goes to the Vatican since she loves to hear about it."

"Maybe he just didn't want her to know it involved a case and felt it was best not to mention it at all. Speaking of which, do you want to fill me in a little about what is happening? Having worked as a detective, I always hate going into a situation without information."

"This case is kind of unusual, and you probably wouldn't believe me if I told you."

"Since your 'partner' is a succubus, I am assuming that the client is highly placed in Hell?"

Tom's jaw dropped.

"I know a hell of a lot about what goes on at the office. Oh, not everything to be sure, but in my early days, working as a detective, we did have a few unusual cases that had some connection to ungodly forces. So as soon as Ms. Luss insisted I hold on to something for her, I sensed it was strange. When she wasn't looking, I took out the cross I wear around my neck and put it close to the thing, and it started to steam. Only something from Hell would do that, and judging by how she looks, and the sex appeal she tosses out as if it were her natural charm, I knew what she was."

"You continue to amaze me, Amy. Yes, she is a succubus, although she prefers to be called a demoness. I can't give you much in the way of details, but let's just say something is missing from Hell, and we have to find that something before a little hell is raised on earth."

Boarding was quickly completed. Tom noticed that Amy had booked first-class seats, something that did not usually happen with the agency, but Amy just smiled and quipped that having control of the booking gave her a little leeway.

They were an hour into the flight when Amy noticed the worried expression on Tom's face.

"Something bothering you?"

"Just that the more I think about it, the more I wonder about Tom not telling our mother that he was going to Rome. It is just not like him."

"You said he was the one who told you to meet him in Rome. Why would he call and tell you that if he didn't have information you could use?"

"He didn't call, he sent me an email. But you raise an interesting question. Why didn't he call me?"

Tom pulled out his phone, set it to Wi-Fi, and then scanned his emails. The email from his brother was no longer there. He went through his deleted files in case he had accidentally deleted them, but nothing was there either.

"Do you have a laptop with you?"

"Well, not a laptop, but I do have an iPad that has Wi-Fi connectivity if that would help."

Tom nodded, and Amy pulled it out of her purse.

Tom accessed the internet, then went to a site he and his brother had once used to send secret messages to each other. He hadn't used it in a while, but knew that the system the site used sent a tone to their cell phones when a message was left and would notify John right away. It did not allow long messages, almost like Twitter, but he only needed to send a short one.

"John, heading to Rome as per your email. Where should we meet?"

It didn't take long for a reply.

"I sent no email. Whatever you do, don't leave the airport. On my way."

"Trouble?" asked Amy.

"Big time. John did not send a message. We are walking into a trap in Rome. He told me not to leave the airport, but that may not be safe either. I need to think of something else. Can you send a message to your brother? They may be walking into trouble as well unless our deception worked."

"Fortunately, this airline allows texting using Wi-Fi. I will send him a message that it could be a trap. He is a very good detective. He will know what to do."

****

"You might look like my sister, but your mannerisms are way off. Hopefully, we won't bump into anyone who knows her," said Ben to Laura-Luss.

"Well, not much chance of that. It's not like a receptionist travels a lot. I'm surprised that Tom would allow an untrained person to go on such a risky trip."

"I guess your boss doesn't tell you everything."

"You shouldn't know who my boss is. That is privileged information. When my boss hears that there are loose lips at your agency, he might just look for another company to represent his interests. He happens to be quite rich and well-connected."

Ben tilted his head up and roared with laughter.

"What's so funny?" Laura-Luss squeaked out, giving him a funny look.

"My sis and I have worked with the agency for over twenty years. We know everything that goes on, including how your boss is old goat horns himself, and that you are a succubus, or if you prefer, a demoness," he added, seeing the angry look on her face.

"Plus, there are other things that even Tom doesn't know about this case or the agency he works for. It's part of the reason my sister decided to go with him to Rome. She'll be able to watch for certain things that, for the moment, she can't tell him."

"Can't, or won't?"

"Can't. A being in your position must know that there are ways of making sure certain information can't be passed on.

"Also, to let you know, my sis worked as a detective for over fifteen years before she moved to the receptionist position. Trust me, she can take care of herself."

The boarding had gone without complications, and they had just reached cruising altitude when Ben received the text from Amy.

"Trouble?" asked Laura-Luss, seeing the expression on his face.

Ben read the text aloud.

Found out that John did not send message. Heading into a trap in Rome. Be careful, as you may be heading into one too.

Laura-Luss turned pale, something quite unusual for a succubus, and Ben realized that it boded ill.

"You look like you've seen a ghost."

"No, not a ghost, unless you count the holy one."

Seeing the look of puzzlement on Ben's face, Laura-Luss went on to explain.

"My boss would not make those types of arrangements. It is not his style, and he would want Tom to accomplish what he is trying to do. Asmodeus does not have the know-how, nor the thinking process to set something up like that."

"Then who?"

"It looks like the forces of Heaven are entering the fray. Oh, not the top echelon, but some of the angels have been wanting an out-and-out war for a long time. It looks like they have become aware of what is going on and have decided to use the opportunity to put their own plans into action."

"By letting Asmodeus defeat Satan? How does that help them?"

"If Asmodeus becomes powerful on the Earthly plane, he tips the balance of power. So, either Satan makes his presence known on this plane and there is an all-out war between him and Asmodeus, which of course would call forth the full might of Heaven, or he cedes the Earth to Asmodeus, making two of the three planes of existence in the possession of evil, and the forces of Heaven will be called forth again to fight Asmodeus."

"Which, of course, would give your boss a reason to let Asmodeus accomplish his plans."

"I don't follow? Why would my boss give up all the power he currently holds, and forgo the extra power he seeks?"

"Think of this scenario. He lets Asmodeus have Earth. The forces of Heaven come down and, in an all-out battle, finally defeat Asmodeus. In doing so, the forces of Heaven are depleted. Satan musters the forces of Hell in an all-out war against the depleted forces of Heaven."

"Putting it that way, no matter what happens, my boss becomes a winner, as long as he does not go against Asmodeus head-to-head. Yeah, that sounds more like his style."

"Which makes me worry more about you," Ben added.

"Me? Why?"

"Because Satan may have planted you to upset Tom's investigation at the most opportune time."

"I know this may sound strange, but I happen to like Earth just the way it is. An all-out war would ravage this plane of existence and wipe out most of humankind. So, I give you my word, I will do everything I can to help Tom succeed. I will swear on all that is unholy."

This statement took Ben aback. For a demon to swear this was almost unheard of. It would mean her total dissolution if she went back on it. He looked her in the eye and then held out his hand to shake.

"And I swear on all that is holy to work honestly with you to prevent this disaster from happening."

Laura-Luss shook Ben's hand and said, "Not a word of this to Tom. He must not know what I have just sworn, nor its meaning. It may affect the way he works, and so far, he has done an amazing job. That being said, you must send a text to your sister letting them know the type of forces they will be facing."

"I agree. Now let's talk about what happens when we arrive in 'Hell'."

CHAPTER 18

 The plane had begun its descent when Amy's cell phone pinged. A text from her brother. She read it to Tom.

Our hellish friend says this trap is not from her side. Looks like lower upstairs has entered the fray.

"Lower upstairs?"

"She must mean the lesser angels. I can think of a number of them that would love to take advantage of this situation." Seeing Tom's expression, she continued, "You are not the only one with a Catholic background. My parents insisted we attend church and Sunday school when we were young. The teacher I had was a true believer in angels and knew all their names and their positions of power. It was like an obsession with her. She was worse than any fire and brimstone preacher from the Deep South."

"Okay, so that changes things a lot. We now have three different forces looking to turn this the way they want, and we still have no idea where Asmodeus is, or what his final plans are."

"So that is what is missing from Hell!" exclaimed Amy.

"Since you are now stuck in the middle of this, and have knowledge I am going to need, it is only appropriate now that you know the entire story." Tom then proceeded to fill Amy in on all that had happened since that strange meeting in his office a week ago. It had felt, though, like months had passed since then.

"So, to sum it up, Asmodeus somehow left Hell, probably with a little aid, and is planning on some major event to open the gates of Hell, which means he already has a force prepared for his advent into this plane."

"There is something I don't understand, and hopefully my brother can fill me in on this. If Asmodeus is already here, and his boss comes here often, judging by his meeting me for this assignment at our offices, why would they need a major event to invade here? They obviously have no problem going back and forth."

"Your brother, having high connections with the Vatican, will probably have some of the answers you are missing, but you may already have them yourself if you remember your Catholic upbringing."

"How is that?"

"Think of your Bible studies. In each case where goat horns has appeared on Earth, he has either been invited by a mortal or had the way opened up for him. Remember as well that never has his full power been on display here since he was forced out of heaven for disobeying God. The same would be true for even the most powerful of his demons, which, let's face it, are just fallen angels."

"That makes sense, in a weird sort of way. If they had their full power and could come here any time, they would probably rule here."

"Or there would have been a continuous war here between forces that would have decimated humans a long time ago," added Amy.

"I also remember Lucifer telling me that he made an agreement to be allowed here. So, Heaven must have some say in his comings and goings."

"I would not count on anything he says. Oh, maybe there has to be some type of communication for certain situations, but I know he has been here many times before, and I'm willing to bet it was not always with the knowledge of the forces from above."

"How would you know that?"

Amy tried to say something, but could not get the words out. She then said, "I'm sorry I can't tell you that."

"Can't or won't? If you know something that could affect this case, I need to know."

Amy again tried to say something, but after a few moments, all that came out was, "I can't."

Seeing her struggle like that, Tom realized that she was somehow being blocked from speaking about it. He could think of one source that was capable of that, so decided to just file the information for now and let it pass.

"We'll be landing soon, and I still have no idea what to do once we get there. Now, even less so with this new information. I had thought to maybe hide in the chapel at the airport, but if it's a lesser angel doing this, that could play right into his hands."

"Your brother did say to stay at the airport. I think as long as we stay wherever it is crowded, we should be okay. Even lesser angels won't deliberately put humans at risk."

"Won't they be doing that by allowing outright war on Earth?"

"Once the devil or demon has opened a portal on Earth to Hell, the forces of heaven will be forced to answer. It will not even be questioned by the higher angels how it happened. But if a lesser angel were to cause even a single human death by an act of their own, it would be felt in Heaven, and that angel would be banished to Hell. At least that's the impression I got from my Sunday school teacher."

"Well, I sure hope she was right."

"I think even the forces from below are being cautious when they confront you. So far, nothing has happened while you've been in a public place."

"So far. I hope that continues, but the closer the day of reckoning comes, the more chances are that they will act no matter where I am, especially if they think I can hurt their plans in any way."

"We will have to trust your brother. If he said to stay at the airport, he must know something."

"Still, I wish I had my gun with me. I hate traveling without it, especially at a time like this. Being weaponless makes me feel helpless."

"We are not exactly weaponless," replied Amy, pulling out a large crucifix from her bag. It was almost a foot long.

"That may or may not slow down a demon, but if another hellhound comes our way, or an angel looking to do us harm, it won't do much."

Amy looked around to make sure none of the other passengers were looking, then twisted a decoration near the base where the arms of Christ were and pulled on it. As she did so, it separated into two sections, revealing a blade of at least eight inches. She quickly put it back before anyone could see.

"Besides being a blade of pure silver and extremely sharp, it has been bathed overnight in holy water. Not only will it destroy any hell beast it stabs, but it will also cause harm to any angel with ill intent."

"You continue to amaze me, Amy. I think I'm falling for you."

"Don't be a fool. Beside the fact that I am much older than you are, you have already given your heart to someone."

Tom laughed at this. "If you know so much about what happens at the agency, you will know that I am quite single, not even a girlfriend right now."

"The Bible says nothing about falling in love with a demoness. I figure as long as she loves you back, it should be fine."

"Now you're sounding like my brother. There is nothing romantic in any way between that succubus and me. I would not risk my soul for a piece of ... well, you get my point."

"Falling in love is not risking your soul, at least as far as I can see."

"Just drop it. There is nothing between her and me," Tom angrily responded.

They remained silent for the remainder of the trip, and it wasn't long before the wheels of the plane hit the tarmac. Keeping what Amy said in mind regarding crowds, they waited until almost half the plane's occupants had passed their seats before getting up. The lineup at customs was long, but with the crowd around them, they felt safe for the moment.

The Rome Leonardo da Vinci-Fiumicino Airport was a marvel in itself. After clearing customs, they went to the central retail area. Looking up, they saw a dome-shaped roof with a jagged central piece that looked like the aftermath of an earthquake had separated it into two parts. It is considered a marvel of engineering and quite breathtaking. They strolled around the storefronts for a while and then grabbed a coffee and sat in the central court, admiring the view.

It was three hours later that they finally saw Tom's brother walking towards them.

Reaching them, John gave Tom a huge hug and then turned to Amy. "You may look like Laura-Luss, but you are not her."

"John, meet Amy from my office. Amy, this is my brother John."

As they shook hands, John realized why she looked like Laura-Luss. "You know that piece she gave you may fool some of the lesser demons, and of course, almost all humans, but Asmodeus, or most angels, would see right through it."

"You know, when we planned this out, we doubted Asmodeus would be watching us himself, and we had no idea that angels would be working against us."

"Lesser angels, brother. I'm glad you figured that part out. That is why I'm especially glad you stayed at the airport. Too many people around for them to try anything."

"When did you figure out about lesser angels?" asked Amy.

"When Tom sent me that message through our secret virtual room, I did a follow-up check of my emails. One had been sent using my computer and then deleted. Until then, I had thought it was a demon ploy, which is why I told Tom to wait at the airport since it is consecrated ground. But only something holy can access my emails like that. Due to certain safeguards, not even a human hacker can do that.

"Now tell me what in my email convinced you to run to Rome to meet with me, and at the same time, separate from your girlfriend."

"Not you too," snapped Tom.

"Relax, brother, I'm just playing with you. Now fill me in on everything."

Tom told his brother all that had passed since they last spoke.

"So, Laura-Luss and Amy's brother are on their way to Hell, Grand Cayman. I sure hope they don't run into any trouble there. And yes, there may be something there that might help. As for a way to destroy the Devil existing in the Vatican, I find that highly unlikely. I have studied extensively the records within the secret vaults, and I found nothing to suggest that." He held up his hand as John was about to interrupt.

"There have been rumors, though, of something that could change the leadership in Hell. Something that the Church has kept hidden."

"Isn't that almost the same thing?" asked Amy.

"Not really. What it would do, if it is true, is allow another demon to supplant Lucifer as the most powerful demon, giving him control of Hell. So, it won't destroy him, but it will make him subservient."

"If this does exist, why wouldn't Asmodeus be after it, instead of starting a war on Earth?" asked Tom.

"Because he does not know about it. Neither does Lucifer. Even the top officials in Rome have only heard about it as a rumor. I know because I have been given access to what these officials know. There is one person, though, who may know."

"The Pope?" asked Amy.

John just laughed. "No, not even the Pope. It is someone of very little importance in the hierarchy. He is more like a librarian. He has been the keeper of records for the last sixty years. I will take you to him. But we have to be very careful. If the lesser angels have set this up, then they may know more about it than I do, and could be using us to get it."

"So, how do we keep angels from spying on us?" asked Amy.

"That is where you will come in. You will be our decoy."

"No way, John. I will not put her life at risk."

"Not to worry, brother. I have someone local to protect her. They won't be after her per se, they will be following her using the scent of Laura-Luss, thinking that she will lead them to what they seek."

"Be cool, Tom. I have been used as a decoy many times during my investigative days. I know how to play the part."

"Except you are not trying to decoy people. You will be decoying friggin angels and demons."

"Like in the Dan Brown movie, I will have my own Tom to care for me, even if your last name isn't Hanks."

"Very funny. But unlike the movie, it isn't only priests that are in danger here."

"Brother, have I ever steered you wrong? Trust me, the person I have protecting her will be more than up to the task."

Just then, a young lady ran up to John and gave him a big hug.

"It has been so long, Father. I'm glad you called."

"John, Amy, meet Vanessa. Vanessa, this is my baby brother Tom, and his assistant on this case, Amy."

"Ugh, she smells of demon." Nevertheless, she reached over and shook each of their hands.

"Vanessa is a special person. She has angel blood in her. She has also trained with the Demon Hunter squads of the Vatican."

"Angel blood?" questioned Tom. "Won't that be like handing Amy over to one of the parties that are trying to stop us?"

"Your brother has filled me in. I may have angel blood, but I also love this planet just like it is. And I know that look. You think I am too young to have worked for very long hunting demons. But you know what they say. You can't judge a book by its cover."

John laughed at Tom's expression. "She happens to be two hundred and fifty years old."

Now both Tom's and Amy's mouths dropped open.

"It's the angel blood," Vanessa replied to their looks. I will look like this till the day I pass, which is still a couple of centuries away, God willing."

"I see there are a lot of things you have never told me, John."

"Vatican state secrets are just that. Even many at the Vatican are unaware of her. Only the Pope and a couple of archbishops know of her origin. Now you two do, at least somewhat, and I ask that you keep it that way."

Tom and Amy nodded in agreement.

"Now it is time we did some investigative work. Vanessa, please take Amy on a tour of the city, a long, winding tour. Tom and I will slip out the secret exit and meet with my contact."

The secret exit turned out to be a tunnel that was accessed through a reception area reserved for Vatican officials, an area most were not aware of. John used a thumbprint to access the door to enter the tunnel. The tunnel's end brought them to a staircase leading into a garage where several vehicles were parked.

"So this is how Vatican officials come to and from the airport when they are on unofficial business."

"Of course. Being a state unto itself with pull on the Italian government is an advantage."

John led them to an Alfa Romeo sports car with the keys already in the ignition.

"Not worried about someone getting in here and stealing some of these?"

"The only way they could enter or leave here is with the thumb of one who is permitted in here. If I start to see certain people are missing their thumbs, then I will worry," replied a laughing John.

"I wouldn't want to see that."

A remote in the car opened a garage door, exiting onto a small road in a wooded area. Tom noticed as they passed a sign in Italian that he understood to read, No Entrance. Beyond that was a gate that opened again by using the remote in the car, and a smaller road that led them around the airport to connect with the main road leading to Rome.

After a few minutes of driving, John pulled something out of his pocket and handed it to Tom. "Sorry, brother, but I must insist that you put this on."

What this was, was a blindfold.

"You've got to be kidding me."

"Nope. I am taking you on a route that only a handful of people in the world know about. It's a secret entrance into Vatican City. It must remain that way, even for you. Should anyone ever try to get that information from you, you will honestly be able to say you don't know how to find it."

Realizing his brother was serious, Tom put the blindfold on. Once he had it over his eyes, it adjusted itself, forming a complete barrier to his sight.

"This feels weird."

"A mixture of technology and church know-how. It can't 'accidentally' slip off."

It was almost half an hour before the car took a sudden turn. There was the sound of a gate opening, followed by another five-minute drive. Then the sound of a garage opening. A few minutes later, the car came to a stop, and John pulled the blindfold off his brother.

"We are in a section of the Vatican that few people visit."

Tom followed John down a twisting corridor until they came to another door that required John's thumbprint. Once through that door, they continued down a corridor with doors on both sides, all of which were solid wood. At the end of the corridor was another wooden door, which they stopped outside of as John knocked.

"Enter, young one. I have been waiting for you, said a baritone voice from the other side. It was dim as they entered, but Tom could see a swivel chair behind a desk, with its back to them.

"Please be welcome, Tom," came from the person in the chair. As it swiveled around, Tom was surprised to see a wizened and short man sitting there, short enough to be considered a dwarf. He had long flowing white hair with a pencil-white mustache and stared at Tom with crystal blue eyes. He practically jumped from the chair and rushed forward to shake hands. He could not have been taller than five feet.

"I have heard so much about you from John, and I am sure half of it is an exaggeration." His laughter was as deep as his voice.

"Well, if he told you I have a habit of getting into trouble, then no exaggeration at all," replied Tom, taking the offered hand. The handshake was quite firm.

"Tom, this is my oldest friend and mentor, Dom Emmanuel. I studied with him when I first came to the Vatican to learn some of its deepest secrets. The Pope had wanted me to do a special assignment for him, and all the information I needed, I was able to get from Emmanuel."

"And even with all I have taught you, you still have a lot to learn. You were lucky to catch me here with your call, so I was able to hide what you were asking. These topics are not to be discussed in public."

"I understand, Dom, but my business is urgent, and lives hang in the balance."

"I figured as much, based on your questions. But even for you, my friend, I can't provide you with that information, unless I know the entire story, to judge whether information of that import can be released."

"The fate of the world may rest with what you have to tell us," responded Tom.

Emmanuel laughed. "You are right, John; your brother sure knows how to get into trouble. Please have a seat and fill me in."

Tom looked at John and received a nod.

After Tom had completed the entire story, Emmanuel stood up and went to a cabinet. Expecting him to return with a book, Tom was surprised to see, instead, a tray with three glasses and a decanter.

Without saying a word, Emmanuel returned to the desk, poured an amber liquid into each glass, and handed them over.

Raising the glass to toast, he said, "May God protect us," and downed it in one gulp. Seeing John do the same, Tom emptied his glass. It was a quality of whiskey that Tom had never had before. It went down smoothly, but when it hit his stomach, it almost came right back up. He had to force it to stay put.

Emmanuel sat back down, reached into his desk, and pulled out what looked like an ancient notebook. It was maybe seven inches by ten inches and about an inch thick. It had a brown leather-like jacket, but as soon as Emmanuel laid it on his desk, Tom could detect a strong smell of decay.

"This is what you are looking for. It is a book of ancient spells, fashioned in Hell over a thousand years ago. The cover is made of human skin. It has spells laid on it to prevent it from deteriorating. There is one spell in particular that Asmodeus would want. It would take the powers that Lucifer has to command Hell and transfer them to him. But he needs more than the spell located in this book. He needs a certain piece of Lucifer himself, a piece that is located in Hell. He would also need to lure Lucifer to Earth during a special ceremony."

"Does this ceremony include a mass suicide?" asked Tom

"Actually, yes."

"So, if Satan stays in Hell and protects that certain piece, then we have nothing to fear. Especially if you keep that book right here where no one can get it."

"If only it were that simple. You see, several years ago, this book was loaned out. I do not know how or by whom. But it means that someone may very well have a copy of that spell. Furthermore, once Asmodeus starts his ceremony, the force of the ceremony will draw Lucifer forward, whether he wants to come or not."

"Then I have to get Laura-Luss to make sure Lucifer hides the piece of himself needed for the spell somewhere in hell where Asmodeus can't get it."

"From what I can see, this has been in the planning stages for a very long time. The piece we are talking about is in Hell, alright, Hell on Earth that is."

"Grand Cayman," exclaimed John.

"Exactly. I had thought only a few knew of this, but it appears word has gotten out. We can only hope your associates get there first. But be warned. Asmodeus has gone too far to stop now. Even without the piece, he will continue and hope he can defeat Lucifer without it. Maybe with help from some other force, either already on earth or on the way."

Tom was puzzled. "Question. Why would any forces of heaven want Asmodeus to succeed, and why would Lucifer even take a chance of letting Asmodeus out of Hell if it could result in his loss of power?"

"Lucifer has always been prideful and thinks he is smarter than anyone. His purpose is to let Asmodeus start a war with Heaven, to weaken the forces of Heaven. Then he would take control of the Earth. Holding two of the three planes would make it difficult for the Holy Father to battle him without destroying mankind. He thought he was so brilliant, hiding a piece of his heart in a place called Hell, that would have his rivals hunting everywhere but on Earth.

"As for the forces of heaven, we are dealing with a minority of angels that would love to have a final battle with Lucifer. If he were drawn to Earth and under attack by Asmodeus, he would be weakened. As well, once he is drawn to Earth with power, the Archangels, like Michael, would be forced to come here to fight. This would give the lesser angels what they have always wanted: a chance to fight Lucifer and prove themselves, giving them more power. Maybe Asmodeus is counting on this, too."

"But I thought Lucifer came to Earth many times. I have even met with him at my office. Why would this be different?"

"Yes, he can come and go to Earth, as long as he leaves the focus of his power in Hell. Not to say that he is not strong enough to wipe out a city if he wanted, but any use of that type of power would call the Archangels, and that is a battle he knows he could not win. So, he comes and goes without bringing his full power with him. But the ceremony that Asmodeus would use to draw him out would bring all his power with him. Then, Asmodeus could use the spell in this book to take Lucifer's power from him. No matter who wins, Lucifer, Asmodeus, or the Archangels, the use of that power on earth would pretty well wipe out humankind."

"The question is, how do we stop this from happening?" said John.

"It will be up to Tom and his succubus."

"What?!!!"

"You two must finish this case. You must catch Asmodeus before he finishes his plan."

"And just how are we supposed to do that? Is there a spell in that book of yours that will somehow allow us to trap Asmodeus without him killing us?"

"I'm afraid not. It is something you two will have to figure out. However, I have made a copy of that spell that Asmodeus will try to use on Lucifer. Maybe it will help." He handed a piece of paper to Tom and then, turning to John, he added, "And your part in this has to end today. You will only draw the attention of the lesser angels to your brother as long as you are helping him. Even now, I can feel their presence heading towards us. Tom, you must drop John off somewhere outside the Vatican and let Vanessa take him to the airport as soon as possible."

"But how can I abandon my brother at a time like this?" John demanded.

"You must or you will bring about his downfall."

****

"I had forgotten how hot it is in the Caribbean," said Ben as they disembarked.

"We are visiting Hell, so what did you expect?" replied Laura-Luss, a grin on her face.

"You demons have a twisted sense of humor."

"I could demon-strate how twisted our humor can be if you like," replied Laura-Luss, emphasizing demon as a separate word.

"I don't know how Tom has been able to tolerate you so long. He must care about you not to have throttled you by now."

"More like he's lucky I haven't done something to him."

"I am sensing a lot of caring between the two of you."

"You humans always read your stupid emotions into everything." Even as she said it, she was beginning to wonder what was happening to her. Not long ago, she would have done something nasty to any human who talked to her like Ben just did. It must be Tom's influence. Being forced by her boss to handle him with kid gloves was making her soft. Once this assignment was finished, she needed a good dose of mayhem to get herself back to normal.

Ben rented a car, it being easier to make a quick getaway, if need be, than trying to find a cab while being chased by any opponents they should come across. Since the only mid-size available was a Kia Rio, he decided to spend a little more for the Jeep Wrangler. More the type of vehicle they could use for escape should the situation arise.

"Once we get there, we will have to figure out not only where to look, but how to do it." Ben's voice rose an octave higher as they hit a bump.

"How?" the demoness replied. "Simple, we walk through the Limestone field and search for something unusual."

"Not so easy, Ms. Luss. There will probably be lots of tourists, as well as security, who will not want us to possibly damage their precious tourist trap. You might be interested to learn that although the unique formation is technically limestone, there are various scientific names for this formation. Listen to what it says in this pamphlet I picked up at the airport:

> Hell is a unique formation that is characterized by jagged, spongy pinnacles of black-covered limestone. This phytokarst formation is produced when attacking filamentous algae interact with the Ironshore Formation limestone present at this location.
>
> Phytokarst is a distinctive landform resulting from a curious type of biologic erosion. Filamentous algae bore their way into limestone to produce black-coated, jagged pinnacles marked by delicate, lacy dissection that lacks any gravitational orientation. Ordinary rainfall-produced karst and littoral karst are characterized by flat-bottomed pans

and vertically oriented flutes, thus differing from phytokarst. Algae attack by dissolving calcite preferentially to dolomite.

The ironshore karst is a special type, both in terms of its texture and origin. First, texture – it is a black, random spongework of pits, jagged ridges, and pointed pinnacles. It is developed in a narrow strip just above the tide line on ancient limestone rocks. If you break off a piece, you will see that the black color is present near the surface, and it grades to gray inside. Second, origin – it is being dissolved largely by algae, bacteria, and fungi, so it is often called "biokarst". These tiny (microscopic) organisms bore into the rock and dissolve the calcite crystals. They are most dense within a centimeter or so at the surface, causing the black color. Why this results in the characteristic macro-texture is not fully understood, but you always see the two elements together, so they must be linked somehow. Proximity to the marine environment is key. Maybe the splash, spray, and mist from the waves breaking provide just enough moisture to sustain the algae.

Laura-Luss gave a dismissive sniff. "Sure. Or there may be another explanation for it, but I won't know until we see it. Speaking of which, it is almost three. Since most cruise ships depart around this time, a lot of the tourists will no longer be there. I have certain abilities that will allow us to pass unnoticed."

Seeing the look on Ben's face, she added, "With no harm to them. Don't worry."

"If you use any of your special abilities, won't that draw attention to us from certain forces we don't want around?"

"It is a chance we will have to take."

"Maybe not. You can pass by anyone without being noticed, and without using any special power, can't you?"

"Yes, but I will need that power to hide you."

"Then don't hide me, I will hide myself."

"How will you do that?"

"Why in plain sight. No one will notice just another tourist."

Laura-Luss gave him a quizzical look.

"You'll see when we get there."

It took less than thirty minutes from the airport, as the demoness was correct in her statement that most of the tourists would either be gone or heading back to the ships. Ben pulled into the parking area and found a somewhat shaded spot in front of a sign that appropriately read, 'Devil's Only Parking.' This even got a smile from Laura-Luss.

"Now, are you going to tell me how you will remain invisible?"

"More like show you." Ben fished his bag out from behind the seat and started pulling out objects. First was a pair of binoculars, which he proceeded to hang around his neck. Next were two walkie-talkies.

"I'll hold this like it's a phone so people will think I am talking to a friend somewhere and describing what Hell looks like. But what I'll actually be doing is using the binoculars to see if I can spot any irregularities and letting you know."

"That is quite ingenious, for a human."

Not bothering to respond to that, Ben then pulled a small box out of his bag and handed it to her.

"What is this for?"

"More 'human' ingenuity. Whatever is out there can't be large, or it would have been spotted a long time ago. Once you find what we're looking for, put it in this box. It's made of lead and embedded into the case are symbols and 'spells' that will hide the object away from any forces of Hell, or Heaven."

"You did come prepared. But how would you know about any of this?"

"My sister and I have worked with the agency for a long time, and yes, this agency has handled many unusual cases, shall we say. My sister, knowing who you are and the nature of the case, made sure I had what I needed."

"I guess Tom did ask the right person to help."

They exited the car and each went their separate ways. Within seconds, Ben could no longer see Laura-Luss. He proceeded past the gift shops and towards the limestone fields. Picking a spot where he could see a good portion of the two-acre plot, but where few others were standing, he lifted the binoculars and looked for any formations that might be a little different.

The walkie-talkie issued some static, and then Laura-Luss' voice came through loud and clear.

"I am nearing the center of the field. So far, nothing. Have you spotted anything?"

Ben tried to find her amongst the formations but could not see her. He did, though, see an area that occasionally bubbled for no reason.

"Your ability is perfect. I can't spot you at all. But I may see something that is unusual. Give me some indication of where you are so I can guide you."

For just a second, a hand appeared and waved, then was gone. Any tourist who might have spotted it would have thought it was a hallucination.

"Perfect. Now go about five feet to your right and look down. Notice that near that darker-than-black flat-topped piece, there is bubbling every once in a while?"

While he could not see her, Ben saw a disturbance in the small puddle of water he had indicated to Laura-Luss.

"There is something here. Is this case water protected? I don't want to pull the thing out of the water as I can feel the power coming from it only when my hand is near it, but I think the water is somehow muting it."

"Not to fear, the water will not diminish the case's protective abilities in any way."

A minute later, she was standing next to him.

"Got it!"

"It's a piece of Lucifer, isn't it?"

"A piece of his heart."

"I wonder how that got here."

"Most likely, when Lucifer was cast from Heaven in the fight with the Archangel Michael, it was cut out of him by Michael's sword. When it fell to Earth, it landed here, and that is what probably created this unusual formation, despite what geologists might say, and what you saw in that brochure you read to me. Lucifer may not have wanted to retrieve it for many reasons, part of which may be that it gives him access to Earth.

"But the real question should be, what do we do with it?"

CHAPTER 19

Tom was sitting at a café near the Vatican, waiting for Amy and Vanessa to arrive. He knew John was still upset that he couldn't help and had to abandon his brother at a time like this. But he also knew that John's mentor, Dom Emmanuel, would not have said to do so if he weren't sure. John had hugged him and then gone in the opposite direction, hoping to lure any watchers away.

Shortly, a small red sports car pulled up, Amy sitting up front with a big smile on her face, while Vanessa was signaling him to hurry up and get in back. The back seat of the car had almost no leg room, so Tom had to sit crossways on the seat, pushing aside bags to do so.

"What did you girls do, go shopping or something?"

"Of course," laughed Amy. "What else would you expect when I'm in a foreign country with a company credit card and an unlimited expense account?"

"We must hurry to the airport," said Vanessa. "I can sense the lesser angels closing in. They know you are here and probably know why."

"Once we're on the airplane, we'll be vulnerable," said Amy, picking up on the urgency in Vanessa's voice. "What's to stop them from just crashing the airplane?"

"Don't worry," Vanessa replied. "No matter what, they're still governed by certain rules. The lesser angels can't in any way directly cause harm to a person, and if they see evil trying to harm a human, they have to intervene to protect the human or be cast into Hell. They'll probably follow the plane back to New York, which in turn will protect you from the forces of Asmodeus who don't care so much about collateral damage."

"But if they are governed by these rules, wouldn't helping Asmodeus go against the rules?" asked Tom.

"That's the irony of the situation," Vanessa explained. "As long as forces of evil go directly against a person, they have to intervene. But if the forces of evil are fighting other forces of evil, they do not."

They had lapsed into thoughtful silence and were nearing the airport when a car coming towards them suddenly swerved into their lane. Vanessa was able to maneuver quickly enough to avoid that car, but almost immediately, another did the same thing. Everyone was instinctively bracing for the head-on collision when the oncoming vehicle suddenly lifted into the air and flew over them. Amy glanced at Vanessa, about to ask if she was responsible for saving them, but before she could say a word, Vanessa spoke up.

"Looks like the lesser angels are nearby. It must have been lower-level demons taking control of the cars."

Neither Tom nor Amy seemed prepared to comment further, and soon they arrived at the airport. "The demons can't touch us here," Vanessa assured them. "These are sanctified grounds." She pulled up in front of the Departures terminal and whipped the car into a space marked Reserved. She pulled out a sign and put it on the dashboard.

"This area is for Vatican personnel, so no need to worry about tickets. I'll go with you to the boarding area, and then you'll be on your own. From here on, you should be okay to New York."

When they reached the gates, Vanessa gave both Tom and Amy a two-cheek kiss. "It has been fun. Next time you come through, I will take you to some places where you can have a blast." She smiled and then turned away, moving out of sight in moments.

"Well, I don't know what her idea of a blast is, but if it is anything like her fun, I think I'll pass," said Amy.

Tom laughed. "I am with you on that."

****

"Don't look now, but I think we have company," said Ben, looking in the rear-view mirror. "That sedan has been behind us since we pulled out of the parking lot, and it's now closing on us."

Laura-Luss looked back. Using her abilities, she was able to see not only into the car but into the person driving it. "Not exactly the company we want to have. The driver is a half-demon. Not a full-blood, but still strong enough to cause trouble."

"Can you do something to stop him?"

"Not without calling attention to ourselves. There are too many cars around now. I would have thought there would be less traffic on the road at this time."

"Is it possible that other demons are driving those cars?"

"I find it unlikely. Asmodeus would not want to draw that much focus onto himself here, and Lucifer would not want to light a big arrow onto where he was hiding what we have in the box. Most probably, Asmodeus has sent out some type of message telling people to head to a certain place. He does have influencing abilities. Not strong enough to get people to murder for him, but maybe give people the desire to get a meal at a certain restaurant, for example. It would have to be people, though, who have sinned considerably. It could be a lot of thieves or other low-life individuals."

"I'm open to suggestions."

"Give me your phone."

Ben reached into his shirt pocket and handed it to Laura-Luss. "Code is 2525."

She opened the phone and Googled maps.

"Okay, take the next exit. Most of the cars should keep going. We can circle around and then back onto this road. At least it should separate us from the pack."

Ben followed her advice, and sure enough, most of the cars kept on going. Only the sedan stayed on their tail.

"No other cars around, so I can act now." Then she was gone.

Shortly after, Ben saw the other car veer off the road and flip over into a ditch. A moment later, Laura-Luss was back in the car.

"What did you do?"

"Just appeared beside him and put my hand on his lap. It helped that I had no clothes that he could see."

Ben laughed. "That'll teach him to take his eyes off the road."

They were able to return to the road leading to the airport soon thereafter.

"I think we have another problem," Ben said, pumping the brakes as they came up to a traffic jam featuring all the cars they had let go by, now just parked on the road.

Ben pulled over, trying to see a way around it. But as soon as he stopped, the thugs started getting out of their cars and walking towards them.

"Okay, this is not good," Laura-Luss said, her tone reinforcing the gravity of her observation. "If I use too much of my power here, it could cause problems."

"Then it's up to me," replied Ben. He jammed the jeep into reverse, raced backward a few hundred feet, then pulled the wheel hard over, shifted into drive, and floored it off the pavement. "Fortunately, this baby has off-road abilities."

It was a rough ride, but Ben's driving abilities got them through the worst of the terrain. They were able to get past the blockade and then re-enter the road.

"Nice driving," said Laura-Luss, letting go of her grip on the dashboard and grab handle. "Let's hope there are no other obstacles."

They were approaching the airport, but there looked to be security stationed at the entrance.

"Give me my phone," said Ben, holding out his hand.

Laura-Luss handed it back to him. "What's your plan?"

Ben did not reply as he one-touch dialed a pre-programmed number.

"What do you need?" asked the male voice that answered.

"Quick access into the airport."

"Is that you coming in the Wrangler?"

"Yes."

"Take the exit lane on your left. I'll clear the way."

Ben moved into the exit-only lane, and as he approached the gate, it raised.

"Now, park the car right where you are. Someone will pick you up." The phone went dead.

"Who was that?" asked Laura-Luss.

"Someone I paid when we arrived. He used to do work for our company."

A few minutes later, a small white car pulled in behind them. A large black man exited. How he could fit in that little vehicle, the demoness had no idea. Ben jumped out and hugged him.

"I could always count on you, Henry."

"It's been a long time, Ben. But no time for reunions. I need to get you to your plane before my boss knows you're here. A call came into the office to detain a white man with a beautiful woman, driving a jeep. Since it means trouble, I know it had to be you. Not to worry, though. Once you're on the plane, they can't touch you."

"Yeah, but the terminal, it is another story," said Laura-Luss.

Henry nodded. "Which is why we are not going into the terminal."

He gestured for them to squeeze into the small vehicle with him, then raced between the back hangars and out onto the runway. "I got two tickets for you on that plane over there. The pilot is a friend of mine, and he'll let you board from here."

He pulled up beside the plane where a stairway already stood in place. When they got out of the car, Ben gave Henry another hug, and Laura-Luss kissed him on the cheek before boarding the plane. As soon as they entered, the ramp was pulled away, the door closed, and the plane moved into the take-off position. A steward guided them to their seats in the front executive section before taking his seat. Within minutes, they were airborne and on their way to New York.

CHAPTER 20

 "My brother just texted me," said Amy. "They're at the office waiting for our arrival."

The flight from Rome had been uneventful, and with little luggage, Tom and Amy cleared through customs and baggage quickly.

"Did he say if their trip was successful?"

"I think he's being cautious. We know that somehow emails are being tampered with, and he doesn't trust even texts at this point. However, he did say enough for me to know that they found something."

"Good. Send him back a text. Just say 'likewise.' That should be enough of a clue."

They were heading towards the exit doors when Tom's cell phone buzzed.

"That must be Laura-Luss. I hope she realizes not to say too much." But when Tom pulled the phone out of his pocket, he didn't recognize the number. It only showed three digits. Wondering if this could be another setup, Tom answered cautiously.

"No time to talk, Jonas. Get your succubus and go to Chatham Square Cemetery. We will speak then." The call disconnected.

Seeing Tom's expression, Amy asked, "Trouble?"

"Maybe. That was the golem, Vince Faustelli. For some reason, he wants Laura-Luss and me to go to a cemetery."

"Maybe he's made a choice."

"Yes, but what choice? Is he helping us or setting us up? Only one way to find out for sure. Send a text to your brother and tell him to have Laura-Luss ready at the front door. No time to go home for my car, and I don't trust hiring a cab right now, so I'm going to get a rental. I will drop you off when I pick her up."

"Maybe Ben and I should go with you for backup."

"No. I've put your lives at risk enough. From here on in, it will be up to Laura-Luss and me. We won't put any others in harm's way. Dom Emmanuel said that it was up to the two of us to stop Asmodeus. I trust him. Between the demoness and myself, we will find a way. As for Vince, if this is a setup, there isn't much we can do about it, except be prepared. But I just have this feeling that he's chosen the right side."

Even though it was midday, it was almost an hour later by the time they checked out a car and fought the New York traffic to get to the offices of the agency. Laura-Luss saw them pull up and opened the car door for her and Amy to change places.

"Good luck, you two. I know you don't want to get anyone else involved, Tom, but if you need anything, just call. If you two fail, then it will still affect all of us."

"Will do, Amy. Thank Ben for us."

As soon as Laura-Luss was belted in, Tom pulled away and headed towards the cemetery.

"So, where are we headed and why? Amy's message was quite cryptic."

"We think someone is tapping into our communications, and the call I received is more evidence of that. Vince just said one sentence before hanging up. To go to Chatham Square Cemetery."

"That makes sense."

"In what way?"

"It is a Jewish cemetery. Also known as First Shearith Israel Graveyard. So, no chance that Christian angels will hang around there. Yet it is also sanctified ground, so it should keep demons away."

"What about you? You're a demon."

"It will bother me to be there, but it won't stop me from entering the grounds, nor cause me serious harm. Did he say where he wanted us to go?"

"Not really. The funny thing is, though, for some reason, he called me Jonas. I guess to throw off anyone who might be listening."

Laura-Luss laughed. "He is quite brilliant. I know exactly where to go."

Tom gave her a puzzled look.

"He wants to meet at a certain gravestone. That of Dr. Walter Jonas Judah, the second Jew known to attend an American medical school (King's College, now Columbia University) and the first native-born Jew to do so; he died at the age of twenty of yellow fever in 1798."

"How do you know this?"

"I was there when he died."

"Did you—?"

"No, I had no part in it. I was there for other purposes."

When she did not elaborate, Tom decided not to pursue it further.

The entrance to the cemetery was closed, so they had to park on the street and climb over a fence. Laura-Luss knew exactly where to go and led Tom exactly to the gravestone. Tom bent down to read the inscription but could not make heads or tails of the language.

"It is written in Russian," said a voice from nearby. Tom jerked up in surprise and even Laura-Luss was startled, as she had sensed no presence nearby.

"For your information," said Vince Faustelli, it reads:

> *Walter Jonas Judah grew up in a wealthy Sephardic family and was known to be the first American-born Jewish medical student. In 1795, he entered King's College (later Columbia University), where he studied medicine. When a yellow fever epidemic broke out in New York in 1798, he could easily have left the city, as most wealthy citizens did, but he chose to stay to help his sick fellow citizens. Unfortunately, he became infected and died at the age of 20.* The English name Walter comes from an ancient Germanic word that means "commander". The name Jonas is the English version of the Hebrew name Jonah, meaning "dove". Surname Judah—from the biblical name Judah.

"And there's no need to worry," said Vince, bringing them back to the current situation. "The fact that I am here, and you two are still alive, tells you I have made a decision, and it is not in support of Asmodeus."

"Thank you," said Tom.

"Don't thank me yet. First, though, please check your emails."

Puzzled, Tom pulled out his phone and saw several emails that had not appeared before, including one with no return address, just a symbol showing goat horns.

Looking over his shoulder, Laura-Luss exclaimed, "That's from my contact in Hell, doing the research I asked. I was wondering why we had not received it yet. It was just a simple search that could not have taken more than a few hours."

"I can explain," said Vince. "One of the first things Asmodeus did when he came to our plane was to use the knowledge of a certain demon, who works in Hell's communication room, to set up a program that mixes technology and magic to intercept and block any emails going to and from certain people. Once he knew you were on his tail, Tom, he had his helper use the program on both your emails and your phone. However, it has its limitations. Since it uses Hell magic, it won't work on sanctified grounds."

Tom nodded his understanding. "Well, let's see what this has to say." He opened the email and began to read aloud:

The program worked. The computers in Hell keep a record of all the passing of demons onto the human plane. I know most of Asmodeus' followers and ran a program to see where they have been over the last year. They did not all go to the same place, but many did, and the others almost all crossed the same area. All we need to do now is see what cults are in that area.

Tom looked up. "Hmm, upper New York state, near the Canadian border."

"More explicitly, near the Quebec border," replied Vince. "Which makes sense since he knew I had been living in Île Bizard for several years, so I would be nearby when he needed me."

Tom typed in a search for cults in that area and was surprised at how many there actually were. But one, in particular, stood out. He read the entry, then gave them a summary.

"Word of Life, Christ Church, a splinter group from the Word of Life Church. So radical that even the founders of the original church cut off ties with them. Led by Jeremiah Irving, the cult has seventy-seven member families, and the size of each family is seven. According to one former member, Jeremiah insists that each couple has five children, no more and no less, so the family always adds up to seven.

"Divorce is not allowed, and if a family member dies, they are to be replaced, either through a forced marriage with a kidnapped outsider in the case of parents, or forced adoption in the case of children. If a woman gets pregnant after they reach their limit, an abortion is performed. The exception is that once a year, an extra child is allowed, or one is procured, to perform a sacrifice to a demon.

"It is also said that many of the children in the various families are those of Jeremiah Irving, as he insists on 'sampling' each member's wife at least once, to purify her.

"After an investigation, they were unable to find any proof of this, so the claims of the former members were said to be revenge, as he, according to cult leader Jeremiah

Irving, had been kicked out of the cult. Just a few months after the investigation, the former member disappeared under mysterious circumstances."

"That sounds like the type of cult that Asmodeus would use," said Laura-Luss. "He is probably even the demon they are said to sacrifice to."

"But that's a lot of people for a mass suicide," replied Tom. Seven times seventy-seven is five hundred and thirty-nine. Is there a special significance to that number?"

Vince Faustini responded. "As you are aware, Tom, the number of the beast is said to be 666. That is the number of Lucifer. However, Asmodeus, being the most powerful of demons, next to goat horns himself, has his own number. It is 777. Also, for a mass suicide to open a portal, the number of deaths has to exceed five hundred."

"Does the article say where exactly this cult is located?" asked Laura-Luss.

"Nothing specific. Just upstate New York, near Lake Champlain."

"Can you enlarge a map of the area on your phone?"

Tom opened up the map app and set up the display of Lake Champlain. Since it could not be too close to a city, but close enough to get supplies, they were able to narrow it down. Using the information from the computer program Laura-Luss had created, and crossing all the paths taken, they were able to narrow it down to a few square miles.

"If we have it right, then there is only one road that goes into that area. We follow that road, and it should lead us right to them."

"But we can't follow that road," said Tom. "They probably already know we'll be coming and will be watching the road. However, I could rent us an ATV and we could follow along the road until we figure out exactly where their encampment is and go in the back door, so to speak."

"What about backup? Maybe get the police involved?" Laura-Luss asked.

"You don't have time for that," answered the golem. The ceremony will commence at midnight tonight. You will never be able to convince the authorities to act by then, especially after the last investigation went nowhere."

"We also don't want to get too many innocents involved," said Tom.

"I won't be able to assist you either," said Vince. "Asmodeus put a tracker on me. If I were to head there, he would know I was going against him and act accordingly. Since I was due to come to New York and always visit this cemetery, it is unlikely that Asmodeus made a connection with you two."

"Out of curiosity, why do you visit this cemetery?" asked Tom.

"My creator is buried here," was the answer.

"Any ideas on how to stop Asmodeus, or at least the mass suicide?" asked the demoness.

"No," said the golem. "But that being said, I can tell you two things. Asmodeus fears you for some reason, Laura-Luss. There may be something that you have, or can do, that at this moment you are not aware of. I would concentrate on that if I were you."

"What is the second thing?" asked Tom.

"A mass suicide is essentially a sacrifice to evil. To stop this sacrifice, a sacrifice of another kind is usually the only response."

"What sacrifice?"

"That is for you and your succubus to figure out. I have done all I can. Now I suggest you get going, as it is a long drive from here to where you need to be. Time is running out." With that, the golem walked away.

"You have an idea?" said Laura-Luss, seeing the expression on Tom's face, like he was working a puzzle.

"Not quite, but something is germinating in the back of my brain. We might have the tools now to do something. You still have the piece of Lucifer with you. We might be able to use that."

"Didn't Amy tell you that they locked it in the safe at the office?"

"Yes, she did, but I know you, Laura-Luss. Something that would give you leverage in Hell would be too hard to resist."

Tom did not see where she'd had it hidden, but Laura-Luss produced the box containing the piece.

"I'm sorry, Tom. I shouldn't have taken it. There is that part of me that just can't stop myself."

"Not to worry. It's that part of you that I was counting on. Let's hit the road. It's a good six-hour drive to where we're going. That will put us nearby with just a couple of hours to spare. I'll call the office from here and have them arrange for us to pick up an ATV. We have until then to make a plan."

Once Tom spoke with Amy and arranged their future transport, as well as a few other items he requested, they left the cemetery and got back in the car.

"From here on, we are traceable. I have no idea what forces will be aligned against us and if they will be trying to help or hinder us. So, we will have to stay alert. You wouldn't happen to know how to drive, would you? Do they teach you that in Hell?"

"Sorry, Tom, no. And I realize lack of sleep will slow you down, even with the boost you have received, but there is not much we can do about it now."

"Then we'll stop and pick up some food. A few burgers, a couple of hot dogs, a family-sized fry, and about a dozen Cokes should do."

"I know you think that having the piece of Lucifer with us will help in some way, but it was stupid on my part since it makes us a target."

"Au contraire, my dear. The piece will help us get there with less interference."

Seeing the look on her face, Tom explained.

"The lesser angels will stay away as they will know you will detect them, but the forces of Asmodeus, believing we may have the piece, will let us pass so that Asmodeus can acquire it. We just have to make sure that doesn't happen."

They pulled into a Sonic's drive-through and Tom ordered four burgers, three hot dogs, fries, cheese fries, onion rings, and some Chili cheese tots, along with a half dozen Cokes.

"This should last me a little while."

Laura-Luss held the food for Tom as he drove, passing him items as he asked for them.

Halfway through the trip, she asked, "Has the food helped your thinking process? I sure hope so because we need a plan and we need it fast."

"I do have an idea, and it stems from my visit to the Vatican. I haven't had a chance to tell you what happened, and most of the details are unimportant; however, there is one thing that I think will help.

"It is true that there is something hidden at the Vatican that can harm Lucifer, though not something that can destroy him. It's a spell that Asmodeus now has, but I also have a copy."

"What does this spell do?"

"Used, with the sacrifice, and with that piece of Lucifer, it can transfer power from Lucifer to Asmodeus, basically making Asmodeus the new boss in Hell. Of course, Asmodeus wants more than that. He will then use that power to try and take over Earth and then Heaven."

"That helps us how?"

Tom pulled a piece of paper out of his pocket and handed it to Laura-Luss.

"I can't read it, since it's in a language I don't know, but I figure it will work just as well for you as for Asmodeus."

She was aghast.

"You want me to take on Lucifer!?"

"No. I want you to use that spell, at the opportune moment, to take the powers of Asmodeus. I understand it transfers power from a stronger power to a lesser power. Well, Asmodeus is a stronger power, and you are a lesser power."

Laura-Luss looked at the paper.

"Yes, I understand this. It is a type of ancient Latin that was modified."

She read the entire spell.

"I think you are right. But we will need a piece of Asmodeus for it to work."

"Once we have a piece of him, how fast can the spell work?"

"I can have the spell prepared in my mind before we arrive. Once we have a piece, I will just need to say one word. The problem, though, is getting a piece of Asmodeus."

"Leave that to me. I will need the piece of Lucifer that you are holding."

"No, Tom! Asmodeus will tear you to shreds in seconds. You can't stand up to him."

"Neither can you until you cast the spell. I will bait Asmodeus using the piece of Lucifer, and when he gets close to me, I will take a chunk out of him with one of the tools I asked Amy to arrange for me."

"You plan on being the sacrifice that the golem mentioned, don't you?"

"Not if I can help it, but if that is what it takes, so be it."

"I won't let you!"

"You have no choice, Laura-Luss. Besides, I'm only an assignment. Why should you care?"

Laura-Luss sat back in her seat and did not respond for a little while. Finally, she did.

"You are right. I was being stupid. Let's just get this over with."

The remainder of the drive went in silence. About an hour outside of Plattsburgh, Tom pulled off the highway.

"Why are we getting off here?"

"There is a Catholic church near here called Sacred Heart. We will pull onto the grounds so I can check my emails. Amy should have sent me the information on where to pick up the ATV and other equipment."

As they neared the church, Laura-Luss said, "Pull over here. We are now on sanctified ground. I can feel it. You should be able to check your emails here."

The sun had set, and it was quiet where they stopped. Tom pulled out his phone and scanned his emails. There were several, including one from his brother, but the only one he had time for now was the one from Amy.

"Okay, there is a place called Chesterfield. We'll get on to the 87 and then exit in about forty-five minutes onto the 22. Off the 22 is a road called Shunpike. Just before, an ATV has been hidden in the bushes. I have the exact location, so it should not be hard to find. There is a place nearby where we can park the car and it won't be noticed."

Whether it was nerves or anticipation, the time seemed to pass quickly as they hit the exit for the 22 and then spotted Shunpike Road. Tom spotted the parking area Amy mentioned in her email and pulled in. It was very quiet. Even the homes they had passed were dark at this hour. He checked the clock as they left the car.

"Ten-fifteen. We don't have much time. Let's hope the encampment isn't far."

"We are close. I can feel the evil from here."

Tom soon spotted the ATV behind some bushes beyond where they had parked the car. Next to it was a bag and what looked like a long pole.

"Thank you, Amy," said Tom, going through the bag. Inside was a pouch with blessed silver bullets that would fit his gun, as well as a cross, holy water, a knife sharpener, and flashlights. The pole turned out to be a hoe."

"What do you need a knife sharpener for?"

"This." Tom picked up the hoe and used the sharpener to bring an edge to the hoe that would cut paper.

"As you said, I don't want to get too close to Asmodeus. I will swing it at him when he nears me, and with luck catch a chunk of him which I can toss to you on the follow-through."

"That might work."

"Do you know how this ceremony he will perform works? Does the mass suicide take place before or during the ceremony? I want to save as many of the innocents as possible."

"They are not innocents, Tom. You would do well to remember that. They chose to be in this cult and follow its rules."

"Maybe the parents did, but the children didn't."

"'The sins of the fathers are visited on the children to the third and fourth generation.'—Exodus 20."

"'Permit the children to come to Me; and do not hinder them; for the kingdom of God belongs to such as these.' Matthew 19:14," replied Tom. "As well, I have my own. 'The children shall not perish because their parents made a mistake.' Tom 1:1."

"I understand your desire, Tom, but if Asmodeus succeeds, it will be all the children in the world who will perish. We will try not to harm them, but we must not let our fear for them prevent us from doing what we came to do."

"I will do all I can to prevent harm coming to them. You know that Laura-Luss. So, if there is anything you know about the ceremony that can help me, you'd better tell me now."

Surprised that Tom had used her name rather than calling her demoness or succubus, which he was wont to do when he was upset, she softened her stance.

"If it is what I think it is, the ceremony must be complete before the deaths. When Asmodeus finishes his calling, the congregation must then all die at the same time. On their deaths, Lucifer will be called forth, and the battle will begin."

"For them to die at the same time, it must be by some strong poison in a drink. I can't see the parents getting their children to shoot themselves or something like that."

"It is the only way that I can see as well. The poison would have to be extremely powerful, though, to kill that fast. I don't know of any man-made poison that can do that. Therefore, it must be some Hellish concoction."

"If we could slip some holy water into the drinks, would that somehow nullify the poison?"

"It should. But how will you manage to get it into seventy-seven glasses at the same time?"

"We have to get there before they start pouring. There must be some large container that the liquid is in since I can't see Asmodeus trying to poison seventy-seven different glasses either."

"Then we had better get a move on. Time is running out."

They jumped onto the ATV, and Tom started it up.

"This is kind of noisy. They will hear us coming."

"Can you use your senses to pinpoint exactly where they are?"

Laura-Luss concentrated, turning her head in different directions and focusing her mind each time she turned. It only took her a few seconds to find the area they would be in.

"About two miles that way, next to a small body of water."

Tom drove a little over a mile and then pulled the ATV off the road. It was heavily forested, but they were able to find a path large enough for the ATV to follow. After ten minutes, Laura-Luss said to stop.

"Asmodeus is nearby. I can feel him. We must go on foot from here."

Tom unloaded the supplies and followed Laura-Luss through the woods. Soon they came to the edge of the woods, which opened onto an encampment that was not marked on any map.

"Eleven o'clock. He is about to start the ceremony. Can you see where the poison is?" asked the demoness.

Tom looked around and soon saw a table with a large jug and a row of Dixie cups.

"Over there," he pointed out.

She looked where Tom indicated. "Yes, I can see the evil emanating from the jug. Asmodeus must be nearby if he has already put the poison in."

From his angle, Tom was able to see someone standing near the jug, but could not make out who or what it might be, as the figure was a shadow. A moment later, he moved away from the table and into the light.

Tom saw a tall man wearing a white suit. He had long silver-brown hair and a well-coiffed beard. "That must be the cult leader."

Laura-Luss followed Tom's gaze and gasped. "That is Asmodeus. He has taken on human form. No wonder the people were so easily swayed into the cult. He has the power of persuasion far beyond anything a human could do."

"As long as he is standing near that table, I will not be able to put the holy water into the jug."

Just then, they saw a line of people approaching the table. As each person passed it, they picked up a Dixie cup.

"No time now. I will distract Asmodeus, and you put the holy water into the jug."

"How are you going to do that?"

"Just be ready." And with that, she disappeared.

Sensing her presence from her use of her Hell-based abilities, Asmodeus looked around and called her out.

"I know you are here, Laura-Luss. Now I can feel your presence. If you surrender to my will now, I will let you survive, and you may even hold a high place in my council."

"There won't be any high place or any council if you follow through with your plans. There will be nothing left of this plane or its people." She appeared at the opposite end of the clearing from Tom.

"You think not," said Asmodeus, walking towards Laura-Luss. "But you would be wrong. I have made some arrangements. Once Lucifer is mine, I will control all of Hell and have a place on this plane as well. The lesser angels I am working with will negotiate a treaty with Heaven, in exchange for certain favors."

With Asmodeus' attention turned away, Tom made his silent approach towards the table. Worried about betrayal from the cult members, Tom kept careful watch on them as he edged forward. But studying them, he realized he had nothing to fear. They were in some sort of trance, their eyes only on the jug. One member was moving forward to take the place of Asmodeus to pour the liquid.

Out of time, Tom ran the remaining distance, flipped the top off the jug, and poured in the entire contents of the bottle of holy water. Immediately, there was a spark and then a small poof as the jug came apart, pieces narrowly missing Tom, although a few of the bits struck the member next to the jug. That member immediately fell to the ground and went into convulsions.

Hearing the noise, Asmodeus turned towards Tom.

"YOU! For delaying my plans, you will die a horrible death—and do so over and over again."

Pointing to one of the cult members, he said something Tom could not make out. Thinking that the member was going to attack him, Tom prepared himself, not wanting to use his gun to kill a person. Instead, the member turned away and went to a shed nearby.

"I am always prepared. I have more of the poison handy. Do you have more holy water?" Seeing Tom's expression, he added, "I see not."

Grabbing tightly onto the hoe, Tom walked towards Asmodeus.

"You think you can beat me with a garden tool, you puny man? I will make mincemeat out of you."

Before he could reach Tom, he was hit from behind by something tossed by Laura-Luss. Asmodeus let out a roar as he had been hit by a spelled rock, causing minor pain, but no real harm.

"I gave you a chance, succubus, and you threw it away. Prepare to be dissolved."

The distraction was all Tom needed. Lunging forward, he swung the hoe, taking a chunk out of the arm of Asmodeus. The coating of holy oil he had put on it ensured that the hoe would penetrate the skin. This time, Asmodeus felt real pain, for the first time that he could remember. His roar was magnified because of it.

He turned back to Tom, grabbed the hoe, and tossed it into the trees. Then he grabbed Tom, throwing him across the compound.

Tom heard the snap and then felt the pain in his left leg. Looking down, he could see the bone coming through the skin. He was on the verge of passing out, but Asmodeus had no intention of making it that easy for him, as he marched through the clearing towards him.

"Stop, Asmodeus. I have what you want."

Asmodeus turned to face Laura-Luss and saw the box she held in her hand.

"Is that the piece of Lucifer I was looking for?"

"Yes. You let Tom go, and I will give it to you."

"Ah, the succubus is sweet on the human. I have a better offer for you. I will kill the human, and when I take over Hell, I will allow you all the time you want to play with him."

"He won't be in Hell. His soul is too pure. But you will be." With those words, Laura-Luss pulled out her other hand. She held the piece of Asmodeus that had been stuck to the hoe. She completed the memorized spell and tossed the piece back to Asmodeus.

Asmodeus tried to sidestep the object, but it was too late. As soon as it hit him, the power transference spell began.

"NOOOOO."

Asmodeus began a counterspell of some sort, slowing the transference. But he could not stop it completely.

Instead, he turned back to Tom. "I may not be able to send you to Hell, but I can certainly end your miserable existence."

The power emanated from his hands, like lightning bolts, heading straight for Tom, who knew he was done for. He managed to yell out, "My sacrifice will end this," before the bolts of power could reach him, and then he closed his eyes, waiting for the end.

When the end did not come, he opened his eyes. But standing between him and Asmodeus was Laura-Luss, absorbing the bolts.

"You have not absorbed enough of my power yet to stop this, succubus. It will only mean your annihilation."

"Then I will take you with me. As Tom said, a sacrifice will end this."

Laura-Luss pushed back on the flow of power from Asmodeus. As she pushed, she was also drawn forward toward him. She reached for him as she got closer, then, when close enough, grabbed his wrists.

Now, Asmodeus screamed, in pain and fear. The power had looped back and was flowing into him at a rate he could not contain. He tried to break the grasp of Laura-Luss, but her strength had increased enough from his power that he could not force her away. His physical form started to expand and glow brighter and brighter. Soon, the façade he had taken on was gone, and the demon's form took over.

Still, it did not stop there as he kept expanding until he was twice his normal demon size. Then suddenly it did stop. For seconds, there was no change. Then his form started to contract, getting smaller and smaller until he reached the size of the human form he had taken. Laura-Luss looked him in the eyes and said, "Adios, great-great-grandfather. May we never meet again."

With that, Asmodeus exploded. Laura-Luss stayed between him and Tom, ensuring that none of it harmed Tom, yet knowing the consequences.

She turned to Tom as she started to fade away.

"Goodbye, Tom. I have enjoyed being with you. I love you."

Then she was gone.

Tom sat there, stunned by what had happened. He realized he must be heading into shock from the pain, but was it possible for a demon to love, or was that just another trick of hers? With this thought in his head, he passed out.

Around him, the community slowly started coming back to life. As husbands looked at wives, mothers at their children, and children at their parents, none of them understood where they were or what had happened.

CHAPTER 21

When Tom regained consciousness, he opened his eyes to bright lights and a familiar face standing next to the bed he lay in.

"Good afternoon, brother. It's about time you woke up."

Tom looked around. "Where am I, and how long have I been here?

"You are in the hospital, or to be more exact, the Champlain Valley Physicians Hospital. Since it is in partnership with the Grey Nuns, we were able to arrange it quickly. You have been here for two days."

"What happened, John? The last thing I remember is Laura-Luss blowing up Asmodeus, then fading away."

"To sum it up, you two managed to defeat Asmodeus. The cult fell apart when Asmodeus was vanquished, and the police arrived not long after, following an anonymous tip, which I think was sent by Amy from your office. As well, the piece of Lucifer is now safely in church hands."

"And Laura-Luss?"

"Returned to Hell, most likely."

"Are you sure? The way she faded away and said goodbye, I felt that somehow it was permanent."

John looked his brother in the eyes.

"What were her last words, Tom?"

"First, she said, 'Adios, great-great-grandfather. May we never meet again,' to Asmodeus, before he blew up. Does that mean Asmodeus was truly destroyed?"

"If he blew up, then yes, it will be permanent. Tom, what were her last words?" Tom was surprised at how insistent his brother was about this.

"Before she faded away, she said, 'Goodbye, Tom. I have enjoyed being with you.'"

"Is that it?" John's voice was even more forceful.

"I thought I heard something else, but it could have been my imagination."

"What did she say, Tom?" John practically yelled it.

"I thought I heard her say the words, 'I love you.' But I was kind of concussed at the time, so maybe I did not hear correctly, or maybe it was another game of hers."

"No, Tom, it would not be a game. It is very rare for one of demon blood to love a human, but impossible would for one of them to say it and not mean it. She truly fell in love with you, and now she is suffering for it."

"What do you mean by suffering?"

"If a demon falls in love and returns to Hell, they are vanquished to the pit of despair, where the worst punishments are inflicted on sinners. For a demon to fall in love is the worst crime a demon can commit against Hell, and for that, she will be made to suffer."

"Why would falling in love be the worst of crimes for a demon?

"You must remember who their master is, and his arrogance. His servants must only worship him, and loving someone would put him in second place, in his mind."

"Is there anything we can do for Laura-Luss? She saved my life, and maybe humanity. She does not deserve that."

"There might be a way, but only if you can admit to the truth."

"The truth about what?"

"About how you feel for her."

"I liked her. She was okay for a succubus. And she saved my life."

"That is not enough, Tom."

"There can be no more. She is from Hell, and I am a Catholic. My soul is not for sale."

"You will be released later today. Amy said she would send a car. Other than some stitches on your leg and a headache, you are fine." The change of subject did not go unnoticed by Tom, but he ignored it.

"What do you mean, fine? I fractured my leg. I saw the bone come through."

"That would explain the stitches. They X-rayed your leg, Tom. Your bones are fine. Maybe a last gift from the demoness you don't care about."

"Stop going on about that. She is a succubus that I worked well with. Nothing more."

"If you say so, Tom. I must be leaving now. If you realize something different, give me a call."

Before Tom could respond, his brother was gone.

A short while later, a doctor entered his room. After a quick exam, he informed

Tom that he was free to leave and that there was someone by the front door waiting for him. A nurse showed him where his clothes were and left the room for him to get dressed. Tom first went into the bathroom, splashed some water on his face, and ran a comb through his hair. As he dressed, he looked at his leg. It was bandaged exactly where he had seen the bone come through. Other than some mild discomfort, it didn't bother him. He finished getting dressed and then looked around the room. The only item that was his was the cell phone sitting on the table next to the bed. He picked it up and left.

When he got to the lobby, he saw Amy and Ben waiting for him.

"You guys drove all the way here just to pick me up?"

"Yes and no," replied Amy. Yes to we came here, but no to driving." She pointed to a limousine as they exited the doors.

Once they were comfortably seated, Ben pulled out a bottle of cognac and poured three glasses. "To a successful case."

They clinked glasses and downed the liquid in one sip. Ben poured each another glass, and this time they sat back and enjoyed it at a slower pace.

"So, what now, Tom? A nice vacation? You sure earned it," said Amy.

"I couldn't have done it without you two."

"You would have found a way. All we did was go along for the ride," replied Ben.

"Too bad Laura-Luss couldn't be with us now. Without her, none of us would probably be here. Did she go back to Hell?" asked Amy.

Tom realized that they had not yet been filled in on what had transpired. He sighed and then told them how the confrontation with Asmodeus had concluded, neglecting again the final words of the demoness.

It was silent for a few minutes. It was Ben who broke it.

"The funny thing is that during the time I was with her, I came to like her. Maybe even trust her. Not once did she even make a pass at me, and that is rare for a succubus."

"You know, when she put that piece of herself on me, not only did I look like her, but I felt like I knew her a bit. I think she must be part human or something because it seemed like she had real feelings."

Before Tom could respond to their comments, his phone beeped. It was a one-line text from his brother.

If you want to know more, speak to Mom.

"Tom, it's okay to say that you like her, you know," said Amy.

"Or maybe a little more," put in Ben.

Amy expected a sarcastic response to that from Tom, but instead, he remained quiet. Not wanting to provoke anything, she said nothing further.

Ben picked up on her silence and followed suit.

For the next two hours, they continued that way. Then Tom picked up his phone and texted his brother.

Where is Mom staying?

The response was almost immediate.

Sisters of the Catholic Apostolate. Have them drop you there on the way. She is expecting you.

Tom then checked his phone to look up the address. It was on their route, about an hour and a half away. He checked the exit and the stores in the area.

"Amy, I need you to drop me off on the way. Tell the driver to take exit 131 and drop me at the Nike Factory Store."

"You have a sudden urge to buy shoes?" asked Ben.

Amy, however, did not question his request. She gave Ben a look to keep quiet and turned to the driver to give him instructions.

When she turned back to Tom, all he said was, "Don't worry about me. I have a destination in mind. I'll grab a cab."

****

Tom watched the limo carrying Amy and Ben drive away. Before he could phone for a cab, a white SUV pulled up beside him.

The man inside lowered the passenger window and said, "Mr. Wilkins, please get inside."

Tom hesitated, and then his cell phone beeped, indicating a text message. A glance showed it was from his mother.

I have sent this car for you. Love Mammy.

Knowing it had to be from his mother, as few knew his childhood nickname for her, Tom climbed into the front seat and buckled up.

The driver did not speak again as they pulled out of the parking lot. Tom sat back and pondered everything. He was beginning to think he knew nothing about anything when it came to his own family.

They drove for about half an hour, then the car pulled over into a small park.

"You will be met here. I'll be back to pick you up when you're finished."

Knowing that was his cue to get out, Tom unbuckled and left the car. He had no sooner closed the door when the car drove away.

Looking around, Tom studied the park. It was more like a small picnic area with a couple of picnic tables and a few park benches. There were no people around at all. Tom was beginning to wonder if he had been set up when he saw a nun approaching. It was only as the woman got closer that Tom realized it was his mother.

She walked up to him and hugged him.

"You have grown since I last saw you."

For the first time in days, Tom laughed.

"You say that every time you see me, Mom. Yet each time you give me a hug, your head touches my chin at the same spot."

"I wanted to hear you laugh, dear. I can feel, though, that you are conflicted. I have come because something troubles you."

"Much troubles me. Starting with the family that I no longer know."

"We are still the same, son. But life has caused changes in all of us."

"First John with the knowledge he has never shared, then cousin Dominic with the experiences he has never spoken of, and now you, knowing I needed to speak with you before I even had a chance to talk with you. Mother, what is going on?"

"I know that is not what is bothering you, but I will tell you a story so you can understand."

Tom was about to say something further, but his mother stopped him.

"I must tell you something that you never would have believed before today, and you must hear this before I can help you."

She took Tom's hand and led him to the park bench, where they could sit comfortably under the shade of a tree.

"When your father passed, I was in a dark place. I had even considered taking my own life."

His mother held up her hand before Tom could speak.

"Let me finish.

"You were away on an assignment with that other company you used to work for. John was in Rome on Vatican business. I did not know who to turn to. As you know, the Church has always been my strength, and yet I felt like I had been deserted by both the Church and by God.

"I stood at the edge of the cliff near our house, looking down at the surf far below. I was moments away from taking that final step. I thought I had no purpose left. I lifted my foot to take that final step when a strong wind blew in from the water and pushed me back hard. I tried to move again towards the cliff, and the wind again came up and pushed me away, this time knocking me onto my derriere. As I sat there looking up, I realized that the clouds above were moving in the opposite direction from the wind that had blown me over. How could that be, I wondered.

"Then I heard the wind whispering to me. It said; 'It is not your time, Shirley. There are still works for you to do. Speak to your son, the priest. He will guide you.'

"I was not sure if it was my imagination or just an inner will to survive, but I heeded it and went back to the house. I had just walked in when the phone started ringing. I picked it up and sure enough it was John."

"Before even saying hello, he said, 'Mom, I just had a feeling that I had to call you right now.'

"I won't go into the entire conversation, as we spoke for hours. I told him how I was feeling, about having no purpose. That was when he told me about his real work at the Vatican. I knew then that I did have a purpose. It was then that I decided to become a nun.

"Since starting the process, though, I have had more visions and heard that same voice from the wind many times. It is that voice that told me that you needed me now. But I can only do something for you if you tell me everything."

Tom took a deep breath and then went ahead.

"Her name is Laura-Luss."

"The succubus."

"You know about her?"

"John filled me in while you were hospitalized."

"Mother, she has been banished to the pit of despair in Hell, and it is my fault."

"Why is that? Is it because of love?"

"Love has nothing to do with it. It is because of guilt."

"I see," she said, raising an eyebrow. It was a look she had often given Tom when he was younger. It was the look she gave him when he was not telling the real story.

"Yes, mother, guilt. She is banished there because I failed."

"And how did you fail?"

"When we faced Asmodeus, I was supposed to call for you know who to come and get him. I froze because I was dumb. If I had studied my Bible like I should have, I would have known the real name of Lucifer and called him. He would have captured Asmodeus, and Laura-Luss would not have been banished, since she would not have had to fight Asmodeus. All I thought of at the time was using the spell Dom Emmanuel had supplied. John had given me enough hints that I should have figured it out, and Lucifer himself told me to call him when we had Asmodeus."

The anguish on her son's face was almost more than she could bear, yet she knew she had to press further, or her son would be lost.

"You know as well as I that old goat horns would not have honored his word. Not when it came to Asmodeus, since he had let Asmodeus free to enter our plane. Had you called him then, he would have used the opportunity to take the souls of those poor cultists, as well as yours, since you would have been the one who called him.

"That is not why you feel guilt, and that is not what is bothering you. You must be truthful if you want to save her."

"But mother, she is a succubus, a demon from Hell. I can't have feelings for her. If I were to admit that, my soul would be lost."

"Yet if you don't admit it, still your soul will be lost, just in a different way."

Looking her in the eyes, he finally admitted the truth to himself.

"Yes, mother, I have fallen in love with a demon. I am bound for Hell."

A voice came to them from nearby. Tom looked up and saw a woman approaching them. She was dressed all in white and shone as bright as a searchlight.

"You are bound for Hell, just not in the way you are thinking."

For a moment, she shone brighter than ever, and Tom had to turn his eyes away. But when he looked back up, he was able to see clearly again. Now it was just a woman of indeterminate age. He was baffled by all that had passed, and yet he knew that this lady before them was special.

"Thank you for coming," his mother said to the lady.

She then turned to Tom to introduce her.

"Tom, this is Saint Mary."

"The mother of Jesus?" Tom stuttered out.

"No, Tom. I am Mary Magdalene, the wife of Jesus."

Tom just stared—at a complete loss for words.

"I can't spend much time on your plane, Tom, so you must listen closely."

Tom just nodded.

"Laura-Luss may be a demon, but she is also part human. Somewhere down her bloodline, a demon mated with a human. An offspring rarely comes from that, but it does happen. If she didn't have at least some human blood, she could not have fallen in love with you."

Tom was surprised. "You mean she meant what she said?"

"Yes, Tom, and for that she was banished to the pit of despair. She will stay there for a thousand years unless you can bring her out."

"Me?"

"Yes, Tom, you."

"But how?"

"I can show you how to get there, but you will need a guide once you are there to get to the pit of despair. There is an imp in Hell named Ilyish. My guide will get you to him, and you will need to convince him to lead you to the pit."

"I see many problems with this plan, but two stand out. One, how do I convince the imp, and two, how do I remain undetected?"

"The imp is a friend of Laura-Luss, and yes, some demons can have friends in Hell. You will need to convince him that you are willing to sacrifice everything to help her."

"If I can admit to myself that I am in love with her, I think I can convince the imp of that. But the second problem remains."

"You can pass through Hell, undisturbed, by calling Lucifer by his real name."

"Wouldn't that just put a neon sign over my head saying, 'Here I am, come and get me'?"

"If you call his name on earth, then yes, it will attract him. But if you call him by his real name in Hell, it is a name forbidden in Hell, and all will turn away and ignore you in fear. Lucifer himself laid that spell out, and even he is not immune to it. Ironic, no?"

"But I still have not figured that out yet. I guess I'm not a good enough Catholic."

"Being a good Catholic has nothing to do with it. In truth, few Catholics, even amongst the majority of the priests, know this. No, I can't speak his name, but I can give you the final clue you will need to figure it out.

"The timeline in the Bible is messed up because Lucifer played a trick and went back in time, for which he was cursed. You see, although it is true that he was the serpent that convinced Eve to lead Adam to the tree of knowledge and to eat the fruit there, in reality, he had not yet existed. And yes, Lucifer is a fallen angel who became a human, and then committed the ultimate sin by murdering his brother."

"Once you get to the pit of despair, it should be easy to find Laura-Luss. You must take her by the hand and exit the pit, then you have to find a secluded place. However, there will be one final act you must perform, or she will be drawn right back into the pit."

"And what act is that?"

"You must consummate your love."

"How do I do that?"

It was his mother who responded.

"You must have sex with her. Or do I have to tell you how to do that, too?"

Tom stared at his mother, dumbfounded.

"I must leave now. Your mother and brother will make the arrangements. Go back home and prepare. Then you must catch a flight to Montreal."

"Montreal?"

"Under Mt. Royal, there is an entrance to Hell. You will be met there tomorrow." With that, she faded away.

"Time that you got going, son. I will call your brother and have him meet you at your house. He knows what you will need. Be careful!"

His mother gave him a final hug and walked away. She had just left his sight when the white car pulled back into the park. Sighing, Tom headed over to it.

CHAPTER 22

"From here on, we will not mention his name, so as not to draw his attention in any way. He guards the paths to his domain and will not tolerate those who use them without his permission, especially humans."

Tom listened carefully to his brother's instructions. John had been waiting for him when he arrived home, and sat in his living room, quietly patient, while Tom showered and changed.

"John, you probably know the answer to this better than anyone else on this planet, and I am not sure if I even want to know, but what are the chances this mad plan can succeed, and that in the end I won't lose my soul?"

Looking his brother in the eye, his response was not the least what Tom expected.

"Brother, your soul is already lost, unless you do this and succeed."

Tom just stared at his brother in shock and disbelief.

"It was what I was afraid of when you and Laura-Luss first came together to see me, but there was no way I could prevent it. This was a trap by you know who from the very beginning. He always has multiple levels to his duplicity, so no matter how things turn out, he gets a win.

"He knew that the odds of finding and trapping Asmodeus and surviving it were low, but at the same time, he was aware of the ties your family has to his adversary. So, on the chance you succeeded in your mission, he had set up other possible scenarios where he could get a win. One was that you called him when you found Asmodeus. Depending on the situation, he could either entrap Asmodeus and declare that part of the Earth as his own, or destroy Asmodeus, have a brief confrontation with the forces of Heaven, proving that he was acting in concordance with the covenant, and leave with the souls of the cult that followed Asmodeus. Of course, in his arrogance, he never believed that Asmodeus could defeat him.

"However, on the off chance that you could defeat Asmodeus yourself, with the help of Laura-Luss, he had his final winning card ready. He knew that no matter how hard you want to resist, the allure of a succubus, over some time, is hard to avoid. If you could resist her physical charms, working closely with her, you could fall for her in other ways. It's why he specifically chose Laura-Luss from his gaggle of succubi. He knew enough about you to know that you would be attracted to her in that way.

"One thing he wasn't counting on was the human bloodline of his chosen succubus. He never really expected her to fall in love with you.

"That being said, the fact that you have fallen for her heavily taints your soul. If you ignore your feelings or allow the one you love to suffer, then he has you. The one way to cleanse your soul of this is to sacrifice everything in the name of love."

"If he knows all this, won't he be expecting me and lay a trap?"

"Once again, his arrogance is in the way. He will not know for a while yet that Laura-Luss is in the pit of despair. Despite what everyone thinks, he does not have God's powers. He can't see everything, everywhere, even in his own domain. Unless he specifically goes looking for her, it could be weeks before he knows where she is. He may even believe she was destroyed when Asmodeus was. And yes, Asmodeus was completely destroyed and will never appear again. That can happen to both angels and fallen angels like Asmodeus, although it takes a lot for it to happen."

"You could still have warned me. I could have dropped the case then."

"It was already too late. If you dropped the case, that would have been a broken contract, and a taint on your soul, although of course not a major one, and one that could eventually have been washed clean.

"The role that I have, both in the Vatican and in my covenant with the demon hunters, comes with responsibilities, which even surpass my commitment to my own family. When you came to me with your story, I knew then that you had been chosen for this, not just by him below, but by those above. They can be just as manipulative as the other one, but I can't go against their wishes. All I could do was prepare you and hope for the best."

"So, Heaven set me up to be damned."

"No, brother. Free choice is always yours. You put yourself in that position with your choice of a profession and the company you decided to work for."

"John, that doesn't make any sense. If Heaven chose me for this, where was my free choice?"

"The Lord's ways are not easy to understand. Let me put it to you this way. Once you chose your profession and company, Heaven used the opportunity to make sure you came to the notice of their adversary. They were well aware of his connection to that company and would one day give an important case of this type to someone who had had dealings with the supernatural. They just made sure that he was aware of it."

"So damned if I do, and damned if I don't."

"More like damned if you don't, and possibly damned if you do. There is a chance that you can succeed, and I am here to help with that."

John pulled items out of the bag he had brought and handed them to Tom one at a time. The first item was a wooden flute.

"What in hell am I supposed to do with this? Charm the demons away?"

"Have you never heard that music has charms to soothe the savage breast? Well, this works similarly. Once you are in Hell, you will use the flute first and then call out you know who's real name. The combination of the two should keep you practically invisible. As a backup, there is this."

He handed Tom a case that, when opened, revealed a half-dozen darts.

"Look at the other end of the flute."

Tom turned it and saw grooves on the inside of the flute, grooves that matched the shape of the darts.

"Hopefully it won't come to this, but if you are in a situation where a demon sees you, and has you trapped, insert the dart, then give a good blow. It has certain properties that will act like an old-fashioned blow dart instrument used by native tribes around the world for years. These darts are specifically made to stop any demon in hell, except, of course, their boss, so try and avoid him. It won't destroy them, as that would draw the attention of the wrong party, but it will freeze them for five minutes, and when that wears off, they will forget what they had seen and go about their business."

The next item was a wooden cross.

"You will have to leave that silver cross around your neck here. Silver in Hell is like a beacon. This cross, though, has been especially blessed. Keep it under your clothes, and next to your heart."

John then handed Tom a roll of tape.

"I mean next to your heart."

Then John pulled out a set of priest gowns.

"I am going disguised as a priest?"

"No, Tom, these are for me."

He put on the gown, pulled out a small bottle of oil, and told Tom to get on his knees.

First, he anointed Tom with the oil, then proceeded with a ceremony, the likes of which Tom had never seen before, even after years of going to church. Yet, as soon as the ceremony was finished, though, he did not remember any part of it.

"It is the only real protection I can give you," said John. "This ceremony is only performed on demon hunters before they leave on a hunt. Few know how to perform it, and no one upon whom it has been performed can remember it. There is special training required to do this. It is like armor, but it won't stop everything. It is just an extra layer of protection.

"I contacted your office and told them that you would be staying with me for a few days, to recover from your ordeal. I have used Church resources to arrange your flight to Montreal. From there, take a cab to the observation deck on Mt. Royal. Mother told me that someone will meet you there and that you will know who it is."

"I see Mother and you even keep secrets from each other."

"There are things that neither of us needs to know about each other."

"Did you ever stop to think that if Heaven were more open about things like this, and stopped keeping secrets, there might be less evil in the world?"

"It goes back to free will, Tom. As long as humans have free will, then some secrets must be kept."

"Is there an entrance to Hell on Mt. Royal, or is that more of a metaphor, and somehow I will be transported into Hell from there?"

"It's a real entrance. Laura-Luss had just returned from Hell using that entrance when you met her that day you faced the hellhounds. Mt. Royal is an extinct volcano. There is a hidden entrance that leads into a lava tube. At the end of that lava tube is an entrance to Hell. You need to know, though, that it is there and how to open it. Whoever you are meeting at Mt. Royal will probably show you how. There must be something different about it since I know of no human who has been able to enter Hell through one of these portals."

John pulled his brother into his arms and gave him a bear hug that felt like it was sucking the air out of Tom.

"Good luck, brother. Please return."

John then picked up his bag and left Tom's apartment.

****

Tom stood on the observation deck of Mt. Royal, taking in the beautiful spring day, the sun shining brightly. Most of the snow had melted since he last stood here, waiting for Laura-Luss, not that long ago, though it seemed like a lifetime with all that had happened since then. He realized that, in a way, it was another life ago. Back then, all he'd had to worry about was capturing a demon and avoiding the seduction of a succubus. Now he was planning on entering Hell to rescue said succubus and declare his love for her.

"We meet again, Mr. Wilkins."

The voice was not one he expected to hear.

"Although I am grateful for what you did for us, Vince, I have other matters to attend to right now."

"Like saving your succubus from Hell?

"What would you know about that?"

"I am to be your guide."

"I had expected someone else."

"A creature of Heaven can't enter the gates of Hell. Whereas I can. I was asked to come here."

"Not that I am ungrateful for this offer, but why should I trust you?"

Vince smiled.

"There was a time I would have taken offence at that and torn you to pieces. Maybe it is true what she told me, that I have changed in ways that are unusual for creatures like myself.

"As for your question, there are many reasons. First, the fact that I am here. Your adversary would not have contacted me to stop you. Second, the fact that I was asked by a being that you have put trust in. Third, well, that is not easy to explain, especially for me. I was originally created to protect a village that has not existed for a long time, and for the last centuries, I have existed only for self-preservation. I had had enough of that existence and only wanted it to end—until I met you and your demoness. For the first time in a long time, I wanted to help someone else for no other reason than that I care for them.

"Yes, Tom, for a golem to care for anything other than what he was created for has not happened before. I do not understand it, but here I am."

"I think I do understand," replied Tom. "That is also the reason you were asked to help. You may be closer to your desire to become human than you realize."

"How is that?"

"For a long time, you have been looking for a magic spell to make you human so you could end your existence. Yet the only magic you needed was what you could create within yourself.

"And so much has happened that is magical since I was assigned this case. From defeating a demon to avoiding the adversary's traps, to falling in love with a demon, and now a golem discovering his humanity. Maybe I need to cast aside my doubts and commit myself as my brother and mother have done."

"No, Tom, you are wrong on two counts. First, your path is not the same as that of your brother or your mother. If you had chosen that path, then Asmodeus might have succeeded in what he was doing."

"You may be right about that; I will have to think about it. What's the second thing I am wrong about?"

"It is not a demon that you have fallen in love with. All that I have learned over my existence shows me that pure demons and humans can never truly love one another. What you have fallen in love with is the human part of Laura-Luss. I have also done my research and have access to information you don't, information that may be useful in your quest."

Vince pulled a piece of paper out of his pocket and handed it to Tom. It was a simple genealogy chart.

Laura-Luss: great-granddaughter of Lilith and Asmodeus, granddaughter of Yuki-Onna and Shadow, a shapeshifter from the union of Lilith and Asmodeus, daughter of the union between Linkus (half-human and direct descendant of Mara (the agent of death—Hindu) and Lilus, the daughter of Shadow and Yuki-Onna.

Summary: Lilith and Asmodeus begat Shadow:

Shadow and Yuki-Onna begat Lilus

Lilus and Linkus begat Laura-Luss

"It is rare for a mating between a demon and a human to produce children, but it does happen. If raised as human, they will essentially become human and lose almost all of their demon qualities. However, some of the evil stays, and those who can't overcome it end up becoming serial killers, drug addicts, or politicians.

"If raised in Hell, they usually lose all traces of humanity. What can happen, though, is if they spend time on our plane and associate with humans, the human part can become temporarily ascendant. In the case of Laura-Luss, not only did her humanity become ascendant, but she also met you, and because of the human part of her, she fell in love."

Tom thought back to his first meeting with Laura-Luss. "So, what she told me was true. I had thought she was just trying to impress me with her ancestry and make me feel at ease because she has human blood."

Vince nodded, understanding Tom's mistrust.

"Now that she is in the pit of despair, though, her demon part will have taken over completely. It is a self-preservation tendency, since the pit of despair is the worst part of Hell, and the demon part is what she needs to keep any sense of her identity.

"Tom, you will somehow have to get past her demon part and reach her human part, or you will not even be able to get her to leave the pit. You will have very little time to do it. Once you have entered the pit, the door will only remain open for moments."

"How do I even get into the pit?"

"The imp will show you the way there. He will know how to enter. Know this, though: a demon won't help another demon out of the pit, as by doing so they would be consigned to the pit themselves. Being human, though, you do not face that fate unless you get trapped in there by not leaving quickly enough. Once trapped there ... well over a thousand years, you will be stripped of your humanity.

"So, Tom, are you ready to face the horrors of Hell to win your love?"

Putting his hand on the wooden cross taped to his heart, Tom looked up to the sky and said, "Forgive me, God, but yes, I am ready to enter Hell."

Making sure no one was observing them, Vince led Tom over the side and into a wooded area. From there, they followed a path that only the golem was able to see.

"Should you survive this, the path will remain within you, and you can return to it if you so desire," the golem said over his shoulder as he led the way,

It took almost half an hour, but they came to an area that few others traversed. Nestled against the side of the mountain was what looked like a shallow cave. Entering it, they came to a dead end. Tom looked at Vince as if to ask what next, but Vince was already acting. Waving his hands, he said, "To Hell with life."

Moments later, a section of the wall seemed to fade away, revealing a tunnel. The way forward was pitch black. Tom reached into his bag to grab a flashlight, but before he could reach it, Vince turned, grabbed Tom by the shoulders, and breathed into his face. Suddenly, Tom was able to see clearly as if the place was brightened by daylight.

"A flashlight might make your presence known to those you don't want. I have given you an ability that will always be with you. Seeing in the dark will now be second nature to you. Call it a parting gift. As well, this will allow you to pass the gargoyle guardians. They would normally destroy any humans that came this way, but since I am not human, I am allowed to pass. Now you will be too. I will lead you to the door to Hell, but then I must leave."

Amazed by this ability, Tom did not know what to say, so he followed the golem in silence. He looked at the gargoyles as they passed them, and shivered inside, thinking of what would have happened to him if the golem had not been with him. Soon, they arrived at a large iron door. The golem knocked once, and the door opened, revealing a small creature.

"Did you bring my payment?"

Vince handed the creature a small leather pouch.

"You will find more than enough fairy dust in this bag to pay for your job as a guide many times over, Ilyish."

The little imp then noticed Tom for the first time.

"There was no arrangement to guide a human, golem. I was to guide you, and only you."

Vince turned to Tom.

"I must leave now. The rest is up to you." He turned and walked away.

Ilyish was pushing the door closed, but Tom shoved his foot in the way, preventing him from completing the act.

"Human, leave now before I call on the demon guards to come and get you."

"And in doing so, letting them know that you are making deals with the outside world? I think not."

"Even should I choose to guide you, it won't be long before the master of this domain will sense your presence. A golem he might not bother with, but a human in his domain he will, and if I am caught with you, I will be severely punished."

"I have the means to avoid his detection."

"Then where am I supposed to guide you to, should I choose to do so?"

"I need to get to the pit of despair."

The imp gasped.

"Only a fool would want to go near that place, and I am no fool."

"But you do know how to get there."

"Of course, I do. I know where everything in Hell is. But there is nothing you could say that would convince me to take you there. The risk would be too great, even for one such as me. No matter how much payment the golem made, it would not be enough to go there."

With that, the imp once again tried to push the door closed. Tom pushed back, forcing his way in. Fearing what could happen if he allowed a human in, the imp was ready to yell for help until he heard the one thing that Tom could have said that would give him pause.

"Laura-Luss."

"What about her?"

"She has been banished to the pit of despair. I have come to get her out."

The imp was stunned.

"How do you know she is there? And why would you care?"

"She is there because she declared her love for me. I am here because I love her."

Ilyish fell to the ground, the shock of what he had just heard being more than he could handle. Tom rushed over to him.

"Are you okay? Did I hurt you when I pushed the door against you?"

Ilyish looked Tom in the eyes. Seeing that he cared about whether or not he was hurt surprised him, but also convinced him.

"Yes, I can see that you could fall in love with one of our domain, and I can see why Laura-Luss could fall in love with you. I was wondering why she had not come to see me when her mission was over, but I had not thought she was in the pit. Human, if you are ready to risk your soul to save her, then I am willing to risk punishment to help her. Now, if you truly have a way to turn our masters' eyes away from you, then you had better do it now. Soon, the stench of human will reach others who will carry word to him."

Helping Ilyish to his feet, Tom reached inside his shirt and pulled out the flute. He blew a note and then whispered, "Cain, your eyes will not see me, and you will not sense my presence in your domain, nor will any you command."

He faded out of Ilyish's sight for a moment.

"You do have the means to avoid detection," whispered Ilyish.

Tom reached over and touched the imp's shoulder, once again becoming visible to him.

"I had heard that those who know the true human name of my master could avoid his presence—or call him. I now see that the rumors are true. Yet I was unable to hear what you said."

"It is the nature of the summoning. One has to figure it out for themselves, or so I have been told. Now I ask again, will you guide me to the pit of despair?"

"Being an imp, I am one of the lowest demons on the hierarchy tree. As such, I am ignored or mistreated by all except those at my level. Laura-Luss was the only demon, not of my level, that treated me with any type of respect. She has helped me many times over and even protected me when an angry higher-level demon tried to take out their anger and frustrations on me.

"The advantage of being ignored is that I can travel throughout the domain of hell without anyone noticing me. Out of boredom, I have been all over Hell, and yes, I have seen the pit of despair. I will help you, but you must promise me one thing."

"That is?"

"That you won't give up on her once you get to the pit. She will not be as you remember her."

"I was told that once I get in the pit, I will have no problem finding her."

"Most assuredly, since she will come right to you. Because you have shared time with her, your presence will attract her. It will be up to you, though, to convince her to leave the pit with you. Demons that are cast there have a spell put on them that works on their willpower. You must find a way to overcome that—and do so while she is trying to tear you to pieces."

"That was not a part that I was made aware of."

"Which is why I have that one condition. If you give up at any time, her fate is sealed. Besides being stuck in the pit for a thousand years, when she is finally released, she will have no memory of who she is."

"I have no intention of giving up, at any time. I would think the fact that I have come to Hell to get her should tell you that."

"Hell is one thing. The pit of despair is another. Still, I see in you a strength and will that is unusual in humans. I will guide you."

"I need one more thing from you."

"You humans. One huge favor is never enough, is it?"

"Once I get her out, I will need a place where I can have some privacy with her."

Ilyish smiled. "Now that I can understand. Not to worry. Ilyish knows of many places like that."

He took Tom's hand and led him on.

Time seemed to have no real meaning in Hell, at least not to a human. They passed through tunnels and empty spaces until they came to an area that Tom could make no sense of. He felt dizzy and lightheaded.

Ilyish stopped and pulled out a bandana.

"I will have to blindfold you from here. The places we will pass through are just too overwhelming for a human's senses."

Tom did as Ilyish suggested, and held the imp's hand as he led the way. With his eyes covered, Tom started to feel better.

Tom had no idea how long they traveled, but finally, Ilyish came to a stop and told Tom to remove his blindfold. They stood at the end of a tunnel with only a stone wall in front of them.

"Do you have rope in that backpack?"

Tom reached in and pulled out a roll of cord, about a hundred feet long. Ilyish took one end and tied it around his waist, then told Tom to do the same.

"Once you enter the pit, you will only have minutes to get Laura-Luss and return. This rope will be your guide back to the door, but if you do not return quickly, it will close, and you will remain inside. Are you sure you are ready?"

"As ready as I'll ever be. Now, where is this door?"

"Just keep walking to the end of this tunnel and you will pass through it."

"Walk where? I only see a stone wall there."

"That is the door. Now hurry. It is only a matter of time before someone comes here."

Tom walked to the end of the tunnel and put his hands on the wall—or tried to—but his hands sank right through. Tom followed his hands and passing through the wall, came upon a scene that once again challenged his senses. He heard groans and screams; he felt a sticky substance like blood washing over his body, yet could not see the cause of it, nor did any of it remain on him. The smell was beyond even the worst slaughterhouses imaginable. Colors seemed to change constantly, and he could never get his eyes to focus. He realized that if he did not get out of here soon, this place would drive him into lunacy.

A roar, and then his body was picked up and tossed aside like yesterday's garbage.

He got to his knees and saw a large, red demon, horns glowing and large teeth gnashing, heading towards him. Although it bore no resemblance to the demon he came to rescue, Tom knew that it was Laura-Luss.

"Laura, my love, you must listen to me."

The creature responded with a raspy, deep voice.

"I know no Laura, and love does not exist in Hell. You have been sent to torment me further, but it is I who will torment you, as I rip you into a thousand pieces, for you to reform, so that I can do it again and again."

Tom knew that there would be no appealing to her as long as she was in the pit. He had to use another method to get her out. He could think of only one way. The risks were great, for by speaking the name he was about to, he could be discovered.

"You have been summoned by Lucifer. I have been sent to get you."

The demon grabbed Tom, bringing its face right up to Tom's, the smell from its breath almost overpowering.

"You are lying, puny demon. I will now tear you to pieces."

"I am not a demon. I am a human."

This caused the demon to pause.

"Humans do not get tossed into the pit of despair until they have been turned into a demon. You lie."

"Smell me, and tell me that I am not human."

The demon stared at Tom, then bent closer and took a strong whiff.

"It is not possible."

"Unless I was sent. We do not have much time. Come with me, and I will explain it to you."

"I can't leave this place. It is not permitted."

"It is not permitted that I can be here, yet here I am."

"Hurry, Tom, the way is closing." Ilyish's voice came from beyond.

"Who is that?" roared the demon. "I will tear it apart."

"If you want to know, you will have to follow me."

Tom felt the tug on the rope and knew it was now or never. He grabbed the demon in a full-body hug. The demon's skin was burning him like fire, but it did not resist. Pulling as hard as he could, and with Ilyish also pulling on the other end, Tom hauled the demon to the wall and then through.

Once they passed through, the burning on his skin stopped. Instead of the large, red, monstrous demon in his arms, he held on to the very feminine form of the succubus he remembered.

"Where, how," was all she managed to say before Tom quieted her questions with a kiss. Ilyish stood there grinning.

When he broke off the kiss, Laura-Luss looked him in the eyes.

"You came for me. You risked the fires of Hell for me. Why?"

"Because I love you too."

"You don't understand. I will be returned to the pit of despair as soon as we are discovered, and you will be cast into the fires of Hell to turn you into a demon."

"Not if we are married."

Tom pulled out a piece of paper from his backpack.

"Ilyish, would you do the honors?"

The imp took the paper from Tom's hand and read it. Then, beaming a huge smile, he said, "It will be my pleasure."

Tom took Laura-Luss' hands in his own and looked her in the eyes, as Ilyish read aloud.

"Tom, do you take this demon to be your wife, knowing that with her nature, she still has to follow Hell's decrees? To let her live in Hell while you live on Earth, to honor her, and to return to Hell from time to time as the situation warrants, to state your love again."

"I do."

"Laura-Luss, do you take this human to be your husband? To take no joy out of your role as a succubus, except when you are with him. To protect him whenever he should return to Hell to be with you. To cause no harm to him when you are on the plane of Earth. To state your love for him whenever he returns to Hell."

She stared into Tom's eyes, not believing that this could ever happen.

"I do."

"Then by the power invested in this document, by the covenant recognized by the leaders of both Heaven and Hell, I now pronounce you husband and wife. Laura-Luss, you may kiss your groom."

Wrapping her arms around Tom, she gave him the most sensual kiss he had ever received.

"You know what must happen now for this to become valid."

"Ilyish says he knows of a place where we can have some privacy."

"Are you sure, Tom? You spent the last number of weeks doing everything you could to avoid this."

"The sacrifices I am willing to make for love," replied Tom, the smile on his face sending a wave of heat through the demoness.

Ilyish led them to a room that contained a real bed, then closed the door on them. Tom turned to Laura-Luss as she jumped into his arms. Being a succubus, she did not need to remove her clothes; she was already naked. Her body felt pleasantly warm in his arms, as she leaned away and started to undress him. Her hands moved in ways he had never experienced with a woman before. Once she had his clothes off, she pushed him onto the bed and climbed on top of him.

The rhythm she used had Tom moaning and groaning in pleasure, but what surprised him was that Laura-Luss matched him groan for groan and moan for moan.

Time moves differently for humans in Hell, and how long their lovemaking went on, Tom had no idea. At last, though, he lay back, the demoness in his arms, both of them satiated.

"It is so much different doing it for love, and not as a job. Maybe that is how prostitutes feel?"

"No, Laura, prostitutes do it for money. You are not a prostitute. When your demon nature takes over, and you are forced to act like a succubus because you are ordered to, that is not you. Here now, holding me, that is the real you. Never forget that."

"That is the first time you have ever called me Laura. I like it better than the full name."

"When you are with me as my wife, you will always be Laura to me."

There was a rap on the door, then Ilyish's voice called in.

"I think you two had better wrap it up. There appears to be some type of disturbance. Larry has come to tell me that there is a search going on."

"They must be looking for us," said Laura-Luss.

"No, they are looking for me. If I understand correctly, you are now back to your previous rating as a demon. Even your boss has to honor that. However, if they find me here, that could be another matter. I must leave as quickly as possible," Tom said as he dressed.

"There is no way you can get out of here without being caught. Every demon in Hell will be looking for you."

"Not every demon, my love," said Tom, kissing her. "Besides you, there is Ilyish and his friends. Be good to him. He is kind, for a demon. As for me getting caught, not likely. I know his true name."

With that, Tom once again whispered Cain's name and faded away from her sight. He touched her shoulder, and she could see him again.

"Ilyish will lead me out of here. Until our next reunion," he gave her one last kiss, then left with the imp.

Ilyish knew secret ways that were quicker than when they had come in, and soon they were once again at the entrance to Hell in the extinct volcano of Mt. Royal.

"Goodbye, Ilyish. I hope that I can call you a friend now."

"It would be my honor to have a human for a friend. Tell the golem to give you the spell to call me, and when you do, I will meet you here again. Goodbye—my friend."

Tom walked toward the daylight, heading back to the life he had in New York, but knowing that life would be quite different from now on.

CHAPTER 23 – EPILOGUE

Tom was sitting at the desk in his office when Amy's voice came over the intercom.

"Tom, you have a visitor."

"Okay, Amy, send him in."

He had been expecting this day since his return from Montreal a week before. He wasn't sure how the devil would react, but he'd made some preparations with the help of his brother.

He stood as Lucifer came through the door.

"Hello, Tom," he said as he crossed the room and shook Tom's hand. "Glad to see you back in top form."

Tom said nothing, but sat back down, indicating with a gesture that Lucifer should take one of the guest chairs opposite.

"You did well," said Lucifer, as he settled himself. "Not quite as I expected, mind you, but overall, I am satisfied. Also, there is no need for those white candles I see on your desk. I have kept my word; the stench I attached has been removed. You can have your brother confirm it if you wish."

Accepting what Lucifer said, and knowing he would be seeing his brother again soon, Tom simply said, "I ruined your plans, destroyed your right-hand demon, and you are satisfied? Now I'm puzzled."

"Oh, Tom, my plans were not in the least ruined. When I discovered Asmodeus was no longer in Hell, I just decided to take advantage of the situation."

"A situation that you created, no?"

"Yes and no. I left the opening, but it was up to Asmodeus to use it. He did, but he failed in his designs and has been eliminated for his failure."

Lucifer laughed. "Do not look surprised, Tom. Let me explain something to you. I do not want the Earth destroyed, nor do I want humankind destroyed. In time, I will come to rule here under my terms and conditions. When I do, well, most people will not notice much of a difference. I happen to like things here as they are. Besides, creating is a pain in the ass. Just ask God if he will deign to talk with you."

Tom could think of no suitable response, so he remained silent.

Lucifer let the silence drag for a beat, then let the other shoe drop. "Time to discuss your next case."

Tom looked startled. Whatever he might have been expecting, this wasn't it. "No," he declared, giving voice to his gut reaction. "No more cases with you as my client. I'll discuss this with my superiors and tell them so. It can't be completely against my contract to refuse one client."

Lucifer just smiled. "I control your superiors, Tom."

"Then I will talk to the owner of the company directly," replied Tom.

"Go ahead and talk. I am listening."

"You own this company?"

"Of course. I would never hire someone I did not already control."

"Since I know who you are, why would you want me working for you? You know that I will not do your bidding if it goes against my own morals, and I have family that will help me if need be."

"As with this case, Tom, you will always have your free will to act as you deem fit. However, there is one request I have of you for which I require your willing agreement, since it is not in your contract."

"You can make any request you want, but if it is not in my contract, it's highly unlikely that I will grant it."

"Oh, this is something I think you will be pleased to act on. You see, I need a liaison to act between our New York office and our Montreal office. It will require you to stay in Montreal for at least one month a year."

Tom was genuinely taken aback. "You know, and you're still willing to let it go on?"

"Tom, I know everything that passes in Hell. Eventually anyway. If it keeps you happy and working well, then it is a price I am willing to live with. Do you accept?" he asked, holding out his hand once again.

Tom reached over and took Lucifer's hand. "I never thought that I would shake hands on a deal with the Devil."

Lucifer laughed.

"I do have one more question, though," said Tom.

"Ah, my presence here. Yes, I lied that first day we met. It is true that for this case, I had to get a special disposition from Heaven, due to the circumstances. Had

Asmodeus used the spell he had to summon me, my powers would have been fully manifest, and I would not have been able to stop it. But as long as I do not use my powers in a major way, there is little that Heaven can do to stop me from coming and going to visit the financial enterprises, of which, of course, I have many. Now you must prepare for your next client," said Lucifer, sliding a file across the desk. "He will be here shortly."

Tom opened the folder and looked at the contents, scanning the first page synopsis. "You've got to be kidding me."

Lucifer rose from his chair and started for the door. "You handled one supernatural mystery so well, I thought another would be just up your alley."

Tom didn't have a chance to say a word before he was out the door, and Amy came in. "So now you know," she said. "Sorry, I could never tell you, but he has this way of making sure we can't talk about it."

"Not to worry, Amy," said Tom, shaking his head with a profound sense of resignation. "I completely understand.'

"So, what's this new case?"

"According to the file, my next client is a vampire—whose coffin has been stolen."

"Oh, great. *Another nail in the coffin.*"

Watch for the next adventure in the Tom Wilkins mysteries. When a vampire's coffin is stolen, it doesn't seem to be a big deal. But Tom is about to learn just how big a deal it could be—not just for the vampire—but for humans around the world. Will Tom solve this case, or will it truly become ANOTHER NAIL IN THE COFFIN?

CAST OF CHARACTERS

Tom Wilkins – Private detective working for P.I. International

John Wilkins – Tom's Brother, and a priest

Shirley Wilkins – Tom's mother, who is in training to become a nun

Dom Dominic Sicone – Tom's cousin, a monk at Oka Abbey

Amy Johnson – Secretary at P.I. International

Ben Johnson – Investigator and brother to Amy

Dom Emmanuel – Records keeper at the Vatican and John's mentor

Vanessa – Human with Angel blood and a friend of John

Mr. Potenkins – Tom's superior at the agency

Vince Faustelli – A golem

Laura-Luss – Succubus, prefers to be called a demoness

Lucifer – Aka Satan, aka old goat horns, etc. – client of Tom Wilkins

Lupus – A small demon and messenger of Satan

Barttle – A bogie in the computer room in Hell

Fox Fairy – A demon in Hell who is feared by some and held in awe by others Thought to originally be one of the Shen – a spirit of the dead rising from the grave. A known seller of information

The Shadow – A deadly ethereal demon that works for the Fox Fairy. Thought to be the dark part of a human's psyche, which has taken real form

Ilyish the Imp – Friend of Laura-Luss, or as close to a friend as is possible for a demon to have in Hell

Larry - dark-colored bogie and companion of Ilyish

Jesses – a demon in Hell